"You're sure you'll be all right with the baby?"

Zach asked, his gaze moving from Lily to John Henry. There was too much here that could tempt a man, too much that could make him forget his purpose.

"Certainly. I may be a little awkward right now, but I'll get the hang of it." Lily didn't know if that were true or not, but she sincerely hoped so.

Zach started toward the door, and John Henry whimpered. Lily looked at him in alarm. She picked him up, being as careful as if he were a carton of eggs.

"See, I told you I'd get the hang of it."

John Henry decided to allow her one more moment of triumph. Then he opened his mouth and proved her wrong.

Dear Reader,

There's so much excitement going on this month that I hardly know where to begin. First of all, you've no doubt noticed that instead of the four Silhouette Intimate Moments novels you usually see, this month there are six. That increase—an increase you'll see every month from now on—is a direct result of your enthusiasm for this line, an enthusiasm you've demonstrated by your support right where it counts: at the bookstore or by your membership in our reader service. So from me—and all our authors—to you, *thank you!* And here's to the future, a future filled with more great reading here at Silhouette Intimate Moments.

And speaking of great reading, how about this month's author lineup? Heather Graham Pozzessere, Barbara Faith, Linda Turner, Rachel Lee and Peggy Webb, making her Intimate Moments debut. And I haven't even mentioned Linda Howard yet, but she's here, too, with *Mackenzie's Mission,* one of the most-requested books of all time. For all of you who asked, for all of you who've waited as eagerly as I have, here is Joe "Breed" Mackenzie's story. This is a man to die for (though not literally, of course), to sigh for, cry for and—since he's a pilot—fly for. And he's all yours as of now, so don't let him pass you by. And in honor of our increase to six books, and because Joe and some of the other heroes I have in store for you are so special, we've decided to inaugurate a special program as part of the line: American Heroes. Every month one especially strong and sexy hero is going to be highlighted for you within the line, and believe me, you won't want to miss his story!

Finally, I hope you've noticed our bold new cover design. We think it captures the sense of excitement that has always been the hallmark of Silhouette Intimate Moments, and I hope you do, too.

In the months to come, expect only the best from us. With authors like Kathleen Eagle, Emilie Richards, Dallas Schulze and Kathleen Korbel coming your way, how can the future be anything but bright?

Leslie Wainger
Senior Editor and Editorial Coordinator

13
ROYAL STREET

Peggy Webb

Silhouette®
INTIMATE MOMENTS®

Published by Silhouette Books New York

America's Publisher of Contemporary Romance

This book is for my niece, Laura Fortune,
on her graduation from high school

SILHOUETTE BOOKS
300 East 42nd St., New York, N.Y. 10017

13 ROYAL STREET

Copyright © 1992 by Peggy Webb

ISBN: 0-373-07447-6

First Silhouette Books printing September 1992

All the characters in this book have no existence
outside the imagination of the author and have
no relation whatsoever to anyone bearing the same
name or names. They are not even distantly
inspired by any individual known or unknown
to the author, and all incidents are pure invention.

Printed in the U.S.A.

Books by Peggy Webb

Silhouette Intimate Moments

13 Royal Street #447

Silhouette Romance

When Joanna Smiles #645
A Gift for Tenderness #681
Harvey's Missing #712
Venus de Molly #735
Tiger Lady #785
Beloved Stranger #824
Angel at Large #867

Silhouette Books

Silhouette Christmas Stories 1991
"I Heard the Rabbits Singing"

PEGGY WEBB

grew up in a large northeastern Mississippi family in which the Southern tradition of storytelling was elevated to an art. "In our family there was always a romance or a divorce or a scandal going on," she says, "and always someone willing to tell it. By the time I was thirteen, I knew I would be a writer."

Over the years Peggy has raised her two children—and twenty-five dogs. "Any old stray is welcome," she acknowledges. "My house is known as Dog Heaven." Recently her penchant for trying new things led her to take karate lessons. Although she was the oldest person in her class and one of only two women, she now has a blue belt in Tansai Karate. Her karate hobby came to a halt, though, when wrens built a nest in her punching bag. "I decided to take up bird-watching," says Peggy.

Acknowledgments

Art is never created in a vacuum. There are always special people, places and events that influence a work. And so it was with *13 Royal Street*.

I want to thank all the people who helped bring this novel to life. Some of you provided information, some inspiration, some emotional support, and some provided all three.

My particular thanks to my daughter, Misty Webb Griffith, who has been my confidante, my sounding board and my major source of encouragement since the beginning of my career. It was Misty who first heard my idea for this book and who encouraged me to write it. She was also tireless in supplying legal information, although I'm not certain I understood all of it. If I've made any mistakes in presenting the legal aspects of this book, they are entirely my own.

To my son, Trey, who is equally supportive and proud of his mother, I express gratitude for information on weapons . . . and for the wonderful bear hugs that keep me going.

And to my agent, Eileen Fallon, whose gentle persuasion and encouragement prompted me (finally!) to try this book, I say, thank you.

Also, thanks to Caroline Willis at Deposit Guaranty National Bank, Tupelo, Mississippi; Jacqueline Estes, Attorney at Law, Tupelo; Dennis Voge, Attorney at Law, Tupelo; Johnny Ashe, Tupelo Police Department; Catholic Charities, Inc., adoption agency, Jackson, Mississippi; and finally my editors at Silhouette Books, Tara and Leslie, who believe in me enough to let me give voices to a dog and a baby.

Thank you, my dear and special friends.

Chapter 1

Bentley hated her.

The thought of going into her sister's apartment after a hard day's work and facing that pampered pooch who thought he was people was almost enough to make Lily turn around and go back inside her own cool, peaceful apartment. But Rose had called to say she needed her. And so Lily left her elegant upstairs apartment and started across the courtyard to her sister's apartment.

She paused in the courtyard, inhaling the mingled scents of gardenia and wisteria, drinking deeply of the sweet fragrance that was so typical of New Orleans in the summertime. Although the French Quarter, with its strange mixture of elegance and gaudiness, was right outside the wrought-iron gates, the flower-bedecked courtyard gave the impression that the apartments within its confines were entirely isolated from the rest of the world.

Sometimes Lily felt as if she, too, were entirely isolated from the world. Not always, but sometimes. Days like today, for instance. It wasn't that anything had gone wrong.

On the contrary, her day at the bank had been unusually successful and productive. The market had rallied and some investments she had made proved to be brilliant, even if she did say so herself. Her clients had said so, too. "Lily," one had told her, "you're positively brilliant. But then, you always did have so much potential." Maggie Carouthers had said that. Maggie was an old friend of Lily's Aunt Bonnie Kathleen. Aunt Bonnie Kathleen, who had three degrees and was therefore considered wise and knowing by the family, had always said, "Lily has so much potential. She'll go places. You mark my words."

Everybody in the family had marked her words, and they had all watched as Lily had lived up to her potential. She was the twin who won the National Merit Award and who was on the debate team and who was named Most Likely to Succeed. She was the one who had gotten the best job.

No, it wasn't her work that had bothered her today. It was the coffee breaks that almost did her in. Two of the bank tellers were talking about vacation cruises with their husbands, and one of the secretaries from the Loans Department told everybody she was pregnant. She'd even paraded around the lounge in her first maternity outfit.

Not that Lily minded maternity outfits or even babies. She didn't mind vacation cruises, either. With a few husbands she could take exception, but still... All she had wanted today was coffee. Instead, she got several recitals of marital bliss.

Marital bliss had eluded her. In fact, bliss of any kind with the male of the species had eluded her. Even her sister's dog, who was stridently male, took exception to her. She didn't know why she could never sustain a successful relationship with anything male. Maybe it was because she'd always had so much potential.

Lily sighed. She took a deep breath, one designed to fortify her for the confrontation with her sister's dog, then crossed the courtyard and punched her sister's buzzer.

"Come in," Rose called. "The door's open."

That was just like Rose, to keep her door unlocked. Lily's sister went around in a merry fog, trusting guardian angels and her husband, George, to take care of her.

Shaking her head in fond dismay, Lily went inside. Bentley was waiting for her behind the door, growling.

"Don't you dare bite me, you spoiled brat." Keeping one eye on him, Lily closed the door, expecting at any moment to have him attack her legs. That's the way Bentley always greeted her, with a feint to her legs, then a vicious snarl. Sometimes he scored with a small nip, but usually she was too quick for him.

"Pet him, Lily." Rose came from the bedroom, her purple caftan and her scent of lemon verbena floating around her.

"Are you out of your mind?" Lily hung the jacket of her business suit on the hall tree and smoothed down her skirt. "He's ruined more stockings than I care to think about. I wouldn't touch him with a ten-foot pole."

"I'm afraid you're going to have to. George and I are going to Spain. It's some exchange program between Loyola and the University of Madrid."

"How long will you be gone?" Lily's jacket was askew, so she reached over and rehung it.

"He's been asked to conduct a three-week seminar."

"That's great, Rose." Lily smoothed one last fold in her jacket, then turned to face her sister. She had the eerie sensation of looking into a mirror. No matter how often she came face-to-face with her twin, it was always the same. Rose's green eyes, heart-shaped face and ivory skin were the exact duplicate of her own. It was the hair that was different. Rose wore her long red hair loose and curling around her face. Lily's hair was tamed into submission by many hairpins and a clever French twist.

Lily felt her nape for stray curls. Satisfied that there were none, she continued. "The change will do both of you good."

"A change *will* be nice," Rose agreed. "Especially for George." She forgot she was keeping her sister standing in the hall as she launched into her favorite subject, her beloved husband. "I worry about him, cooped up in that classroom with air-conditioning that never works right, always worrying over his students, running back and forth to that chemistry lab at night. He never has time to exercise. He doesn't eat right, either—all that greasy fast food."

"Maybe you can get him on a good health routine in Spain. And I'll be glad to take care of everything while you're gone. Except Bentley." Lily eyed the culprit, who was skulking behind the coat tree in the hallway, awaiting his moment to strike. "I'm not keeping that dog."

Rose merely smiled and led the way into the den. She knew her sister. Lily liked for everybody to think she was all business, but she was an old softie deep down where it counted. Rose sat in her favorite chair with the needlepoint cushion and folded her hands on her lap.

Lily shoved aside a fringed shawl and one pink ballerina slipper, and sat on the sofa. Bentley sidled up to her, heisted one leg and wet the rug just on general principles.

"Good grief, Rose. Why don't you keep that mutt outside?" Lily glanced around the cluttered den for something to use to wipe up the puddle.

"I don't want him to get heatstroke." Rose lifted a towel, still damp from her bath, off a leather footstool and tossed it to her sister. "Here. Use this. A little tiddle never hurt anything. He's just upset. He'll settle down when the baby comes."

"Have you heard from Mrs. McGruder at the adoption agency?" Lily asked, scrubbing the rug.

"Yes. About a month ago. She's cautiously optimistic. I just know a baby will turn up soon."

"I hope so, Rose." Lily cast a critical eye at her sister to see if she showed the strain of waiting. Rose and George had been trying to adopt a baby for two years. Ever optimistic, Rose already had the nursery decorated. Though she had been disappointed time and again, she was still as cheerful and smiling as if she expected Christmas to be around every corner.

Satisfied, Lily leaned back on the sofa. "A baby will make your life complete, Rose."

"And what about yours?"

"I have a beautiful apartment, a full social calendar and a wonderful job at Belle Chasse Bank. What more do I need?"

"A man would be nice."

"You're not going to start that again."

"I just keep thinking you'll find somebody wonderful and get married again."

"Once was enough."

"I never did understand what went wrong between you and Howard. I always thought he was such a nice man."

"He *was* a nice man—handsome and clean and neat and polite. Things just didn't work out between us. That's all." Howard Blassingame had accused Lily of having an adding machine instead of a heart. He had said making love with her was like sleeping with the whole damned bank. He'd even said she was not capable of turning off her computer mind long enough to be a flesh-and-blood woman. But Lily had never told Rose any of that, and never would. Some things hurt too much to tell, even to a twin sister.

"I always suspected it had something to do with your job." Rose warmed to the subject. "You *do* spend a lot of time working. Maybe if you occasionally took more time off and dated some nice men—"

"Ha! I haven't dated a nice man since Ricky Simmons took me to the sandpile in his backyard. I was three years old at the time."

"Lily, you're impossible." Rose held her sides, laughing, then she sobered, remembering Lily's long history of failures with men, going all the way back to their high school prom. Her prom date had skipped out on her midway through the dance with an old girlfriend, leaving Lily with a wilted corsage and no ride home. As Lily got older, her problems with men got worse. Rose was getting worried. She wanted her sister to be as happily married as she and George were.

"What about that nice man you met at the Jazz Festival, that tax consultant? George and I thought he was very pleasant, and he was quite taken with you."

"Stop." Lily held up her hand. "I'm not about to be pulled into any more of your matchmaking schemes."

"It's been five years since your divorce, Lily. I've tried to keep my mouth shut—"

"Not only have you *not* kept silent, you've dragged every Tom, Dick and Harry in New Orleans to my doorstep, hoping I'll fall in love. I wouldn't be surprised if you haven't resorted to a gris-gris bag under my bed."

"The love potion is under mine—but it has your name on it."

The sisters laughed together as they always did. The discussion of Lily's failed marriage was not an argument between them: it was a ritual. Every so often Rose felt compelled to steer her sister toward the waters of marital bliss, and just as often, Lily refused to be steered. Her life was peaceful and uncomplicated, just the way she liked it. Glad that the ritual argument about marriage was behind them for a while, Lily relaxed.

"Tell me what you want me to do while you're gone."

"Sign these." Rose retrieved some rumpled legal papers from underneath the telephone and handed them to Lily. "I'm in the process of selling that little piece of property Aunt Bonnie Kathleen left me. This will give you power of attorney in case my real-estate agent completes the sale while

I'm gone. Also, keep up with the mail—and keep Bentley.... Now, Lily, get that look off your face. I'm not going to put this precious little fellow in a kennel. He'd go into a decline.''

"He'll chew up the legs on my antiques and shred all my cushions just for spite. He hates me."

"He does not. Look at those soulful eyes. He loves his Aunt Lily, don't you, pookums?" Rose made kissing noises toward her dog.

Ignoring her, Bentley ripped the cover off a new issue of *Vanity Fair*.

"See, what did I tell you? He's already practicing."

"Maybe I have indulged him a little...and your apartment is much more stylish than mine." Rose chewed her bottom lip. Suddenly she smiled. "I know. You can move in with him. Why didn't I think of that before? It's just across the courtyard, and the change will do you good."

Lily failed to see how moving into an apartment that looked like a cross between a fun house at the carnival and a garage sale about to happen would do her any good, but she didn't tell Rose so.

"All right, Rose. I'll do it." She reached for her purse, muttering to herself. "After all these years, you'd think I'd know better." Keeping a sharp eye on Bentley, she stood up. "When are you leaving?"

"The day after tomorrow. Three whole blissful weeks with George in Spain. It will be heaven."

"Anywhere without Bentley would be heaven."

Rose laughed and walked with Lily to the front door. Lily hugged her sister, slung her jacket over one shoulder and stepped into the courtyard.

The gutsy strains of jazz drifted down Royal Street. New Orleans always sounded as if it was on the verge of a party. That's one of the things Lily loved about the city, that and its continental flavor. Her apartment building, like most of the others in the French Quarter, had a delicately scrolled, wrought-iron balcony that overlooked the courtyard and part of the street.

That's where she headed, straight up the stairs to her second-floor balcony. Although she didn't often loll around on her balcony, today she felt the need to sort of drift along in the summer air.

She leaned over the balcony. Below her, the courtyard was a riot of scent and color and sunshine. It had been just such a day when Howard had left her, a beautiful sunny day not meant for harsh words and angry recriminations.

Lily felt a twinge of irritation. She hadn't thought about Howard in a long time, and she wished Rose hadn't let that particular skeleton out of the closet. Howard's parting words echoed in her mind. *You don't know how to be a woman, Lily. No man wants to go to bed with a damned bank.*

She pushed Howard Blassingame from her thoughts. He was completely out of her life. After the divorce, she'd even taken her maiden name back—legally. She was Lily Cooper now. She would always be Lily Cooper. The past was finished. What she had to do now was plan for the future— and that included the indomitable Bentley.

Lily went inside and made herself a fortifying mint julep.

Bentley was every bit as bad as Lily had predicted he would be. For three days after Rose and George departed, she endured snarls, sulks and outright temper tantrums. He turned over his water dish at every opportunity, deliberately mutilated her favorite pair of bedroom slippers and submitted to the leash and his afternoon walks only under threat of being sent to a kennel.

Lily had come to dread five o'clock.

As she let herself into Rose's apartment, she decided the only good thing to come of her experience was that she had learned she was not cut out to be a mother, even if Bentley was only a dog. She picked her way through the day's clutter—a shredded newspaper, George's baseball cap minus its visor and one of Rose's ballerina slippers.

She hung her jacket on the hall coat tree, then bent down and started picking up the mess.

"Why don't you play with that nice new rubber ball I bought instead of tearing up the place every day?" There was no reply, and she felt rather foolish when she discovered that she'd cocked her head, listening for one. "I'm getting as crazy as Rose, thinking you're human." She stood up and dumped the torn newspaper into the wastebasket, then she got his leash. "Time for your walk, Bentley." She attempted a whistle, but it came out a squeak. She never could whistle.

Hiding the leash behind her back, she walked into the den. "I know you're in here somewhere, Bentley." She looked behind the sofa. "You might as well quit sulking and come on out."

The telephone interrupted her quest for Bentley.

"Collect from Rose Taylor," the operator said. "Will you accept the call?"

"Yes." The word was barely out of Lily's mouth before she heard Rose burst into tears. "Rose...what's wrong?" Rose sobbed louder. *"Rose. What's happened?"*

"George." Rose choked out her husband's name, then went into a fresh gale of weeping.

"Is he sick? Hurt? Rose...stop crying, honey, and tell me what's wrong."

"I'm at the hospital, Lily." Rose sniffed loudly. "It's George's gallbladder. I kept telling him all that greasy food was bad for him."

"Take it easy, Rose. Tell me what's happened, step by step."

Rose launched into a tearful recital of George's gallbladder attack and the mad rush to the hospital. "He has to have surgery, Lily."

Her sister never had been brave in the face of emergencies. Lily would have to take charge, just as she always did. She made some quick calculations. She could call her secretary at home and arrange for all her business appointments to be rescheduled.

"I'll book the next flight and come over, Rose. Don't you worry."

"There's no need for you to come." Rose's voice took on a new firmness. Lily could almost see her squaring her shoulders and plucking up her sagging courage. "We'll be fine. The doctors here are excellent, and George is in good spirits. You just stay home and take care of Bentley."

"Are you sure, Rose?"

"Yes. But, Lily... there is one thing you can do for me. Call Zach."

Lily's hand suddenly tightened on the telephone. Zach Taylor was the last man in the world she wanted to call. What had happened between them more than four years ago was as vivid as if it had been only four days. She still burned with rage and shame at the memory.

"Lily... are you still there?"

"Yes." Lily blocked out the memories and turned back to the matter at hand. "Of course, Zach will need to know about his brother. Give me the number there at the hospital." She grabbed a pen off the telephone stand and searched in vain for a pad. How like Rose not to keep a writing pad beside the telephone. Finally, Lily flipped open the telephone book and wrote on the corner of the area-codes page.

With a final caution to Rose not to worry, Lily cradled the receiver and stared into space. Her brother-in-law would be fine; she felt certain of that. But as insurance, she decided to call the family doctor, who was also a good friend. He wouldn't mind consulting with George's doctor in Madrid just to make certain George was getting the best of care.

After that was done, Lily faced the problem of Zach Taylor.

She'd never known two brothers as different as Zach and George. Granted, they looked alike. Or used to, if photographs didn't lie. George was a big, strapping, black-eyed, black-haired man who, in his heyday, had been head-turningly, heart-pumpingly handsome. He still was, except that he was beginning to lose his hair and go a little to pot. Not that she would ever tell Rose such a thing, of course. Rose still thought George was God's gift to women.

No, it wasn't in looks that Zach and George were different. It was in reputation. Zach was a rake and a scoundrel. Even worse, he made no apologies for his wicked ways. In fact, he seemed to take delight in flaunting them. His showplace house in the Garden District was the scene of such debauchery and decadence that decent people never spoke of him except in whispers and behind closed doors.

What was more, everybody knew that he supported his life-style with family money. Oil. The Taylor family rigs had done more offshore drilling than any other oil company in the South. When George Taylor, Sr., and his wife had died in a plane crash, their vast estate had passed to their children.

George had quietly invested his share of the family fortune and gone on with his chosen career, teaching chemistry at Loyola. But Zach was a wealthy bum. He had ditched his law practice years ago. His ambition in life seemed to be drinking and debauchery.

And yet Rose loved and respected Zach. In fact, she was fiercely protective of him. "He has his reasons for living the way he does," Rose would say.

"What are they?" Lily would ask.

"I don't know," Rose would reply. "But George says they are good ones and we must not question him."

If George told Rose the moon was made of cheese, she'd believe him. Lily sighed. She guessed she would never understand people.

Postponing the call wouldn't make it any more pleasant. She thumbed through Rose's address book, looking for Zach's name. Her fingers shook only slightly when she found the listing and dialed his number. She was proud of herself.

She let the phone ring eight times, and she was glad when Zach didn't answer.

"Coward," she said to herself when she hung up. For the moment, she was spared speaking to the man she despised.

Lily picked up Bentley's leash once more and made a halfhearted effort to find him. But her mind wasn't on walking the dog. It had suddenly drifted backward in time, back to a sultry night four years earlier, a night of pulsing jazz and flashing colors and bright, hot passion, a night before she'd ever known of the existence of a man named Zach Taylor.

It had been Mardi Gras, a February night so uncommonly hot that all the world seemed to have gone mad. Lily walked to the window and leaned her head against the windowpane, remembering....

It had been so hot that night. So hot. Lily had been sitting at her desk, studying the latest performance of blue-chip stocks.

Sweat trickled down the side of her face and into the collar of her white blouse. She stood up and opened the French doors, hoping to catch a night breeze. Not a breath of air stirred.

She went into her kitchen and made a tall glass of lemonade. Holding the cool, iced glass against the side of her face, she returned to her study. Sounds of revelry drifted through the open French doors. Walking onto her balcony, she leaned against the railing. She could hear the laughter of the crowds and the low, pulsing beat of jazz as the Mardi Gras floats swept through the city, trailing hordes of gaily costumed partygoers in their wake.

"A bit of madness," she said, her voice barely heard above the din. Then without warning, she heard another voice. Howard's voice, echoing from her past.

You don't know how to be a woman.

She closed her eyes against the memories. Dear Lord in heaven. It had been a year since her divorce, a year to forget, a year to get over the pain.

You don't know how to be a woman.

His words taunted her, mocked her, accused her.

She opened her eyes and took a long drink of lemonade. It didn't help. She felt restless, discontent.

"Was he right?" she whispered.

Her only answer was the distant sound of laughter and the mesmerizing beat of the music. A nameless fear grew in Lily until it exploded. Suddenly she flung her glass of lemonade over the balcony. It shattered with a faint tinkle against the cobblestones of the courtyard.

"I'll show that scoundrel. I'll prove him wrong."

She stalked into her apartment, leaving a trail of clothes and hairpins all the way from the French doors to her bathroom. She took a long, hot shower, halfway hoping the water would clear the madness from her mind. It didn't. Intense need drove her—need and a fear that had no name.

With water still beading her skin, she rummaged in her vanity until she found what she was looking for—a bottle of expensive French perfume, a Christmas gift from Rose. Lily ripped off the cap and slathered herself with fragrance. The scent of gardenias wafted around her. How like Rose to choose something so blatantly feminine.

Out of habit, Lily gathered her long hair and started twisting it into a knot. Then, feeling reckless, she shook the heavy mass loose. Tonight was not the time for convention; tonight was the time for fantasy.

It took her fifteen minutes to find something suitable for a costume in her closet, but after she was dressed, she was satisfied. She had found a swath of silk, silvery blue and as sheer as moonbeams. Another gift from Rose.

With the silk knotted on one shoulder and belted by a length of gold cord, Lily had fashioned a Grecian costume. Never had she bared so much flesh to the public. She felt naked. Instinctively she reached for her shawl.

"No." She pulled her hand back. "This is a party, not a wake."

She took one last look at herself, then she locked her apartment and joined the Mardi Gras revelers. The crowd surged around her when she stepped into the street, bearing her all the way from Royal to Bourbon street.

"Heeey. Ain't you a doll?" A very tall red devil with whiskey on his breath leered at her. "Where you been hidin', honey?"

Her courage wavered and she almost turned and went back to her apartment. But she pressed on. Ignoring him, she ducked into the open doorway of a small, smoke-filled bar. The front end of a zebra handed her a glass of wine and the back end handed her a sequined and feathered mask.

"Put this on. You need it more than I do." The voice was muffled under layers of black-and-white striped canvas.

"Thanks." Lily took the mask, fastened it in place and searched the crowded room for a place to go. Everywhere she looked there were masses of people, clowns with red, bulbous noses and yarn hair, queens with sequined crowns and feather boas, tarts in black garters and backless red heels, pirates with long swords and drooping mustaches. There was even a huge Humpty Dumpty, sitting on three chairs shoved together and flirting with a pink rabbit.

Suddenly she heard a voice behind her, a deep voice rich with the subtle shadings and musical timbre of the South.

"Wine is far too common for a goddess."

Lily felt the wineglass being lifted from her hand. She tried to turn around, but the press of the crowd prevented her.

"You must be Aphrodite," the voice continued, "the goddess of love."

"I am, and you have taken my wine."

"You deserve champagne and soft music and candle-light." Large hands bracketed her bare shoulders and a large, muscular body pressed against her back. The stranger's warm breath caressed the side of her cheek as he leaned closer, speaking in that mesmerizing musical voice. "Come with me, Aphrodite."

Another time, another place, she might have been cautious. But tonight was Mardi Gras, and the stranger was giving her something she needed, a sense of her own sexuality.

"Who are you?"

"Your rescuer."

The stranger whisked her through the crowd and back onto Bourbon Street. She saw him, then, for the first time. He was dressed in black opera clothes and a long cape that was solid black except for a swath of red satin lining the upturned collar. The upper half of his face was covered by a black silk mask.

At first Lily thought the mask was entirely black, and then she noticed the small spot of glitter as her self-proclaimed rescuer bent closer. A single diamond, shaped like a teardrop, rested on his left cheek. It made him look so sad that sympathy rose within her.

"Who are you?" she asked again. Her voice was no more than a whisper, for whispering seemed the proper respect to pay to this strangely powerful, strangely sad man.

"Who do you want me to be?"

Who *did* she want him to be? A nice, ordinary man with an ordinary name? Someone she could know after Mardi Gras was over? Someone she could date? Someone else who would prove that women with potential couldn't hold a man? No, she decided. This was not the time for reality and caution—this was the time for magic.

She reached out and ran her fingertips over his lips. They were beautifully sculpted and unexpectedly sensual.

"You look like the Phantom of the Opera."

"I admit the passion—and the madness."

Her fingertips wandered up his face and touched the diamond on his cheek.

"You also look sad."

"This is not a night for sadness."

"No." Her hand lingered on the sparkling teardrop. "This is a night for revelry." She felt bold and reckless. "Carry me to a place of music and champagne. I want to dance all night."

"Well said." He covered her hand, pressing it so hard, the diamond bit into her soft flesh. "Come. Let's revel."

Without waiting for her consent, he circled her waist with one arm and beckoned with the other. An open horse-drawn carriage materialized. He lifted her onto the seat, then climbed in beside her. With one muscular arm draped over her shoulder, he told the driver their destination, naming a ritzy bar Lily knew.

Some of the tension eased from her and she leaned back. In spite of setting out to prove she was a woman, she had no intention of ending up in trouble. As long as she stayed in the Mardi Gras crowd, she was safe.

As the carriage made its slow progress through the packed streets, the man leaned close to her.

"We will dance, my love goddess." Through the holes in the mask, she could see the dark glitter of his eyes. They were mesmerizing. "I will hold you close enough to feel the music of your body." With one hand, he traced the plunging neckline of her gown, sending shivers along her skin. "Such a beautiful body."

She felt the powerful pull of his passion, but she didn't want to give in too easily. Part of proving herself a woman was proving herself desirable enough to be pursued.

"I'm not yours."

''Before the night is over, you will be.''

A breeze drifted in from the Mississippi River and Lily shivered. But it was not the chill; it was from the spell of sensuality the stranger was casting over her.

The carriage stopped at a small, elegant bar beside the river. Inside, the music was soft and bluesy, the lights were low and the champagne was cold.

They sat at a corner table, drinking champagne until the enchantment of the music pulled them onto the dance floor. He held her close.

''We were made for each other,'' he whispered.

''We do fit well.'' Heady with power, she snuggled closer. Being a woman with this man was so *easy.*

''Your hair is like fire, and you smell of summer flowers.'' He pressed his face into her hair and inhaled deeply. ''Does someone else tell you those things?''

''No.''

''I'm glad.'' He ran his lips down the side of her cheek. ''Tonight, I want you all to myself.''

They stayed in the bar for hours, alternately dancing and drinking champagne, speaking in rhymes and riddles and telling each other nothing.

Unexpectedly, the conversation took a different turn. They were on the dance floor, warm with champagne and the heat of each other's bodies. Suddenly he removed her mask and cupped her face.

''Tell me your name.''

''Lily.''

''Just Lily?'' His fingers traced her cheeks, her jaw, her mouth.

''Cooper, now.''

Before she knew what was happening, she was telling this unexpectedly compelling man all about Howard and her divorce. He swayed with her on the dance floor, holding her close, urging her with soft caresses and gentle murmurs to confide in him. She later figured it had to be the champagne talking, for she would never have revealed so much of herself, especially to a man she didn't even know.

"He's a fool," the man said after her confession. Pressing his lips against the side of her cheek, he whispered, "An absolute fool to throw away such a treasure."

Her head was beginning to spin from the heat and the champagne. She peered at her dance partner through blurred vision.

"Who *are* you?"

"If a law degree and family money can create respectability, I'm a respectable man."

She swayed a little. He lifted her into his arms and carried her off the dance floor. "Too much champagne, my sweet?"

Holding her cuddled against his chest, he summoned the waiter to call a cab.

"Where do you live, Lily Cooper?"

"I don't want to go home. I want . . ." Her thoughts were muddled. She frowned, trying to remember what she wanted.

Her dark-eyed stranger smiled. "And what is it you want?"

"To be a woman," she whispered.

He carried her to an elegant suite of rooms at the grand old Monteleone. Candlelight made shadows on the dark carpet and danced on the white silk curtains that draped the bed. It was into that gleaming lair of silk that he carried her. Her hair fanned across the pillows, and her bodice rose and fell with the force of her breathing.

"You want to be a woman, do you?"

They were the first words he had spoken since they left the bar.

"Yes." Her whisper echoed around the large room.

"Do you know what you're asking?"

"I do. But first . . ." She reached for his mask. "Let me see who you are."

The diamond felt cold under her fingertips. Suddenly he caught her hands.

"Not yet. Allow me one more blessed moment of anonymity."

She felt his eyes burning into hers as he gazed down at her. Her breath came in shallow pants.

"Who are you?" she whispered.

"I am the man who is going to make you feel like a woman." His voice caressed her, seduced her and held her captive. "But not in the way you think." He smiled then, a sweet, sad curving of his lips. "If you ever know me completely, your senses will not be blunted by too much champagne."

He tore aside his mask and cast it onto the nightstand. She sucked in her breath. His was a face that would cause swooning and fainting, riots and wars. It was both uncommonly handsome and uncommonly fierce. In awe, she traced his high cheekbones, the flat planes of his cheeks, the full curve of his lips.

"You have a scar." She touched the tiny, Z-shaped scar at the top of his cheekbone, just under his left eye.

"A souvenir from my enemies."

"Do you have enemies?"

"Shh . . ." He put a hand over her lips. "Tonight there is no one on earth except you and me. No one and nothing—neither the pain of the past nor the pain of the future." He became brooding and still, and it was almost as if he'd left her. His eyes glittered so terribly, she drew a long, trembling breath, afraid to speak.

"No one. . . ." he whispered, and then his eyes focused on her. "I've frightened you." The terrible fierceness left his face, his eyes, and he gently touched her cheek. "We're all alone in this room, Lily, all alone with our need and each other."

"Yes," she said. "I need you."

He rose from the bed and unfastened his cape. It fell like a dark omen onto the carpet. Next he cast aside his jacket and loosened the top buttons on his white shirt.

Then, fully clothed, he lay down beside her and took her into his arms. The fierce man with the haunted eyes she had glimpsed so briefly disappeared, and in his place was a debonair Mardi Gras reveler. Lulled by champagne, the deep, hot magic of the night and the touch of his hands upon her body, she would gladly have embraced the devil.

"Kiss me, Lily. Kiss me with your heart, your soul."

She gave herself to him completely, not once thinking his request unusual or herself incapable of fulfilling it.

The kiss was only the beginning. He made love to her with his eyes, his hands, his lips. Ever so slowly, he seduced her, peeling away the layers of silk until she lay naked upon his bed.

His touch was all over her, and everywhere he touched, she burned. Still, he didn't remove his clothing. And yet...she felt more loved than she ever had, more cherished, more desirable, and much, much more a woman.

When dawn tinged the sky pink, she lay in his arms languorous and satisfied. He smiled down at her.

"Do you feel like a woman now, my Lily?"

"Yes. But you never—"

"Shh..." He interrupted, putting one finger over her lips. "Perhaps there will be another time for us...." Pausing, he gazed through the window across the room. "Perhaps we will meet again under very different circumstances." Turning his attention back to her, he tenderly brushed her hair back from her forehead. "If there is any justice in this world, any hope, someday I'll be free of this darkness that consumes me. Someday I will..."

She wanted to hear all he was saying, but lulled by champagne and love and the rich sound of his voice, she fell asleep in his arms.

When she awoke, he was gone. Sunlight fell across the tangled sheets and gilded her bare legs. Her Aphrodite costume lay in a silken heap on the floor.

There was no sign of her masked lover, no forgotten cape, no pearl shirt button, no indention upon his pillow. No sign at all save one—the mask with its single diamond teardrop....

Chapter 2

She remembered as if it had been only yesterday. With her face still pressed against the windowpane, Lily gazed out into the courtyard. She still burned at the memory, burned with shame at her champagne-induced madness and burned with the residual flames of passion at the memory. There, she had admitted it. Even after four years, the mere memory of Zach Taylor's hands upon her body set off minor fireworks along her nerve endings. She thanked a just God that Zach had been as scrupulous about avoiding her as she had about not seeing him. Denial that an evening and a subsequent rejection never happened might be a cowardly way, but it was the way she chose to deal with Zach Taylor. Being a woman of potential was burden enough, she didn't have to add heroics to the burden.

For four years she and Zach had managed to live very much apart, in spite of being cast by fate into the same family. But now... She sighed.

Something warm and fuzzy nudged her legs, bringing her out of her trance. Bentley. She bent over and absently patted his head.

"So you've finally decided to come out of hiding? Are you ready for your walk?"

He woofed twice, and she'd have sworn it sounded like a yes. She hooked the leash on to his collar and led him from the apartment. The sun was low in the sky, painting the streets with pink and gold. It was Lily's favorite time of day.

She walked with Bentley down Royal Street, giving him time to prance and sniff and lift his leg on the antique iron hitching posts outside Brennan's famous restaurant.

"If only the customers knew, Bentley. Have you no respect?"

Bentley's antics kept her mind occupied for a few moments, and then her memories intruded again....

After that strange and passionate Mardi Gras night, she had thought she'd never see her masked lover again. In fact, she hadn't really wanted to see him again except to return the mask. He had served his purpose and proved Howard wrong, and for that, she supposed she should feel grateful. But he was also a reminder of her total loss of control, and Lily didn't like to think of herself as anything except in charge.

For three weeks she tried to find out his identity so she could return the mask. When all efforts had failed, she put her phantom lover out of her mind and went on with her life.

Three months after Mardi Gras, she was standing in the rose garden of her parents' house, celebrating Rose's engagement to George Taylor, a man Rose had known only six weeks. She had fallen in love the way she did everything else, spontaneously. Caught up in her usual whirlwind, she waltzed blithely through a brief romance with a man she never mentioned by name, let alone brought home to introduce.

"I'm in love. I'm in love," Rose would say, spinning through Lily's apartment on her brief visits, hugging herself.

"Who is this mystery man?" Lily would ask.

"Mr. Wonderful. Mr. Marvelous. The man of my dreams."

Lily dismissed Rose's ravings as another of her impulses, until the day Rose suddenly announced her engagement.

And now here Lily was, holding a glass of champagne, making her way through the crowd to meet the man she would soon be calling brother-in-law.

"Excuse me," she said as she squeezed past a tall man.

"Certainly."

The familiar voice sent shivers dancing along the backs of her arms. She glanced up and froze. The masked stranger was smiling down at her, his eyes as incredibly black as she remembered, and his tiny, Z-shaped scar white in the sunlight. "It's you," Lily said, squeezing her glass so hard, she was afraid of breaking the stem.

"I beg your pardon?"

Lily was confused. There was no mistaking the man: he had the face, the voice, the body, even the scar of her masked lover. How could he not remember that night?

"I'm Lily Cooper." Holding out her hand, she watched his face for signs of recognition. For a moment she saw a brief flicker in his eyes, a bright flame of passion and memories and something else, something she couldn't quite define. Was it pain? Regret? She didn't have time to analyze, for the light was gone almost as quickly as it had come. His eyes became the unfathomable darkness of an ocean under siege by storm, and his face a careful, polite mask—without the teardrop diamond.

"Then you must be Rose's twin sister." The man took her hand and brought it up to his lips. His touch was cool, impersonal. The memory of his touch three months earlier washed over her, and Lily thought she might be losing her mind. But how could she be mistaken about a man who had stamped his imprint on her as clearly as if she had been branded?

"I'm Zach Taylor, George's brother. Rose told me she had a sister as beautiful as she is intelligent. She was right." He turned his face and a shaft of sunlight caught his scar—the same scar she had touched, caressed. She could still remember how it had felt, slightly ridged and altogether dangerous.

A flush of anger darkened Lily's cheeks. To have been spurned by Howard was bad enough, but to be denied by this man was beyond enduring.

"Did she also tell you that I have something that belongs to you?" she asked, knowing she was being completely irrational, but not caring. How could Rose possibly have told him? No one knew of that evening. Not even her twin. Still, the humiliation of denial hurt, hurt more than Lily would have imagined. And she felt the need to strike back.

Zach Taylor's eyes crinkled at the corners and his lips curved upward in a smile of unrelenting sensuality.

"Most beautiful women have something that belongs to me sooner or later."

"Damn you."

"Many women have."

The arrogant, womanizing bastard. Rage and a strange kind of pain blocked out Lily's self-control and common sense. Blindly, she set her champagne on the tray of a passing waiter.

"Is a diamond-studded black mask your calling card?"

"A mask? What an interesting idea. Perhaps I'll use one on my next foray into a lady's bedroom."

"Does honor mean nothing to you?"

"Nothing means anything to me except my family."

His words were a sharp reminder of what she had done. Not only had she made a scene in public—her sister's engagement party, of all places—but she had insulted her sister's future brother-in-law, her sister's *family*. She wished to be at the bank, in her apartment, in China—anyplace except where she was. She also wished for something to drink, but she had foolishly given away her champagne.

She spun away from him, her face hot and her color high.

"Miss Cooper..." His voice commanded her to turn around. "I believe I have something you need."

"I wouldn't need anything from you if you were the last man on earth."

"Take this." He pressed his own champagne glass into her hands. "It appears you are suffering from too much sun."

"On the contrary...I'm suffering from an overdose of men."

He had laughed, then patted her on the back and sent her on her way as if she were a stubborn and somewhat naughty child.

Her face still burned at the memory.

She tugged Bentley's leash, and the dog immediately let her know that she had tugged too hard. He sank onto his fat bottom in the middle of the sidewalk and refused to budge.

"Bentley, I have too much to do this evening to get into a fight with you."

She tugged once more. Bentley remained staunch.

"If you don't get up from there right this minute, I'm going to leave you and call the dog pound to pick you up."

The little devil rose from the sidewalk as if a tug-of-war had never entered his mind. As he trotted along, he looked up at her with such a hangdog expression, she had to laugh.

"You little con artist. No wonder Rose treats you like people."

Back at Rose's apartment, Lily renewed her efforts to call Zach. His line was busy. She fed Bentley and prepared her own meal, going into the den from time to time in order to call Zach.

His line stayed busy for three hours.

"He's communicating with his horde of women, no doubt. Or maybe he has one of them in the bedroom and doesn't want to be disturbed." The phone could be out of order, of course, but she wasn't about to give Zach the benefit of the doubt. No use getting generous hearted with him after four years of enmity.

Bentley woofed to let her know he was enjoying the conversation.

"Good grief, I'm going to be totally crazy before all this is over. Talking to myself... carrying on like some demented fool."

By the time ten o'clock came and she still had not been able to reach Zach by phone, she decided she'd have to do it in person. She cringed at the thought. Although Zach had been a part of the family, so to speak, for almost four years, she had avoided all contact with him. For a while after her marriage, Rose had tried to press the issue, throwing parties on various occasions and inviting both her sister and George's brother.

But Lily had refused to be manipulated. The first time she arrived at Rose's apartment and saw Zach there, she left immediately. After being caught off guard once, she did some simple sleuthing and found out what kind of car he drove—a black Corvette, as sleek and expensive and panther-like as its owner. She even found out his license plate number.

From that time on she never entered a building if Zach's car was parked outside. She'd missed a few ballets and concerts because of that car and its owner, but sanity and self-esteem had been worth any price.

Rose finally took the hint and stopped trying to force a friendship between Lily and Zach. Rose loved them both, and if they wanted to be enemies for reasons unknown to her, she could accept that.

Cursing the fate that made it necessary for her to go out into the night seeking Zach Taylor, Lily tucked Bentley into his doggie bed and left the apartment. A light rain had begun to fall two hours earlier, and the city was shrouded in mist.

Lily drove carefully. The streets, usually rowdy and crowded at this time of night, were practically deserted. Fog hung over the streetlights and swirled around the doorways. Neon shot dim reflections of blue and orange and green onto the rain-slickened sidewalks.

The somber mood of the city matched Lily's own. She was worried about Rose and George, and angry at Zach for being the kind of man who left his phone off the hook so he could cavort and carouse. Didn't he have any sense of responsibility?

She had no trouble finding Zach's house, even in the dead of night. It sprawled among huge, moss-hung oak trees and carefully tended flower gardens rampant with color, and it was as brightly lit as the face of a two-year-old on his first carousel ride.

"I should have known he'd be having a party."

Lily parked her car and took a moment to tuck her hair into its pins and her blouse into the waistband of her skirt. Then she got out and reached for the bell on Zach Taylor's front door. What she had to do was best done quickly.

The level of noise in his ballroom had reached epic proportions.

Zach Taylor lounged against an ornately carved mantel, a glass of champagne in his hands, and watched his party through hooded eyes. To the casual observer he looked bored and jaded. Only he and his butler knew that he'd nursed the same glass of champagne for three hours and that nothing in the room escaped his notice.

Throughout the evening, every woman at the party had cornered him, one by one. Most of them had merely batted their eyelashes and pouted their painted lips, but some of them had outright propositioned him. He had turned them all down, and now he was experiencing a moment of regret.

A wave of loneliness hit him as he lifted the glass to his lips. With people and noise and laughter swirling all around him, he felt more lonesome than he ever had. Seven years of isolation was a long time. Perhaps too long.

Best not to think about it, especially not now. He still had too much to do, too many enemies to find and destroy—if they didn't find him out and destroy him first. Sometimes when the nights got too long and his bed felt too empty, he longed for a woman to share his life with, a warm and compassionate companion. But a man in his position couldn't afford to become entangled with a woman. The companion he settled for was danger, and it was neither warm nor compassionate.

He scanned the room again, cataloging the petty intrigue taking place in his huge ballroom. The ringing of his doorbell cut through his concentration.

He was instantly alert. All his guests had arrived hours ago. His adrenaline began to flow and his muscles tightened under his dinner jacket. He didn't like the unexpected. It usually meant complications.

He caught his butler's eye and motioned him over.

"I'll get it, Sam. You tend to the guests."

"Right, boss." Sam knew that tending to the guests meant keeping them off guard and off balance with plenty of rich food and too much champagne. It meant getting tongues loose enough to tell secrets.

Zach set his glass on the mantel and sauntered from the room as if he had nothing more pressing to do than watch the rain from his front windows. Shadowed by a huge Grecian urn, he paused in his hallway to study his unexpected guest. She was standing in profile, her red hair clearly visible through the beveled glass in his front door.

Rose, he thought. But she and George were supposed to be in Spain. What the hell was going on?

Zach's footsteps echoed on the shiny parquet floor as he strode quickly down the hall and flung open the door.

Lily Cooper was standing on his front porch, slightly damp, obviously angry and totally desirable. Seeing her so unexpectedly took him aback. It was almost a replay of that day nearly four years ago when he had met his brother's fiancée. For a moment he had thought he was looking into the eyes of the woman he had taken to his bed. And then George had said, "This is Rose."

Now, taking a moment to recover, he studied Lily. Regret sliced him. In the past seven years, she had been the only woman who had come close to penetrating his armor, to making him forget his dangerous mission and the role he must play.

For one evening he had let his guard down, and she had almost succeeded in coming inside his heart, his soul. Even now, four years after that magic Mardi Gras night, he cursed the weakness that had sent him looking for someone to share his dreadful isolation, someone to take the edge off his gut-wrenching loneliness.

He brought his emotions quickly under control. He had left his Mardi Gras mask behind, but not the mask he wore daily, the mask of arrogant indifference. He had played the role so long, he sometimes wondered whether he had lost the man he used to be and whether he even knew the man he could be.

Silently cursing the fates that made the role necessary, especially with Lily, he clamped his hands on her shoulders and drew her into the hall. "Ahh, the untouchable Miss Cooper. Come in out of the rain, my dear."

He got the reaction he was hoping for.

"Take your hands off me." She twisted out of his grasp and stepped back as if he were a deadly virus and she feared contamination. "I'm not one of your playthings."

Memories stirred in the back of his mind, and he had a sudden vision of Lily in a silk-draped bed with her hair spread across the pillows. She had been vulnerable; he had been lonely.

Seeing her now with her hair damp and her chin thrust outward in defiance and bravado, he was seized with such remorse, he almost groaned aloud. He longed to smooth back her damp hair, to caress the tension from her stubborn jaw. Such dreams were not only vain, they were also foolish—and very dangerous.

He had to stop the dreams; he had to keep Lily at a distance.

"We can remedy that," he whispered as he bent over her hand.

He kissed her hand with practiced ease, holding her fingers as she started to pull away. After a couple of seconds, he released her and smiled at her fury.

"How dare you manhandle me! You don't deserve to be told about George."

In a flash, he saw his sister lying in a pool of blood. Fear grabbed his gut. The thing he most feared had happened. He had been found out. His cover was blown. And now the same people he had sought to put behind bars were getting their revenge on him—through his brother. In his hell-bent quest to avenge the death of his sister, he had sacrificed his brother.

Zach caught Lily's shoulders again and held her tightly. A muscle twitched in his tightened jaw. "What about my brother?"

His fierce expression would have frightened a timid woman. Lily was at first startled by his intense reaction, and then she felt shame. Zach was, after all, a human being, and she hadn't shown him any sympathy. He probably loved his brother as much as a man of his kind was capable of loving. No, she thought. That wasn't fair, either. Who was she to judge?

"I'm sorry," she whispered.

His deeply tanned skin turned a pale gold, and his eyes glittered so brightly, Lily could hardly look into them.

"What has happened to my brother?"

"He's all right. It's just his gallbladder. He's fine."

Zach's fingers bit into her flesh. He still looked like a man on the edge. Lily began to talk, trying to say something, *anything* to change that look on his face.

"I tried to call you, but I couldn't get through. George had a sudden attack in Spain, and Rose brought him to the hospital. She says he's fine. The doctors are very good there, but I've called George's physician here just to be sure..." Her voice trailed off. Zach looked like a man chased by a thousand demons. "Oh, God, Zach, I forgot about your sister's accident. I—"

"Don't say another word."

The fear in his gut eased a little, but he had to make absolutely certain that George had suffered nothing more than a gallbladder attack. In his business, he couldn't afford to make mistakes.

The hallway was no place to talk. He practically dragged Lily into his study. Then he locked the door and flicked on the lights. Gripping her shoulders, he hauled her close enough so he could read her eyes.

"Tell me everything you know about George. Are you sure it's his gallbladder? Was anyone besides Rose around when it happened? Were they at the hotel or in a public place?"

"It's just his gallbladder," she said. There was something so deadly cold and dangerous about Zach Taylor that a shiver ran through her.

"Is that all you know?"

"Yes. That's all."

"Damn." He strode to his desk and picked up the phone. "Dead." He slammed it back onto the receiver, walked to his window and gazed out into the darkness.

His brother was hospitalized halfway across the world, and he had no way of knowing if it was from natural causes.

He was overreacting. Maybe seven years was too long to be haunted. *Haunted.* The word drifted through his mind, and with them the burden of a past too painful to remember. Focusing his attention on a small pinpoint of light in his darkened garden, Zach shut his mind to the past and slowly turned back to Lily. She was hugging her shoulders. Guilt slashed him.

"Did I hurt you?"

"Only my pride. I don't get manhandled every day of my life."

He admired her spirit. Even more surprising, he felt the stirrings of tenderness and regret. He crossed quickly to her and took her face gently in his hands.

"You are exquisite . . . and very desirable."

Lily tried to stop herself from trembling, but she did a damned poor job of it. *Stop,* her mind screamed. Once, long ago, he had touched her this way, with kindness and tenderness, and she had become his willing slave.

His eyes were bright in the centers as his hands moved across her face. She closed her eyes to shut him out, willing the anger she needed to combat her feelings.

"You are the most despicable man in New Orleans," she told him.

He released her, glad for an excuse to slip back into his mask. He had let it drop when he'd heard about George. He couldn't afford to get careless enough to let down his guard. He moved away from her and leaned back against his heavy walnut desk, watching her.

She walked to the door and rattled the knob. "Let me out of here."

"Not yet. Not until I get what I want."

"I've told you everything I know. What more do you want of me?"

Understanding. Compassion. Companionship. The words came unbidden to his mind. He must be tired. Never had the burden of his revenge weighed so heavily on his mind.

"You have nothing to fear, Lily Cooper."

"I'm not afraid."

He studied her intently, and she returned his scrutiny.

"No," he finally said, smiling. "I can see that."

Her breath caught high in her throat. *That poignant smile.* For a moment she glimpsed the haunting sadness that had made her heart ache for him so many years ago on a sultry night during Mardi Gras. A small part of her wanted to pull his dark, curly head down to her bosom and comfort him.

Some power beyond her control was at work. Zach was weaving his spell again, and she was dangerously close to believing in him.

"Tell me what you know about Emily," Zach said, quite suddenly.

And the spell was broken.

"I know only what Rose told me. That your sister was killed in a horrible accident."

"Nothing more?"

"Nothing."

Her answer seemed to satisfy Zach. He turned to his desk and picked up a pad and pencil. When he turned back to her, he was a different man, not tormented, not even dangerous. He was an ordinary man concerned about his brother.

"I'll need to know what hospital George is in and the name of his doctor, if you know."

Lily breathed a ragged sigh of relief, and then she told him all the details. After she finished, he crossed the room and took her hand.

"I'm genuinely sorry you had to come out into such a night. My butler will escort you home."

"No, thank you. I can take care of myself."

"See that you do, Lily Cooper. You're much too beautiful for the world to lose you."

He unlocked the door and held it open for her. She wasted no time in leaving. Her heels tapped a hurried rhythm on the wooden floor as she made her way to the front door.

She didn't say goodbye, and neither did he. She just kept on going.

False courage carried her all the way to her car. But once inside, she collapsed. Leaning her forehead against the steering wheel, she took a shaky breath.

Seeing Zach face-to-face had been even harder than she had imagined. For one thing, he still looked like God's gift to women. She should have known Zach Taylor would stay ruinously gorgeous. The unsuitable ones always did. It was a conspiracy. The scoundrels and rakes and bums managed to keep their mouth-watering good looks, while the dedicated professional men got paunches and bald heads.

"Dammit." She beat the steering wheel with the flat of her hand, then she sniffed. She *was not* going to be humiliated by this man again. She sniffed again, louder.

Then the tears started, first a small trickle and then a deluge. She didn't try to stop them; she just bent her head over the steering wheel and let them come.

Chapter 3

Zach watched Lily from the shadows.

Her car was parked under a streetlight, and while he couldn't see her clearly because of the rain, he could see well enough to guess that she was crying.

He balled his hands into fists. His vision blurred for a moment and he saw not Lily, but an endless procession of filth, the dregs of humanity. *Damn the bastards. Damn them all.*

Taking care not to give away his presence by touching the curtains or showing himself at the window, he stood in his darkened study and watched until Lily lifted her head from the steering wheel, started the car and pulled into the street.

She would be all right now. She was a woman of courage. Crying was not a weakness, it was a sign of strength, a sign of humanity. Only people who could feel deeply allowed themselves the cleansing power of tears.

Zach moved away from the window and sank into the chair behind his desk. Sounds of his party drifted through the locked door. No one would miss him.

He sat in the dark, brooding and cursing the fates. God, if only he could cry. If only he had the luxury of allowing his feelings to show. Just once.

But that was too dangerous. He'd dropped his guard four years ago when he'd taken Lily to his bed, and it had almost been his undoing. He couldn't allow that to happen again; he couldn't allow his feelings to show.

He slammed his fist down on the desk. He would get the bastards, every one of them. And when New Orleans was free of the drug-trafficking scum who had killed his sister, he would be free. He would have his revenge.

He pressed his hand against his forehead as memories rose to the surface of his mind.

"No," he groaned. "No."

But the memories kept coming....

Emily was laughing.

His sister had been only eighteen, and she had always laughed.

They were walking together by the river, eating beignets. She had powdered sugar on her cheek.

"You should see yourself. You have more sugar on your cheeks than on your beignet."

She tilted her face up to him. "Wipe it off."

He took out a clean handkerchief and wiped away the sugar. Then he carefully shook the powdery stuff from the cloth before putting it back into his pocket. He had to be in court in half an hour. He couldn't afford to appear before the judge with powdered sugar on his suit.

"You're all clean now, Em. Try to stay that way."

"Only if you promise to come with me today."

"Where?"

"You remember...I'm going to see about my friend Sasha."

He remembered. Sasha was Emily's best friend, and Emily was worried about her. Four days ago, Sasha had come to school with a black eye and a long scratch on her cheek. She told Emily nothing except that she had family troubles she couldn't talk about. Emily had pressed her, but Sasha had refused to talk.

The next day, she hadn't come to school at all. Nor the next. Emily had not seen her for three days, and she'd asked Zach to go across the river with her. Sasha lived in a small shanty near the warehouse district in Algiers.

"I remember. I'm pleading a case this afternoon, but I'll try to be back in time to take you to see Sasha."

"Thanks, Zach. I knew I could count on you."

"Don't count on me yet. I can't predict how fast the wheels of justice will turn. Listen, Em—" he bracketed her face and gently tipped it upward "—I'll try to meet you here at four, but promise you won't go without me. Algiers is a dangerous place to be."

"What about Sasha?"

"I'll help you find out about her. If not this afternoon, then another time." He tightened his hold on his sister. "You won't go without me. Promise me, Em."

"I promise."

It was the only promise Emily had ever broken with him. And it had caused her death. Zach groaned and tried to shut out the memories of his beautiful sister lying in a dirty street in Algiers, her blond hair plastered to her head with her own blood, her breath rasping with the agony of dying.

He had been an hour late that day, delayed in court, and when he'd reached the river, Emily wasn't there. He'd called home, hoping she'd be in her room studying or out on the tennis courts practicing for the school tournament, but those hopes had been dashed. The maid had informed him that Miss Emily had gone to Algiers.

Zach felt his pulse accelerate as his mind replayed that fateful day. He took several deep breaths to bring his heart back under control, and he closed his eyes to shut out the death scene. But he was tired; his defenses were weak.

He remembered as if it had been only yesterday....

He crossed the river to Algiers, cursing his own folly for promising to take Emily there. He should have told her in no uncertain terms that she was not to go—with or without him.

None of this would have happened if their parents had lived, but they were dead, and he and George had been raising Emily since she was thirteen. The responsibility fell mostly to Zach, for he was older and George was away at graduate school except during the summers. Emily was headstrong, and Zach and George were indulgent. They could never deny her anything.

By the time Zach's boat docked, the sun was setting. Soon the city would be dark. A sense of urgency overtook him.

Tracing his sister wasn't hard to do. She stood out in Algiers like a string of pearls cast onto a garbage heap. Everybody who had seen her remembered her.

He was running by the time he reached the warehouse district, running so hard, his blood was hammering in his ears. But it was already too late.

He heard the gunshots just as he rounded the corner. He saw Emily fall, saw her blood bloom across her chest like a deadly flower, saw the second burst of gunfire that slammed into the side of her head.

By the time Zach could reach his sister, Emily's assailant was already leaving the scene, but Zach would never forget him. Everything about that day was burned into his mind— the smell of rotting garbage, the broken asphalt awash with blood and the way the last rays of sunlight fell across his sister like a benediction.

He knelt beside Emily and cradled her in his arms, sobbing.

"Oh, God..."

In his agony, it was the only prayer he could say.

Emily's breath rasped, and the blood gurgled in her throat.

"Zach . . ." He had to press his ear to her lips to hear her. "Avenge Sasha. Promise . . ."

Even with her dying breath, Emily thought of her friend.

"I promise. Oh, God. I promise." She died then, her eyes fixed on his face. He pulled her close, rocking back and forth. "You're going to be all right, Em. I'm here. I'll take care of you. I promise . . . I promise. . . ."

Sweat popped out on his forehead, and Zach groaned. Emily had been an innocent bystander, an unsuspecting witness in a deadly game played out between a local drug kingpin and a local drug dealer. Sasha's father had been dealing drugs and skimming the profits. Word had leaked out and spread quickly on the street. Neighborhood kids beat Sasha. Her father forbade her to leave the house while he made arrangements to leave the city. On the day Emily went to Algiers, a hitman had been sent to eliminate the problem. Emily had arrived in Algiers in time to witness Sasha and her father being gunned down. Emily had tried to run—her fingerprints had been found inside the front hall near Sasha's body and on the railing of the broken-down stoop—but the assassin had caught her on the street.

Zach had left his lucrative law practice in the hands of his partner and gone undercover with the DA's office in order to help hunt down his sister's killer. It had taken him a year to find him. Crown Mackey was now doing hard time for life.

But eliminating one petty drug dealer had not been enough to satisfy Zach. He wouldn't be satisfied until he'd found the kingpin and brought him to justice. It wouldn't be a complete purge of the city, but it would be a start. And at least he would have the satisfaction of knowing that the man who had ordered the deaths that had brought Emily down would pay a price.

Zach unlocked his desk drawer and lifted out his gun. He was licensed to kill. Holding the deadly weight in his hand, he wondered if he ever could. When he had found Crown, he'd wanted to kill for revenge. He could have set it up so he had killed him in self-defense. But when the time came to bring Crown in, common sense prevailed. If he personally went after Crown, his cover would be blown and he would be useless for further work. In the end, he had stayed behind, never knowing whether he could actually have pulled the trigger.

He sighted down the barrel, picking out his targets, even in the darkness—the grandfather clock, a prized possession of the Taylors for four generations; two nineteenth-century gaslights, standing sentinel over a prized painting by Remington; a Dominique chair covered in a Bianchini brocade.

The metal was cold against his fingers, as cold as the loneliness that invaded him tonight.

His life was full of expensive possessions. And he would trade them all if he could turn back the clock to a time when Emily was alive and laughing.

If only... He stopped the thought before it was fully formed. The two saddest words in the English language were "if only." And they changed nothing. It was too late for regrets.

He put the gun back into his desk, locked it, then rejoined his party. In a few hours it would be morning in Spain. He'd find a phone and call his brother. Then he had one other thing to do, something to satisfy himself that he was, after all these years, human. He had to apologize to Lily Cooper.

Zach waited until dark the next day before he went to see Lily. For the past seven years he'd moved about mostly in the dark, and as he parked his car in front of his brother's apartment, he found himself wondering what it would be like to get up in the morning when the sun was first rising and go to work like ordinary men. What would it be like to go to the river in the noonday sun with a picnic basket on one arm, a pretty woman on the other, and not have to look over his shoulder for enemies? He might never know.

Shaking off his blues, he punched the doorbell.

Lily opened the door. She was wearing slacks and an open-necked blouse, and her hair was down, cascading over her shoulders and damp at the temples from a recent shower. A tiny sheen of moisture beaded her throat, and her white silk blouse clung to her where the skin wasn't quite dry.

He feasted his eyes. He would allow himself to look.

A flush came into her cheeks, the kind of flush a woman wears when she knows a man finds her desirable.

He quickly donned a polite mask. After all, he had come to rectify last night's mistake, not to make another one.

"Good evening, Lily."

"Zach." She acknowledged him with a slight nod of her head. A dozen questions flew through her mind, but she didn't want to detain him with questions. She merely wanted him gone.

"Rose told me you were staying here with the dog," he said, as if he could read her thoughts.

"She shouldn't have."

"May I come in?"

Lily hesitated, torn between protecting herself and giving in to the Southern manners that had been drilled into her since she was a child. Southern manners be damned. She started to close the door in his face; then she had another thought. What if he had news of George, something that was too awful for Rose to call and tell?

"Only for a moment." She held the door wide and stepped back to let him enter.

She knew it was a mistake the minute he was in the hallway. He turned his smile on her, the angelic one that made him look like a little boy who had just stolen all the cookies from the jar but who was absolutely certain that he would not be punished. No wonder half the women in New Orleans had ended up, at one time or another, in his bed.

And she had been one of them. Her spine stiffened.

"Say what you have to say quickly and then leave. I have work to do."

"Apologies are best made over a good glass of Scotch."

"I don't know where George keeps his Scotch."

"I do."

Taking her elbow, he propelled her into the kitchen. She was standing beside the table, watching him rummage in the cabinets before his words sank in. *Apologies?* Had he said *apologies?*

Had he finally decided, after all these years, to apologize for denying that Mardi Gras night?

She pulled a chair away from the table and sat down. She thought it would be best to sit for such an unprecedented event.

"I talked to George and Rose today." He turned around, a bottle of Scotch and two glasses in his hands.

"So did I."

"I'm satisfied that he's going to be all right."

"I am, too."

"Do you want yours on the rocks?" He held the Scotch aloft.

"I take mine not at all. Not this evening, anyhow. I told you I have work to do."

"Ahh, Lily." Smiling, he poured two glasses of Scotch and straddled the chair next to hers. "You know what they say about all work and no play."

"How about all play and no work?"

"Have you been listening to rumors, Lily?"

She flushed.

He pressed the glass into her hand, laughing. "Never mind. I thrive on rumors, the nastier the better."

Lily took a sip of Scotch. The man was going to drive her to drink. She'd be glad when Rose and George got back from Spain and she could get on with her own life—a life that definitely would not include keeping company with Zach Taylor.

The Scotch warmed her going down, and she looked up to see Zach watching her.

"You said you came here to apologize."

"Yes, I did."

He reached for her free hand and lifted it to his lips. The hair on the backs of her arms stood on end, and a shiver walked down her spine.

She held her breath, waiting.

"You did me an enormous favor, and I treated you badly."

Some dark, mysterious force pulled at her until she could see nothing except his black eyes, blazing in the centers with an unholy light.

"Please accept my sincerest apologies," he continued, the music of his voice wrapping around her until she was floating under his spell.

"After all these years . . ." she whispered.

Zach was instantly wary. He wanted to apologize, not to resurrect hopeless dreams.

"After last night," he corrected. He released her hand. It was best to let her go. He hadn't meant to touch her. He guessed that being in his brother's cozy apartment surrounded by things that made George so blissfully happy had gone to his head. For a moment, he'd forgotten that unguarded moments were unbidden to him.

"You came all the way to my house in the rain to tell me about my brother, and I frightened you. I'm sincerely sorry."

Lily felt like a fool for alluding to what had happened between them four years ago. Why had she thought that Zach Taylor would apologize after all these years? A zebra didn't change its stripes. He was an unprincipled rake then, and he always would be. Whatever had prompted his apology for last night was surely only a temporary condition.

"Apology accepted." She slugged back her Scotch. After he left, she might get roaring drunk. Her glass rattled when she set it on the table. "Thank you for coming."

She was dismissing him. Zach was disappointed.

"Rose and George tell me you're an expert chess player."

"I don't play games anymore."

"What a shame. I'll bet you're very good at games . . . of all kinds."

He put his glass on the table and stood up in one smooth motion. It was best to leave. He'd proved he was human. What more could he ask? Certainly not that she would invite him to sit in Rose and George's comfortable den and play a game of chess. Certainly not that she would tip her head back and look at him from under her wonderful lashes and laugh with him at something clever he'd said.

"If you need me, Lily, all you have to do is call."

"I don't expect to need you again."

Something flashed in his eyes, and she knew he remembered. He remembered that night in a silk-curtained bed, and still he pretended not to.

Damn you, Zach Taylor, she thought. *I'll never need you.*

"I know you're a strongly independent woman, Lily, but my brother's life is at stake here. If Rose or George should call for help, no matter what time it is, I'll be there for them . . . and for you." He tipped her face up with one finger. "Just call me. Promise?"

"I'll do everything I can to help Rose and George, and certainly I'll keep you informed if something happens and Rose can't call you herself." She stepped back, breaking the contact. "But I won't make promises to you, Zach."

For a moment his naked heart was reflected in a small, sad smile. "Then you're probably smarter than most women."

Out of a sense of duty, she escorted him to the front door. They didn't touch again, nor did they speak, not even to say goodbye.

After he was gone, she leaned against the door, her fingers pressed against her temples. She had a throbbing headache and an intense desire to kick something.

She stomped back to the kitchen and kicked the table leg. Bentley, aroused by the noise, came scampering from his doggie bed. Annoyed at having his favorite dream of chasing rabbits disturbed, he took a nip at Lily's pant leg.

"Where were you when I needed you, Bentley?" She leaned down and absently patted his head.

He was disappointed. He'd counted on a good chase around the kitchen table. He sat on her right foot and pouted.

Lily polished off the Scotch in her glass and poured herself another. She didn't even bother to add any ice.

"You always attack me when I come in the front door. Why didn't you attack him?"

Bentley didn't know who she was talking about. Nor did he care. He was in a snit, and he planned on sitting on her foot until she made him move.

"Maybe if you had chewed up his pant leg, he'd have gone back home and I wouldn't have made a fool of myself, going on about never needing him *again*. Hell. As if I needed him the first time. Which I definitely did not."

She took another gulp of Scotch. It almost made her gag. But she was on a roll. She was in her sister's apartment with a dog that hated her, and she had to deal with a man she despised, besides. Just this once she was going to give up being strong and smart and noble and self-sacrificing and wallow in a little self-pity. She deserved to feel sorry for herself, and she was going to do it right.

"Everybody else has a brother-in-law with a pot belly and a bald head. But Rose? Hell, no. She has to have one who puts every woman in this city in a swoon." She belted down another drink. "Except me. Damn. He will not make me swoon and sigh...."

She lifted her glass once more and drank until it was empty. She was beginning to feel light-headed and wonderfully liberated. She got up, dumping Bentley onto his fat bottom, and refilled her glass with ice. Then she undid the top buttons on her blouse and held the cool glass to her bare skin. The cold felt good.

She poured more Scotch into her glass, then moved back to her chair. Propping one elbow on the table and her chin on her hand, she held her glass high and watched the dark amber liquid swirl around the ice cubes.

"Not me," she whispered. "I won't sigh for him... not again."

She saw his face, shadowed by silk curtains and gilded by moonlight. Zach had left that night without saying goodbye, just as he had tonight. And last night, the same thing had happened. They had parted without a word.

Slowly she lowered her glass to her lips.

"Why do men always leave me without saying goodbye?"

Chapter 4

Lily had a hangover.

The pounding headache had awakened her. She opened one eye, then quickly squeezed it shut again. The sunlight pouring through the window hurt her eyes.

"Oh, God. What have I done?"

Her voice sounded like thunder in her ears. She rammed a pillow over her head and groaned. A brass band set up a racket beside her bed, trumpets blaring, clarinets wailing, drums pounding. Holding the pillow around her ears, she groped for the baseball bat she kept under the bed for emergencies. She had to destroy that band.

With her hand clutched around the bat, she lifted one edge of the pillow and peeped out. The band was still clanging, only it wasn't the band. It was the telephone.

"Hello," she whispered into the receiver.

"You'll have to speak up. I can't hear you."

Lily held the receiver away from her ear. Some fool insisted on shouting at—she glanced at the clock—eight o'clock in the morning. She groaned. She was going to be late for work.

Pressing one hand over her throbbing temples, she spoke into the the telephone again, stronger this time.

"Hello."

"Mrs. Taylor?"

"No. I'm Lily, Mrs. Taylor's sister."

"This is Opalene McGruder at the Sweet Angels Adoption Agency. I need to speak with Mr. or Mrs. Taylor."

Lily came as alert as any woman with a full-fledged hangover can come. Holding the covers over her chest, she scooted up and propped herself against the headboard.

"They are in Spain, Mrs. McGruder. Can I take a message?"

"We have a baby for them, a lovely little boy."

Tears sprang into Lily's eyes. Her sister was going to have a baby. After waiting so long, Rose was going to have a boy.

"That's wonderful!"

"I think so, too. We believe Rose and George will be wonderful parents." Mrs. McGruder paused, and Lily could hear the clatter of silver against china. She was probably having a morning cup of coffee. When Lily heard Mrs. McGruder take a sip, she knew her guess had been right.

"Will they be coming home from Spain soon?" Mrs. McGruder asked after the coffee had gone down. "We like to place our babies in their homes as quickly as possible."

"I'm afraid not. George is having emergency gallbladder surgery today." Lily's mind raced. There was no way George and Rose could come home, not now. What if the agency gave the baby to somebody else? Was that possible?

"Listen," she told Mrs. McGruder. "I can pick the baby up."

"Oh, my dear, no. We couldn't possibly send the baby home without signing papers. He'd be in limbo." She took another loud sip of coffee. She sounded as though she was gargling.

The gargle gave Lily time to think. When the solution came, breaking its way through the Scotch fog lingering in her brain, it was so simple, she could hardly believe it.

"I can sign for her," she said. "Before my sister left, she gave me power of attorney." When Mrs. McGruder didn't say anything, Lily hurried on. She wasn't about to let that woman turn her down. "I'll bring my lawyer to ensure that everything is perfectly legal. And I'm staying in my sister's apartment anyhow, keeping her dog, so the baby would be coming directly to his own home. In fact, to his own bed. Rose has the nursery ready."

Mrs. McGruder finally agreed, telling Lily that she could pick the baby up at four o'clock the next afternoon.

Lily called Rose to tell her the good news. Both of them cried over the long-distance telephone wires, but Lily didn't consider it a waste, and Rose would never have thought spending money to cry was a waste, anyhow.

Still sobbing, Rose said, "George is so happy…. George, honey, we have a boy. Can you hear me, honey? It's a boy." To Lily, she said, "He's still groggy from the anesthesia. They did his surgery right after lunch."

"He's okay?"

"He's doing great. Oh, Lily, I'm so happy." Rose sobbed for another three minutes, then she began to hiccup. "Call Zach. Take him with you."

"Now, Rose, I don't need to involve him in this."

"He's part of the family. And anyhow, he has a law degree. He'll know if everything is all right."

"Whatever you say, Rose."

They talked some more about the baby, about George's surgery, then Lily rang off. She had no intention of taking Zach Taylor to get Rose's baby. She had her own lawyer, who was perfectly respectable and who would certainly see that everything was done properly.

Rose might be miffed, but she would get over it.

Lily got carefully out of bed and dressed for work. She had a million things to do. Not the least of which was calming down. Now that she thought about what she was going to do—care for a baby, even if it was for only a few days—she was scared to death. She didn't know beans about babies.

She'd pick up a baby book on the way home from work and bone up before tomorrow.

Having decided that, she felt better. Intelligent women cared for babies all the time. What could be so hard about caring for a baby?

Sweet Angels Adoption Agency was on St. Charles Street, almost within walking distance of the side-by-side campuses of Loyola and Tulane.

The next afternoon, at precisely five minutes to four, Lily parked her car in the pea-gravel lot behind the agency and turned to the man beside her.

"Claude, I can't tell you how grateful I am that you could come on such short notice."

"I don't often have such a happy occasion as an excuse to break the dull work routine." He squeezed her hand. "It's my pleasure, Lily."

The two of them got out of the car. Lily was so excited, she didn't see the black Corvette.

Zach Taylor, who had been waiting patiently for ten minutes, watched as Lily made her way toward the front door. She had her lawyer with her. It hadn't been necessary for him to come, after all. Claude Montague would see that everything was legal.

He started to leave, and then he thought better of it. George wanted him here. He didn't even have to see the baby if he didn't want to. All he had to do was make sure his brother got the son he deserved.

Zach adjusted his sunglasses and intercepted them.

"Lily." He nodded toward her, then held out his hand to her lawyer. "Claude."

Lily watched in amazement as the two of them shook hands. She knew Zach had a law degree, but she had figured that nobody in the law community would touch him with a ten-foot pole, given his defection and his history.

She was wrong. Her own lawyer was treating him like a long-lost brother.

"Zach. It's wonderful to see you. What brings you here?"

"My brother's baby. I've come to make sure there are no foul-ups in this adoption."

"I didn't expect to see you." Claude turned to Lily. "You didn't tell me Zach would be here."

"I didn't know it."

"Rose called me," Zach said smoothly. "She was afraid Lily would forget to tell me."

"In that case—" Claude patted Lily's hand "—you don't need me, dear. I'll catch a cab and leave you in Zach's hands."

He walked off before she could tell him that the last place she wanted to be was in Zach Taylor's hands.

"Well, Lily. Let's go inside and see about John Henry."

"How did you know his name?"

"He's my nephew, too. Rose told me a year ago that if they got a boy, she was going to name him John Henry, after her daddy. Henrietta Johnell if she got a girl." He laughed. "Thank God she didn't get a girl."

He took Lily's elbow. "It's four o'clock. We don't want to be late."

"You don't have to lead me around like I'm senile." She politely removed her elbow from his grasp. "I want to make one thing perfectly clear to you—right now, circumstances are throwing us together. But don't take any liberties and don't get any wrong ideas. We're not friends, and we never will be. After all this is over, I don't ever intend to see you again."

A huge void inside Zach yawned a little wider, and for a moment he was tempted to say, "I'm not what I seem. Be my friend." But the moment passed quickly. His nephew was his major concern right now.

Opalene McGruder was waiting for them in her office.

"Well, now." She patted her fat hands together after all the introductions and formalities. "This is the part I like best—introducing a baby to his family. In this case, his aunt and uncle. *If* he doesn't have any strenuous objections to you—" she paused, laughing at what she supposed was a wonderful touch of humor "—we'll come back and sign the papers. Follow me, please."

John Henry was lying on his back in a small crib in the nursery, contemplating his feet. One fat, dimpled fist was in his mouth, and his big round eyes were wide with wonder as he watched his feet flail the air. Tears came to Lily's eyes. Some small miracle had brought that tiny person to her sister, Rose. A series of events unknown to her had made it possible for Rose to be a mother.

"He's an angel," she whispered. She hung back, in awe of the miracle before her.

Zach was equally cautious. He hadn't meant to actually *see* the baby. Babies were helpless little things, always needing something, and Zach couldn't afford to be needed right now. Not that he didn't like babies. On the contrary, he loved them. If his life had been different, he might have had four or five of his own by now.

But his life wasn't different, and he had no intention of losing his heart to nine pounds of helplessness.

"My goodness." Opalene looked from one to the other of them. "Isn't one of you going to say hello to the baby?"

Zach approached the crib cautiously.

"How are you, little tiger?" Instinctively he offered his finger, and John Henry immediately latched on to it, cooing.

Zach could hardly believe what was happening. He smiled at Lily and Opalene.

"I think he *likes* me."

"Isn't that sweet?" Opalene McGruder turned to Lily. "I think he's a natural. He'll be a great uncle."

Lily felt a little jealous. After all, she was the one who would be caring for the baby. It was only right that he love her first . . . and the most.

Trying to act braver than she felt, she joined Zach at the crib.

"Hello, little darling." John Henry turned his round eyes on her. Lily leaned closer. "How's my big boy today?"

John Henry poked out his lower lip. His feet got still for two seconds, then began to beat the air in earnest. He opened his mouth and squalled. It was the loudest sound Lily had ever heard come from such a tiny mouth. She stepped back in dismay.

Opalene hurried forward. "Why don't you pick him up, Lily? He just wants his aunt to comfort him."

Lily doubted that, but she reached into the crib and awkwardly lifted the baby. He kicked and flailed and screamed and made so much commotion in general that she feared he would wiggle out of her grasp. Zach reached over and tucked all the moving parts into her arms, then braced his hands under John Henry's rump for added support. Lily was grateful to him.

"There now," Opalene said. "Isn't that better?"

Before Lily could agree, John Henry set up another round of wailing that was loud enough to wake every wino on Bourbon Street.

Lily jiggled the baby up and down. That started him on a fresh tangent. She leaned closer and cooed at him. He grabbed a fistful of her hair and screamed louder.

"Dear me," Opalene said.

"Let me try." Zach plucked John Henry from Lily's arms. The baby banged his fists on Zach's chest, then gave one big sniffle and a wide, watery smile. "There's my little tiger. You're going to be Uncle Zach's boy, aren't you? Yes, you are."

Zach and John Henry began to coo at each other.

Lily tried very hard to feel grateful, but all she felt was a little jealous and more than a little panicked. She was going to be alone with John Henry for days. What did she know about babies? Right now, she couldn't even remember what she'd read on page two of the baby book, let alone page fifteen. What if Baby John Henry hated her as much as Bentley did? If his screams were any indication, he already didn't think she was such hot stuff, and he barely even knew her.

She tore her gaze away from the absolute adoration on Zach's face and turned her attention to Mrs. McGruder. "I suppose we can sign the papers, then gather his things and bring him home."

John Henry's belongings were meager. He left the Sweet Angels Adoption Agency with two nightshirts, a dozen disposable diapers and enough milk and pablum to get him through three days.

He also left the agency sitting in a brand-new car seat in his Uncle Zach's car—the car seat Zach had meant to insist Lily use before he met John Henry. Zach smiled at Lily from behind the wheel of his Corvette.

"I'll bring him to the apartment, Lily. I'm afraid you can't handle him and drive."

"Neither can you. He's bound to cry and create too much fuss for you to concentrate on the road."

Baby John Henry made a liar of her by giving Zach a radiant smile and blowing spit bubbles.

Lily made a last-ditch plea. "Look, there's no need for you to go all the way back to the apartment. I'm sure you have things to do."

"He's not used to you yet, Lily. You want him screaming his head off all the way home?" Zach looked at her as if she had just driven over an old lady's cat. "You'd have a wreck and both be killed." He paused to kiss the top of John Henry's head. "He's my brother's baby, and I'll take care of him. Get in your car and go home. I'll meet you there."

He put the Corvette in gear and probably would have run over her foot if she hadn't moved out of his way. Damn the man. What he was doing was tantamount to kidnapping in Lily's book. She guessed that was nothing new with Zach Taylor.

She got into her car and started after Zach and the baby. Her hands were trembling. "Calm down," she told herself. "Once you get home, everything will be all right. John Henry will fall asleep, and Zach will go away."

When she arrived at the apartment, Zach was in the den, sitting in the wooden rocking chair, the diaper bag at his feet and John Henry in his arms. He was even singing.

After Lily got over the shock of Zach Taylor sitting in a rocking chair and singing to a baby, she listened to the words. They were like nothing she had ever heard. He was crooning about baby buntings and merry-go-rounds with bird-dog puppies thrown in for good measure. The song sounded suspiciously like something Zach had made up just for the occasion.

John Henry didn't seem to mind. He found everything about his new uncle totally enchanting.

Zach glanced up at Lily, standing uncertainly in the door.

"I thought I'd rock him to sleep . . . since I'm here anyway."

"The baby book says they should be allowed to fall asleep in their own beds. 'Good routines create good habits,'" she added, quoting from page six.

Zach's dark look said what he thought about not rocking babies to sleep, but he acquiesced. After all, he decided, what did he know about babies?

Lily led the way to the nursery. She was glad to have something to be doing. While Zach tucked John Henry into his new crib, she stowed his belongings. Holding his two little nightshirts, she pulled open a dresser drawer. Rose had purchased a complete layette. Folded in neat stacks were tiny shirts and nightgowns and sweaters and caps. They all looked too small for John Henry. And half of them were pink. Lily figured that anybody as opinionated as John Henry would be insulted wearing pink.

She finished putting away his things, then joined Zach. He and the baby were admiring each other.

"Look at that," Zach whispered, smoothing John Henry's blond curls. "I had no idea babies were so beautiful."

John Henry smiled. He loved compliments.

Lily breathed a sigh of relief. The baby was content—at last.

"He *is* beautiful." Lily held out her hand. Now that the baby was happy and she was going to have him all to herself, she could afford to be generous, even expansive. "Thank you for bringing him home."

Zach was being dismissed again. His gaze moved from Lily to the baby. There was too much here that could tempt a man, too much that could make him forget his purpose.

He stepped away from the crib.

"You're sure you'll be all right with the baby?"

"Certainly. I may be a little awkward right now, but I'll get the hang of it." Lily didn't know if that were true or not, but she sincerely hoped so.

Zach started toward the door and John Henry whimpered. Lily looked at the baby in alarm. His face was puckered, and it seemed as if he was getting ready for another crying jag.

She picked him up, being as careful as if he were a carton of eggs. John Henry snuggled against her for a moment and she smiled.

"See. I told you I'd get the hang of it."

John Henry decided to allow her one more moment of triumph. Then he opened his mouth and proved her wrong.

He yelled and kicked and screamed and beat until he was red in the face.

Zach, who was barely out the door, came immediately back to the nursery.

"Good grief," Lily said.

"I think he wants me."

"You needn't act as pleased."

"Who? Me?"

"Yes. You." Lily rocked the yelling baby. "There's not a tear in his eye. I think this child has a temper."

"Maybe he's hungry."

"I hadn't thought of that."

"Do you want me to stay long enough to help you feed him?"

Lily considered his offer. It wouldn't be wise to stay around Zach much longer. He had a charm that she had seen only once before, so long ago, and she didn't want the continued exposure. She opened her mouth to tell him "no, thank you," when Bentley came through the door and got into the act. He didn't understand the loudmouthed little person who was getting the lion's share of attention, and he was going to do something about it. He started running in frenzied circles around the nursery and barking loud enough to be heard over John Henry.

John Henry decided to turn up the volume.

Lily changed her mind.

"If you're sure you have the time," she yelled, trying to be heard.

"I think I can manage."

Lily thought Zach's smile was smug as he plucked the baby from her arms and carried him into the kitchen. John Henry's howls immediately changed to self-pitying whimpers.

"I'll stay just long enough to help you settle him in, and then I'll be on my way."

It didn't turn out that way at all, much to Lily's mortification. Every time Zach tried to leave, John Henry screamed as if he were dying. By nightfall Zach was beginning to be worried and Lily was a nervous wreck.

"Good Lord." Lily stared helplessly into the crib at a red-faced, bawling John Henry.

She was so tired, she was clinging to the back of the rocking chair to keep from collapsing.

"I can't leave him like this." Zach paced the floor, wondering what to do. "He can't be getting much air into his lungs that way. If he keeps up that howling, he's liable to suffocate."

After another turn around the room, Zach lifted John Henry out of the crib. The baby quieted and cuddled against him in complete trust, squirming his fat little body until he was burrowed right next to Zach's heart.

Ancient barriers inside Zach creaked and threatened to break. He began to whistle softly, an old river song he'd learned when he was a boy.

John Henry wanted to stay awake to hear it all, but he was too tired. He'd had a big day, trying to show everybody who was the boss. He nodded his little head and fell asleep on Uncle Zach's shoulder.

Lily was so numb, she couldn't feel anything, not even gratitude. She clung to the rocker and watched as Zach tenderly tucked John Henry into the crib.

"Tonight," Zach whispered, so as not to wake the baby. "I'll stay only for tonight."

Chapter 5

Lily left them in the nursery, John Henry curled in a fat ball in his pretty new crib, and Zach sitting in a rocking chair at his side, leaning close to the railings, watching him breathe.

She went into Rose's bedroom and shut the door, leaning against it as if she expected it to come crashing down at any moment. After today, nothing would surprise her. If anything else could possibly go wrong, she didn't know what it was. She felt as if life had plucked her out of a warm, safe cocoon and plunked her onto a roller coaster. She was getting dizzy from the ride.

Never in her life had she felt so inadequate, not even all those times she'd been stood up and abandoned and denied by the male of the species. Maybe women with potential weren't cut out to be wives and lovers and mothers. Maybe success demanded sacrifice, and not knowing how to take care of a screaming baby was a small price she had to pay.

She had thought all babies were cute and cuddly and dependent and entertaining. John Henry was a complete revelation. He had the face of an angel and the disposition of a wildcat. She figured if he had any teeth, he'd bite her legs the way Bentley did. What was she going to do with him until Rose and George came home?

He wouldn't let anybody except Zach touch him.

"Oh, God." Lily pressed her hands against her temples. "Does everybody in the world crave Zach's touch?"

She walked to the bed and lay down across the covers. Relaxed for the first time since John Henry had come into her life, she allowed her mind to drift. It drifted back to the morning she had awakened in an empty bed and found a mask beside her—a black mask with a single teardrop diamond. She had carried it with her when she left, intending to return it to the owner. Now it was buried deep in a drawer back at her place. Out of sight, out of mind, she had thought.

Lying on the bed now, she pictured the mask as it had been so long ago, the diamond catching the lamplight, as bright as a tear. In her mind it took on magical properties, conjuring music and candlelight and champagne and a passion so hot, the memory of it burned her.

That was insane, of course. It was merely a mask, and Zach was merely a man—one of the worst of his breed. Except... A vision of him leaning over John Henry's crib came to her.

She closed her eyes, recalling the expression on his face. It had been tender and fierce at the same time.

She began to drift, to float closer and closer to that fuzzy realm between sleeping and waking. Her last logical thought was of the mask... and the man who had worn it.

"Fatigue," she mumbled. "Battle fatigue."

Then the dark mask and the dark man slipped from her mind and she fell asleep.

Zach's head nodded, and suddenly he jerked awake. He was sitting in the rocking chair beside the sleeping baby. He stood up, bending over the crib and placing his hand on the tiny chest in order to feel the heartbeat.

He had to make sure. The tiny heart fluttered under his hand, and he breathed a sigh of relief.

What had wakened him? He listened. There was no sound in the apartment.

Restless, he strode away from the crib. He knew what had brought him out of sleep. Old demons were chasing his dreams. He had been given the care of a loved one, and he had failed.

He stood in a patch of moonlight beside the window, gazing out. He should leave. He should go now before it was too late. Lily was a bright, capable woman. She would take good care of the baby until George and Rose got home.

Anyway, there might be risks if he stayed. His acquaintances were capable of becoming dangerous enemies if they ever found out about him.

He turned his head just slightly and looked at the crib. A blond tangle of curls shone in the moonlight.

"Oh, God."

It was part prayer and part agony. Zach wasn't aware of having said anything. Premonition gripped him, a premonition so strong, he couldn't ignore it. For seven years he'd depended on his instincts and his premonitions. And they had never failed him.

"It will soon be dawn," he whispered to himself. "Leave."

But something drew him back to the crib. He leaned over, touching the baby's silky hair. And suddenly he knew he could not leave until John Henry was safely in his brother's hands. He had a terrible feeling that if he left, something horrible would happen, that without him as protector, they would all lose the baby, just as they had lost Emily.

But he had failed Emily. Why did he think John Henry needed him?

The baby stirred, opening his pink mouth in a prodigious yawn and stretching his fat little legs. Then he opened those knowing blue eyes and smiled at Zach.

Zach bent closer and kissed John Henry's soft, downy cheek.

"Don't worry, little tiger. I won't desert you. There's one thing I must do, but I'll be back. I promise."

Zach kissed the baby one more time and left the nursery. Then he let himself quietly out of the apartment.

"Dammit, Zach. This had better be good to get me out of bed at this god-awful hour."

The district attorney ran his hands through his gray hair and poured himself a cup of coffee. His hand shook as he brought the fragile porcelain cup to his lips. He was getting too old for this job.

Zach was too keyed up to sit down. He lounged against the doorway of Rafe McKenzie's study, admiring the oil painting Rafe's wife had hung over the mantel.

"It is, Rafe. It's a matter of life and death."

"I thought things had settled down after that last raid you set up. Damn, that was a big one. Three small-time dealers and one top dog."

He smiled with satisfaction. Zach Taylor was a deadly force for justice in New Orleans. In the seven years he'd been working undercover for the DA's office, he'd brought more drug dealers to justice than the whole damned police department. A few had never made it to trial, gunned down by their own kind before they could squeal, and that was all right with Rafe. New Orleans had become a safer place because of the man standing in his study.

"This is not about drugs, Rafe. It's about family."

The DA didn't miss a thing, even if it was only five o'clock in the morning and he hadn't had all his beauty sleep. He saw the muscles bunched with tension under Zach's shirt, heard the new note in Zach's voice, something between desperation and resignation, as if he'd been given a vision he'd rather not have seen.

"Want to sit down and talk about it?"

"No. I don't have time." Zach paced the floor, talking rapidly. "I'm taking some time off. There's something I have to do. And I don't want a damned soul to know I've gone or where I am."

"Where *will* you be?"

"Keeping my tail as far off the beaten track as possible for the next week or so."

"How long will you be gone . . . so to speak?"

"As long as it takes."

Rafe sipped his coffee, studying the man before him. Zach looked like hell. He needed a rest.

"Go. Take as long as you like. Just be damned sure you let me know when you're back. And Zach . . . one more thing."

Zach's head came up, wary, like a hunted animal.

"Be careful," Rafe said.

"I'll try."

Lily pushed her way slowly out of the deep cocoon of sleep and squinted into the semidarkness. She was hearing strange noises and she knew it couldn't be her alarm clock, because the sun wasn't even up. Still groggy, she started to burrow back under her covers. Then she remembered where she was.

"Good grief. John Henry." She bolted from bed and raced toward the nursery. John Henry was crying in earnest now.

"I'm coming," she called, tucking in her shirt and leaving a trail of hairpins in her wake. Last night she had fallen asleep in her clothes. "Don't cry. I'm coming."

As she hurried toward the nursery, Lily took comfort in the fact that she was not in this alone. Admitting that she not only needed but welcomed help was hard. She had always prided herself on being self-sufficient and equal to any task. But being equal to a job at the bank and equal to John Henry were two entirely different things. A little person who would be only a bit taller than her knees if he could stand was shaking her long-held convictions about herself . . . and about Zach, as well.

For all his faults, Zach was good with John Henry. For four years she had believed he was too arrogant to spare more than a passing thought for another person. On that count, at least, she had been wrong about him. Was she wrong about other things, as well?

The wailing continued. It wasn't like Zach to let John Henry cry. She pushed open the nursery door.

"Zach," she called, trying to adjust her eyes to the half-light in the nursery. "Zach, the baby's crying."

There was no answer except a renewed burst of screaming from John Henry. Lily flipped on the light switch, hoping to see Zach, big and efficient and ready to take charge of the problem. The blaze of light showed a stack of diapers on the new furniture, a plastic circus mobile set atinkle by John Henry's flailing feet and an empty rocking chair. Zach was nowhere to be found.

"Zach," she called again, instinctively knowing he wouldn't answer, knowing he was not asleep on the sofa, knowing he was not in the kitchen getting a bottle ready. Zach was gone. He had left without saying goodbye, sneaked out in the middle of the night like a thief.

Even with John Henry screaming in the crib, Lily had never felt more alone.

"He promised," she whispered, pressing her hands to her throbbing temples. She regretted her earlier generosity in assigning him the sterling quality of caring enough about another person to spare them thought. *I'll stay only for tonight,* he had said, but what did promises mean to a man like Zach?

She had a sudden vision of herself standing alone at the senior prom with a wilted corsage. *Abandoned.* Why did men always abandon her?

She stood by the crib wishing she knew exactly what to do and wishing she could vent her frustration as easily as John Henry did. Not only had Zach abandoned her, he had left his own nephew, as well. John Henry was her responsibility now, and hers alone.

She reached up to brush her loose hair away from her face, and felt dampness on her cheek. She couldn't be crying. She *wouldn't* cry, not about the baby, and certainly not about Zach's desertion.

Be strong, she told herself. And to John Henry, she said, "Everything's going to be all right."

He showed her what he thought of her opinion by giving the crib a mighty kick and screeching as if his britches were on fire. As a matter of fact, that's how they felt to him. He decided the whole business of wet diapers was a pain in the rear. And when John Henry suffered, he wanted everybody else to suffer, too.

Lily leaned over the crib and reached cautiously toward him, trying to catch hold of the parts that weren't moving. He foiled her by wiggling every part of him that was movable. His soggy bottom was too heavy to cooperate.

"Well, my goodness. What's the problem, big boy?"

He thought the question was silly. Obviously he couldn't tell her just yet. He hadn't learned the right words. But he would. By George, just give him time.

"I'll bet you're hungry, that's what."

John Henry's renewed burst of screaming showed what he thought of that silly notion.

"Don't you worry, John Henry. Aunt Lily is here. She'll take good care of you. Yes, she will." Lily hoped she could fool the baby with her brave act. It was a futile hope. He yelled and batted the air with his fists, and then held his breath until his face began to turn blue.

"I'll kill that Zach Taylor when I see him." John Henry quieted for a moment at the sound of Zach's name. Lily took that opportunity to lift him from the crib. She almost smiled with relief. He was merely wet. Why hadn't she thought of that?

"All right, we're gong to get a clean diaper now. Remember how we did this yesterday?" She jiggled the crying baby up and down. It didn't help matters a bit. He yanked her hair and screamed louder. "I'm going to have to put you back down. You won't hold your breath again for Aunt Lily, now will you?" She lowered him to the crib, crooning all the time. "That's a good boy, that's my good baby."

John Henry decided to let her off the hook. He stopped screaming long enough to get a dry diaper, which turned out to be quite a while. It took her four tries to get it right. By the time she had a clean one on him, he was ready to go again. He felt a little sorry for her. He decided to tell her so in his loudest voice.

"Oh, please, baby. Please don't cry." Torn between picking up John Henry and getting the baby book, Lily settled on the baby book. There was a chapter in the book called "What To Do When Baby Cries." She knew, because she had seen it . . . Was it only yesterday? It felt like a week to Lily, a week with no sleep and no sanity.

She sat in the rocking chair with the book, frantically flipping pages. Where was that damned chapter? The book fell from her hands and she had to start all over.

John Henry stopped crying long enough to catch his breath; then he took a fresh start.

"Just a minute, John Henry. Please don't cry for just a minute." She had found the chapter, but she couldn't seem to see the words. Then she realized why. They were blurred by her tears. She was getting as weepy as Rose. If she couldn't cope, how was her sister ever going to manage?

Lily staunchly wiped her eyes and started to read. "When baby cries, he obviously has a problem," the book blithely told her.

"I don't want to be told the obvious. I want to be told the problem."

John Henry tried to tell her, but she didn't seem to be listening. He wished his Uncle Zach would hurry and get back.

It was midmorning by the time Zach got back to his brother's apartment. He let himself in the door, using the spare key George had given him. There were no sounds, no signs of Lily and the baby or even of Bentley.

Zach froze, fear gripping his heart. What if his cover was blown? What if his enemies had found out about the baby... and Lily? Although he had been gone only a few hours, that's all it took to do dark deeds. The years seemed to spin backward, and he was in the courtroom, pleading a case while his sister was murdered.

I should have been here, he told himself. *I shouldn't have left, even to get a few clothes and a safe, unrecognizable car.*

Moving with the stealth of habit and training, he began a slow inspection of the house. Rose's den looked the way it should, with her eclectic mix of the gaudy and the elegant and Lily's neat touch. Magazines were stacked, cushions were lined up straight, ballet slippers and fringed shawls and baseball caps were stowed. There was even a new writing pad beside the telephone table, another of Lily's touches. But there was no sign of John Henry or Bentley or Lily.

A vision of Emily came to him, lying in a pool of blood. He had been too late... too late. Her lifeblood was flowing away, matting the long, blond hair....

Shaken, Zach leaned against the doorframe and passed his hand over his damp forehead. He couldn't afford to lose control.

He checked the bedroom next. The bed was still made, but the covers were mussed, as if Lily had fallen asleep on top of them. A black silk gown hung over the back of a chair.

Zach checked the closets and under the bed. Then he picked up the black silk gown. He didn't know what his purpose was, or even his motive. Maybe touching something that belonged to Lily would prove she was all right. Maybe he needed the feel of something that had touched her skin. Maybe he needed the scent of her, the light floral fragrance that had haunted his dreams since that Mardi Gras night so long ago.

He brought the gown to his cheek and held it there, silk against beard stubble.

"Where are you, Lily?" he whispered.

There was a small, surreptitious sound. The gown slid from his fingers, and Zach was instantly alert. The sound came again, a whispery scratching. He reached into his boot and slid a 9 mm Beretta out of his leg holster.

The sound came again, and this time it was clearly behind him.

With the training that was second nature to him, he turned, gun poised, and saw his assailant—an azalea bush scratching against the window screen. A wind had sprung up since he reached the apartment, blowing up a summer rain.

Zach didn't let his guard down. Caution had served him well for seven years.

The apartment was strangely silent. He inspected each room as he came to it, gun at the ready. The bathrooms and the kitchen showed no sign of intruders.

Quietly he approached the nursery door. Was that a sound he heard inside? The sound of breathing?

He eased open the door with his foot, standing back out of the range of fire. Nothing came through the door except the sounds of breathing. Cautiously he glanced inside.

Relief made him so weak, he leaned against the doorframe, the gun sagging from his limp hand. Lily and John Henry and Bentley were curled up together in the middle of the nursery floor, all sound asleep. Bottles and diapers and baby toys were strewed around them. The baby book lay upside down next to a rubber duck. John Henry's head was on Lily's lap, and Bentley was asleep on her foot. She was propped up on pillows, half sitting, one hand resting under her cheek and one arm across the baby. Her clothes were wrinkled, her hair had come loose from its pins, and her face was smudged from last night's mascara mixed with tears.

Zach had never seen a more beautiful sight. He stayed in the doorway, admiring all of them . . . even the dog. They were safe. He had left them for a few hours and nothing bad had happened. They were all healthy and flushed of face, piled up together, snoring softly. George's family—his baby and his dog and his sister-in-law.

"Thank you, God," Zach said, vowing silently that he would do everything in his power to keep his brother's family safe. Quietly, he slipped the gun back into his leg holster. Then he crept softly across the room and sat down on the floor next to them. Outside, the sudden summer rain New Orleans was famous for pattered against the window.

Bentley slept on, his back legs moving as he dreamed of rabbits. John Henry's mouth curved upward in a fleeting baby smile. Zach dared not guess what he was dreaming of . . . some new devilment, no doubt.

Zach tenderly touched the baby's soft curls, brushing them back from his forehead. A sense of wonder stole over him that such a perfect little being could exist. If his life had been different, he might have children now.

Lily stirred, mumbling in her sleep. He had seen her sleeping once before, in the silk-draped bed at the Monteleon. Her hair had been spread across the pillow like flame, and her face had been flushed with the aftermath of passion. Stealing away from her in the cover of darkness had filled him with regret. Aching and empty, he had left her behind on the love-tumbled bed. Was it a quirk that caused him to leave his mask . . . or a desire to leave a part of himself with her?

He wondered what she had done with the mask. Had she kept it as a reminder of that night? Or had she destroyed it in an attempt to forget?

He wished he could forget. God, how he wished he could forget. The memories were too sharp a reminder of just exactly how much he had sacrificed in his hell-bent quest for revenge.

To have a woman like Lily by his side, in his bed . . . He reached out and gently traced her cheek with his index finger. Her skin was smooth, woman smooth.

Desire rose up in him so sharply, so unexpectedly that he was taken by surprise. Quickly he pulled his hand away from her cheek. It would be a long time before his brother came home, days of forced confinement with the woman sleeping on the floor. If he was to survive with his sanity and his conscience both reasonably intact, he had to back off, had to get himself under control.

The distant jangle of the telephone brought him off the floor. John Henry yawned once, then opened his blue eyes and smiled.

He's smiling at me. Zach picked the baby up, being careful not to wake Lily and Bentley. Then he tiptoed from the nursery.

In the den, the phone continued to ring. John Henry looked up at Zach and blew a spit bubble.

"Hello, little man. Did you think I wasn't coming back?" John Henry cooed.

Grinning foolishly, Zach picked up the phone and said hello. The caller was George.

"Zach? Is that you?"

"How are you doing, George?"

"I hurt like hell, and Rose won't sneak me any french fries in here, but otherwise I'm okay. How's my baby?"

"He has the lungs of a bull elephant. You should see him, George. I think he's going to be a linebacker." John Henry grabbed the telephone cord and hung on. Zach laughed. "I'm holding him now. I think he wants to talk to you."

"Put the little fellow on."

Zach held the receiver to the baby's ear. "How's Daddy's boy, John Henry? How's my little man? Are you giving your old Uncle Zach a hard time?"

Zach took the receiver. "George, he's trying to talk to you."

"Really?"

"Absolutely. He had this little grin spread all over his face, and he's blowing bubbles. I think he's going to be a genius."

"Just like his daddy."

Zach heard Rose in the background. "George, sweetheart, let me talk."

"Here's Rose. She wants to talk to the baby."

Rose came on the phone and spent the next five minutes cooing and talking baby talk. John Henry was totally oblivious to her. He had discovered Zach's shirt buttons and found them much more interesting than his mother.

"He already adores you, Rose," Zach said into the receiver. He was very fond of his sister-in-law and would do and say almost anything to make her happy.

"You really think so?" Rose sniffed once, then lit into a regular crying jag.

"Rose?" Zach said. "What's wrong, honey? Don't cry."

George took the phone. "She's all right, Zach. It's just that I'm laid up here in the bed like a sack of potatoes and she's never held her baby."

"Not once," Rose wailed in the background.

"Is she going to be okay?" Zach asked.

"She'll be all right in a minute. Rose likes to cry. She says it purges her system.... Listen, pal, I'm glad you're there with Lily and the baby."

"I'm planning to stay here until you get home."

"Good. I know Lily's doing a damned fine job, but with both of you there, I *know* everything is going to be all right. And, Zach, if you need anything, you know you can call on Adam Miller." Adam was a staunch friend of the Taylors and a professor of parapsychology at Loyala.

"Don't worry about a thing, George. Just take care of yourself and get well so you can come on home."

Zach hung up the phone and headed back to the nursery, thinking of his brother half a world away.

George cradled the receiver and held out his arms to his wife. Rose buried her head on his chest and sobbed till his pajama top was damp.

"I'm such a big old ba-by," she sobbed.

"Yes, but you're my baby." George wound his hand in her silky hair and pulled her closer. "Go ahead and cry, sweetheart. You deserve it."

Rose sniffed once, then lifted her head. "The baby doesn't even know us."

"He will as soon as we get home."

"He'll probably think I'm Lily."

"No, he won't. He'll recognize his mother."

"You're just saying that to make me feel better, George." Rose's smile told him she was already feeling better. George pulled her down and kissed her.

"Does that make you feel better, honey?"

"Hmm. Try it again and I'll let you know."

George tried it again, kissing his wife until they both were breathless.

"If you keep that up, I'm liable to crawl under the covers with you. Then what would the nurses say?"

"They would probably say if I could do that, I'm ready to go home."

"Oh, George." Rose pinched his cheek.

"I love you, Rose."

"I love you, too, George."

"Enough to sneak me some french fries?"

"Don't you try to con me, George Taylor." She got off the bed and favored him with her most severe look. George was enchanted. When she held her lips tight, trying for severity, she emphasized a dimple in the side of her cheek. And there was no way in the world she could keep her eyes from dancing.

"Would I do that, sweetheart?"

"You'd darned tootin', George Taylor. There will be no more french fries for you. You have a baby to think about, you know."

"I'm thinking about him, Rose. I wonder if he's thinking about us?"

What John Henry was thinking about was how he could get Uncle Zach to whistle that tune he'd whistled yesterday and maybe rock him in the rocking chair again. He liked that.

He pulled on Uncle Zach's shirt button and batted his blue eyes. But his uncle was not paying him any attention.

John Henry started to protest, then he decided to see what it was that held his uncle's interest. It might be something he liked. He followed Uncle Zach's gaze, and all he saw was Aunt Lily and that funny dog. He wished the dog would get up and make that nice, loud racket. Maybe he could learn how to talk like the dog.

He lost interest in the dog and began to study his left foot. He liked the way it wiggled. John Henry burped and sighed, then leaned his head against his Uncle Zach's big chest, content.

Lily awoke to the sound of rain and with the feeling that she was not alone. Squinting through eyes that were puffy from too many tears and too little sleep, she looked up and saw Zach. He was sitting in the rocking chair, holding John

Henry and studying her in a possessive way that made the back of her neck tingle.

That was all she needed: to be attracted to Zach Taylor, the king of love 'em and leave 'em. She quickly closed her eyes in order to get herself under control. She took a few deep breaths, then opened her eyes again.

Zach was looking right at her. Fatigue lines were etched around his mouth, but sparks of humor lit his eyes.

"Good morning, Lily. Playing hide-and-seek?"

"Don't be ridiculous. I'm too old to play games."

He smiled at her. She was acutely aware of the contrast they made—Zach Taylor looking smug and gorgeous while she looked like something Bentley had dragged in, something stale and admittedly *old*. She must look shocking.

But more shocking than the way she looked, was the way she *felt*. She found herself actually wanting to look pretty. And all because Zach Taylor was watching her.

What would her family say about her now? Rose was always the twin who primped, while Lily studied. Rose was the one who took up an hour in the bathroom, while Lily didn't care that she had only fifteen minutes to dress for school. Looking pretty was for the cheerleaders and homecoming queens. Women of potential merely wanted to look neat.

Now she didn't even look neat.

She smoothed the front of her blouse and tried to tuck her hair back into the few pins remaining on her head. It was a losing battle.

Zach continued studying her, no doubt for his own amusement. She hugged the pillow to her chest, putting a small barrier between them.

Bentley came awake, sniffed at her leg, growled in distaste, then trotted off to better things. Even the dog found her unappetizing. Abandoned by Zach, rejected by the dog, thoroughly ignored by John Henry and more than a little disturbed with herself, Lily went on the attack.

"Why are you here, Zach?"

"I told you I would stay the night."

"You should have qualified that. John Henry got up at some god-awful hour this morning, and you were nowhere to be seen."

"Sorry. I had a few errands."

"In the middle of the night?"

"Yes."

In spite of Lily's ups and downs with men, her life had always been orderly, manageable and relatively sane. Now it was a roller coaster out of control. And all because of a nine-pound baby and this man.

"I suppose all your errands had bleached blond hair and wore size-six jeans?"

Zach didn't reply immediately. Seconds later Lily wished he had, for his intense scrutiny was beginning to make her feel uncomfortable... and rumpled, besides. Then he did a most unexpected thing: he laughed. She didn't see what was so funny.

"Ahh, Lily. I would never have suspected you were the jealous type."

"The jealous type! Don't flatter yourself."

Zach sat in the rocking chair, contentedly holding the baby and watching her as if he found great pleasure in her company. Awareness of him spread through Lily until her body was zinging like the plucked string of a violin.

Furthermore, she couldn't seem to take her eyes off him. Plain and simple, he was beautiful, beautiful in the dangerous way of men who are strong and sexy and tender, as well. Maybe it was because he was holding John Henry that she thought of him as tender. Or maybe it was because of the way he had touched her so very long ago.

She had to do something to divert her attention.

Still sitting on the floor, she started picking up the mess—diapers that hadn't worked right, toys John Henry had rejected, the baby book that hadn't told her a damned thing she needed to know. She could feel Zach's gaze on the back of her neck.

Why had he come back? And why was he acting as if he was born to the role of uncle? Didn't he have women to chase and parties to throw and hell to raise?

She sneaked a glance at him. In spite of the amused expression on his face, he looked tired. But he looked contented, too, holding John Henry in his lap, one large hand resting easily on the baby's chubby leg. Maybe she had misjudged him. Certainly she had been rude to him.

Clutching the baby book hard in her left hand, she faced Zach.

"Look…I'm sorry about all those things I said. I was out of line."

"You're just tired."

His kindness almost undid her. She felt her throat clog with unshed tears. She swallowed hard and squeezed her eyes shut for a moment. When she opened them, Zach was smiling at her, this time with tenderness.

"Why don't you go back to bed and rest, Lily? I'll take care of John Henry."

"You're tired, too." She felt an unexpected desire to smooth away the fatigue lines around his mouth, to touch them gently with her fingertips and massage and caress—

Shocked by her own thoughts, she stood up and began to put away the toys.

She could feel him staring at her back. Silence stretched between them, broken only by an occasional coo from John Henry—showing his adoration for Zach. Lily was going to be showing more than adoration if she wasn't careful—she was going to be showing naked desire and a complete lack of common sense.

"Thank you for coming back, Zach," she said as she struggled with John Henry's toys and her composure. "Let me finish putting these things away, and then I'll take the baby so you can go."

She heard the rocking chair creak, heard the fall of his footsteps, felt his body heat as he moved in close behind her. Her breath got trapped in her throat. He touched her shoulder, lightly at first and then with a possessiveness that left her light-headed.

"Lily..." She didn't turn, *couldn't* turn. "Look at me, Lily."

Slowly, she turned to face him.

Their gazes met, held, and for a shining moment they were lifted out of their ordinary lives and into a vision of such beauty, they were both speechless. Lily saw Zach as a handsome knight in shining armor, her rescuer, her hero, her lover. And he saw her as a beautiful goddess, his redemption, his future, his lover.

"Zach..."

"I'm staying, Lily."

His words rushed through her. *Staying. Here in the apartment. Only one bed. Days of seeing his endearing smile. Nights of lying awake with him...*

She knew she should protest, but all she could do was ask, "How long?"

"Until George and Rose return."

Lily felt such a mixture of emotions, she thought she might faint. Gladness came, and on its heels, wonder and finally, terror. Already he was chipping away at the careful wall she had built between them. Already she was getting weaker, more vulnerable. What would happen with days of forced confinement?

She stared at him, mute. He shifted John Henry in his arms, never taking his eyes off Lily.

"Why?" she whispered.

Zach hadn't expected her question. *Why?* he thought. *Because I can't look at you without wanting you. Because I can't bear to leave you here with a baby that could be mine... mine and yours. Because I'm getting soft. Because*

*I'm scared. Because I want to protect you and John Henry.
Because I let my family down once and I need redemption.*

The thoughts tumbled through his mind, but he told none
of them to Lily.

"I could give you a dozen reasons," he finally said. "All
of which you would probably question—or argue against.
The simple truth is, I'm staying because I must."

Chapter 6

Lily accepted Zach's explanation as she accepted all other natural phenomena—the silent deadliness of a tornado, the clash of elements that produced hurricanes, the white blindness of a blizzard, the deep mysteries of the Mississippi River. She tugged at a stray curl, knowing one curl didn't matter in her tumbled mess of hair. Needing the distraction and the reassurance of routine, she fussed with her hair anyway.

"Then perhaps we can work out a schedule so we won't..." She paused, not quite knowing what sort of routine would protect her from this man and her own runaway emotions.

"So we won't both exhaust ourselves," he finished smoothly and not without kindness. "I'm going to take care of the baby now, so you can go ahead and get some rest."

"But you're tired, too."

"I'm used to staying up most of the night."

Lily didn't ask why. She thought she already knew. *Wild parties. The racket of dance bands. Women.* She didn't want to think about Zach being with other women.

Oh, God. His *other* women? As if she were one of them. As if she would ever reach out for a man again...in this lifetime or the next. What was the matter with her? *Fatigue,* she decided.

Retreat was her only defense.

"Thanks. Call me if you need me."

His eyebrows quirked upward, and a devilish gleam came into his eye. Zach was ever the rake, and she wasn't about to get burned again.

Gathering her dignity, she left the nursery.

In the privacy of Rose's bedroom, Lily leaned her head against the door...and almost fell asleep standing up. Quickly she showered and crawled into bed. Wrapped in a cocoon of clean covers, she fell asleep.

The rain had stopped.

With Lily asleep in her bed and the baby asleep in his crib, the apartment was quiet. But it was not the empty silence of his big house, the cavernous, yawning kind of quietness that swallows a man's soul. It was a gentle, tender stillness that said, "Something precious rests here."

Zach sat in his brother's kitchen, drinking from his brother's coffee mug, and felt envy. He envied George his wife, his baby, his job, the very ordinariness of his life.

He had never envied a man anything, and certainly not his brother. The feeling was so foreign to him, Zach turned it over and over in his mind, examining it from all sides.

He could try to blame fatigue, but he was too honest for that. No, it wasn't fatigue that was turning his world upside down. It was tasting the fruits he had forbidden himself—singing to a baby, watching a sleeping woman with tumbled hair and mascara on her cheeks, sitting in a rocking chair whistling an old river song.

There was a time when whistling a song came naturally to him. He had grown up happy. When his parents and Emily were alive, when he was young and full of dreams, he used to run beside the river, with George trying to keep pace, whistling and yelling just for the sheer exuberance of hearing the sound of his own voice. In those days, he had pictured himself as invincible. Nothing could daunt him, nothing could harm him. He was the master of all he surveyed, and he made sure his survey was vast.

And then death had stalked his family. First his parents, then Emily. He discovered he wasn't invincible, after all. He guessed he had known it all along, but to have it brought so shockingly to his attention had shaken him.

He lifted George's mug to his lips. The coffee had become cold, but he drank it anyway. Somewhere in Spain, George was probably holding on to his wife. Zach was holding on to a ceramic mug. He'd had a small taste of forbidden fruits, and he wanted more. Living for revenge was a hell of a lonely life.

Restless, Zach put down the mug and walked to the nursery. Bentley, who had begun to fancy himself quite a watchdog now that a little, loud, helpless person was on the premises, left his place beside the crib and growled at Zach.

"Show-off." Zach bent down and scratched Bentley's ears, then he tiptoed to the crib and watched the sleeping baby.

John Henry was so innocent. So helpless. And so very easy to love.

Tender feelings he had kept bottled up for years flowed freely through Zach every time he looked at the baby. He hadn't intended to lose his heart to his nephew, but he guessed it was safe since he would soon turn the child over to his father. Ultimately George was responsible for John Henry. It was George, not Zach, who would be father, provider, role model—and most of all, protector.

"He looks peaceful sleeping, doesn't he?"

The sound of Lily's voice startled him. He hadn't heard Lily come up behind him until she spoke. That bothered Zach. No one had ever gotten that close to him without his full knowledge. Apparently love caused carelessness.

Instead of answering Lily, he studied her. Her skin glowed from sleep. Or perhaps it glowed from the reflection of the soft, peach-colored silk blouse she wore. Or maybe it was her red hair that made her skin so luminescent.

"You look lovely," he said.

Lily was pleased by his compliment . . . and then vaguely uncomfortable because she was pleased. She had always thought women who sought after the compliments of men were vain and silly. And now she found herself in the same boat. She had dressed with Zach in mind. She had hoped he would notice how well her blouse set off her skin.

He had. And she didn't quite know what to do about it.

Maybe Howard had been right. Maybe she did have an adding machine instead of a heart. Facts and figures and rules and routines were a breeze for her. But one simple compliment from Zach, and she was as lost as if she had wandered into a maze.

Perhaps she had. The maze of male-female relationships. Being lost in that maze was not new to her. What *was* new was wanting to be able to find her way, wanting to know how to get in and how to get out again without leaving bits and pieces of herself behind.

Zach was looking at her with appreciation lighting his eyes. She had to say something.

"Are you hungry?"

"You always make me hungry, Lily." His eyes darkened, and her face began to flush. And then he rescued her. "I'm hungry for one of those big hero sandwiches George says you make."

"The one with the olives?" she asked, relieved.

"And the pastrami."

"I'll make us some." She escaped to the kitchen.

Zach watched her leave, then kept looking through the open door long after she had disappeared down the hall. He was slipping, admitting to her that she made him hungry. Lily was too smart not to know what he was talking about.

And he certainly didn't intend to lead her on or to give her any ideas that there would be a repeat of what had happened four years ago at the Monteleon. Giving his heart temporarily to John Henry was one thing, but giving a part of himself to Lily was another thing altogether. George wouldn't be along to take Lily off his hands.

As tempting as the idea was, Zach couldn't start a relationship he had no hope of finishing. In the safety of his brother's apartment, a temporary relationship might work. But what about afterward? What about all those times he would be on the mean city streets mingling with criminals, looking over his shoulder for a knife or a gun or merely a thug with a strong arm?

No. It was best to forget about starting anything with Lily. He would never subject a woman to the kind of danger he lived with, especially a woman he cared for.

He took one last look at the sleeping baby, then joined Lily in the kitchen.

"The sandwiches look good," he said, spying them.

"They are." Lily set out two plates. "Tea? Soda?"

"Tea. I need a caffeine boost."

"What you need is a nap. Why don't you take one? I thought I'd take John Henry with me when I walk Bentley."

"No." Hot color flooded Lily's cheeks, and Zach knew he had been too sharp. "What I meant to say is, I'll go with you."

"There's no need."

"I insist."

"Why?"

He couldn't explain his need to accompany her on a simple walk without explaining a whole lot more, and he couldn't do that. One of the things he hated most about his job was the lies.

"Call it male ego, Lily. Since John Henry came into my life, I keep having this vision of myself as indispensable."

"You're not indispensable, but you come close—where John Henry's concerned, that is," she added, lest he misunderstand.

"That's settled then. We'll all go for a walk as soon as the baby wakes up." Zach took a large bite of his sandwich. "Mmm. Good."

"Thanks." With the issue of walking the dog settled, an ease came over them. "But don't expect this kind of gourmet meal everyday. A hero sandwich is about the extent of my culinary art."

"I'm a thoroughly modern man, Lily. Not only do I plan to do my share in the kitchen, I also plan to dazzle you with my cooking skills."

"I don't dazzle easily." Lily was surprised at how easy it was to relax and exchange light banter with Zach. This was a side of him she had never seen.

"Wait until you see the way I wield a dish towel," he said.

She propped her elbows on the table and leaned closer to him, laughing. "That's all well and good, but do you do floors?"

"I was born doing floors. I *dance* while I do floors."

They laughed together, surprising themselves so that they stopped and looked at each other almost guiltily.

"I don't want to wake the baby," Lily whispered.

"Neither do I."

"It seems like a gift from heaven that he's sleeping so long. I guess I tired him out this morning trying to get a diaper to stay on him."

"He *is* sleeping a long time. I think I'll go check on him."

"I'll go with you."

Together they went into the nursery and stood beside John Henry's crib, their shoulders touching. It was a companionable touch, and neither of them moved apart.

Nor did they want to. After years of being an independent woman, Lily was astonished that she found so much comfort in merely standing beside a man with her shoulder touching his—especially since that man was Zach Taylor.

And Zach reveled in the simple pleasure of being himself with a woman. No pretenses. No artificial barriers. When had he dropped the mask? In the kitchen while they joked over hero sandwiches? In the nursery when he found Lily and the baby safe? Or had it been earlier? Had he dropped the charade the minute he entered his brother's apartment?

He didn't know. All he knew was that being himself felt good.

"Sleeping like an angel," Lily said.

"A tiger in disguise. It won't last." Chuckling softly, Zach took Lily's arm and led her toward the door.

John Henry woke up just in time to see that he had a large audience... one he was about to lose if he didn't do something in a hurry. Crying always worked with Aunt Lily and Uncle Zach, but he was bored with crying. He decided to try something new.

"Wait a minute. Don't leave me in this crib," he said, but it came out, "Goo...oo."

"Did you hear that?" Lily said, turning.

"He's a genius, just like his Uncle Zach." Zach reached into the crib and lifted John Henry out. "Hello, little man. Did you have a nice nap?"

John Henry smiled and batted his long eyelashes.

"I think he's trying to say yes, Lily."

"I'm sure he did. He seems very advanced for his age. Do you think we should start reading Shakespeare to him instead of Mother Goose?" She was only half kidding. The baby book didn't say so, but she thought she remembered somebody on a TV talk show discussing the advantages of reading great literature to babies.

"It can't hurt," Zach said.

Then, realizing they were talking about John Henry as if they would always be in charge of him, Lily and Zach exchanged sheepish looks.

"Let's get ready for that walk," Zach told her. "I'll get John Henry ready if you'll put Bentley on his leash."

"Let's swap. Bentley hates me." Zach gave her a funny look. "Well…John Henry is not too fond of me, either, but at least he doesn't bite my legs."

"I'm sure they both love you, Lily. They just have a funny way of showing it."

She could have hugged him for that. And almost did. Instead, she smiled at him, and he smiled back. They stood that way awhile until they both became self-conscious.

"Well … Let's get ready," Zach finally said, trying to be brisk. But all he wanted to be was mellow.

"Elephant, John Henry," Lily instructed the baby. "See the big elephant?" She and Zach both pointed at the huge pachyderm standing in his enclosure, eating hay.

John Henry preferred to watch people at the popcorn wagon nearby.

Lily had planned to walk Bentley in the French Quarter, but Zach had suggested Audubon Park. Loading them all in an ordinary brown sedan, he had driven there taking the long way around to make sure he was not spotted and followed.

When Bentley had had his fill, neither Zach nor Lily could resist taking John Henry on his first outing to a zoo.

"He doesn't seem interested in the elephants," Lily said.

"A little man of his persuasions will be much more interested in the tigers."

Looking like an ordinary couple, Lily and Zach went to the big-cat area.

John Henry didn't disappoint them. True to his uncle's predictions, he watched the tigers until his attention was caught by a red balloon attached to the wrist of a small boy passing by.

Zach bought six red balloons and tied all the strings together, then spent considerable time batting them about for John Henry's amusement. Lily didn't think he looked at all silly. In fact, she had never seen Zach look more appealing.

When John Henry tired of the balloons, Lily bought him an enormous stuffed tiger. He didn't get the hang of having a stuffed animal right away, so Lily showed him how to rub the soft, plush fake fur and how to snuggle his head up close.

"See, John Henry. Look." She cuddled her cheek against the stuffed animal. "Hmm. Soft."

To the ordinary passerby, she might have looked besotted, but to Zach she looked charming, more charming, even, than when she had been asleep on the nursery floor.

The afternoon vanished, and neither of them knew where it had gone.

"My, how the time has flown," Lily said.

"But there was no point in leaving," Zach said. "John Henry was having so much fun."

In fact, John Henry had been asleep in Zach's arms for the last hour. But in the carnival atmosphere of the zoo, with the late-afternoon sun shining on them, Zach and Lily had become different people. She forgot convention, and he forgot danger. She forgot being a woman of potential, and he forgot being a man with a deadly purpose. They were ordinary people, united by their love of a small baby boy.

As they settled into the car for the drive back, both thought how right it felt to be going to an apartment that would not be empty. It felt like going home.

Zach didn't go directly to bed when they got back to the apartment—as Lily had insisted. Although he didn't say so out loud, he knew he was better with the baby than Lily. She was still uncertain of herself and somewhat intimidated by the opinionated John Henry.

"But you haven't slept in forty-eight hours," she said.

"Look what I would have missed if I had gone to sleep."

She didn't argue. For one thing, arguing with Zach would be like trying to get the north wind to blow south. And for another, she was selfishly grateful for his help.

By the time ten o'clock came, he was dead on his feet. Lily left him stretched out on the sofa, reading a magazine, while she made one last check to be sure John Henry was tucked in for the night.

When she got back to the den, Zach was sleeping with the magazine still clutched in his hand. Asleep, he looked younger, more vulnerable. The lines of tension and fatigue were eased, and a lock of dark hair fell across his forehead.

Lily was amazed at how approachable he seemed—and at how much she wanted to approach him. Maybe it was the influence of John Henry. Or perhaps it was the influence of the apartment. Lily's own apartment was orderly and carefully appointed...and sterile, she suddenly realized. She had left it only a few days ago, just across the courtyard. And yet now, standing among Rose's cozy clutter and watching Zach sleep, she felt as if it had been a lifetime ago.

His chest rose and fell with his even breathing. If he were George and she were Rose, she would ease onto the sofa, being careful not to wake him, and gently pull his head onto her lap. Then she would smooth back his hair. He would snuggle close and maybe sigh.... If he were George and she were Rose.

Lily sighed. She hadn't fantasized since she was twenty and she and Rose had fallen madly in love with the same boy. They had both flirted with him. At least, Rose had flirted and Lily had tried. He had chosen Rose, of course. And Lily had turned her efforts toward scholastic success. Then later, toward business success.

Zach stirred and the magazine slipped from his fingers. Lily picked it up, leaning close to Zach. She could see the fine pattern of hairs on his darkly tanned and beautifully muscled forearms. She was mesmerized.

Like a moth drawn to a flame, she reached out. Her hand hovered over his arm, so close she could feel his body heat, so close she could almost feel the fine hairs brushing against her fingertips.

There was a sudden whir of movement. Before Lily knew what was happening or could even cry out, Zach had her on her back with his forearm across her throat and a gun aimed at her temple.

She opened her mouth, but no sound came out. Her eyes widened as she felt her breath being squeezed from her throat. Then recognition dawned across Zach's face.

"Oh, my God . . . Lily." He eased his arm off her throat. The gun fell to the floor as he cupped her face with both hands. "Did I hurt you?" Bending close, he examined her face and throat. His touch was exquisitely tender, and his eyes were so dark, they might have been bits of the night caught in his face.

He had not hurt her, and she might have told him so, but she was incapable of speech.

Zach was still stretched out on top of her, his broad chest pressed intimately against her breasts, her legs trapped beneath his. She was achingly aware of every hard muscle and ridge and plane of his body. She sizzled. She burned. She longed. And finally she wept inside for what would never be.

"Lily?" Zach's hand was on her lips now, tracing their outline. "I didn't hurt you, did I?"

Yes, she thought. *You hurt me four years ago, and I haven't stopped hurting since.* She closed her eyes, desperately hoping that shutting him out of her vision would shut him out of her soul.

"I'm so sorry, sweet ... So sorry." He pressed his lips against her temple. "I didn't know it was you." His hands were in her hair. "Reflex action," he murmured.

She thought she might keep her eyes shut forever, just stay on Rose's floor with her eyes closed and Zach spread across her like a banquet. She was starved. She would slowly take all of him into herself, through her skin.

"It's okay," she whispered.

"It's not okay."

Moving with swift purpose, Zach lifted Lily and sat on the sofa with her in his lap. She fit wonderfully well in his arms, he noticed. And he was not inclined to let her go.

"I have to make sure you're all right," he told her, although he knew it was a lie. What he was doing was as straightforward as it was old-fashioned. He was enjoying the simple pleasure of cuddling with a warm and sexy woman. It was not desire he was feeling, though heaven knew that would come soon enough. He was feeling grateful for the small excuse to sit on the sofa holding Lily. He could even pretend that he might do the same thing anytime he wanted to ... say on a Tuesday afternoon when he had come home from an ordinary job. Or on an early Sunday morning while church bells rang across the city and his children slept peacefully in their beds.

"Really," she said, "I'm all right. You don't have to worry."

"Let me worry just a little while longer."

Lily knew she hadn't made much of a protest, and she considered protesting again. But she didn't want to. She was glad to have an excuse to sit on Zach's lap. That was something she didn't want to think about right now. Maybe she'd mull over her motives in the morning when she wasn't so tired. Right now she just wanted to stay where she was.

She gave a soft sigh and settled against his chest with her head resting over his heart. Its strong, steady beat was reassuring.

Zach's arms tightened ever so slightly. Her hair brushed against his cheek. It was soft and fragrant. Until that moment he hadn't realized how much he missed that small pleasure—sitting in a cozy apartment with the touch of a woman's hair against his skin, while the rest of the world scurried madly about doing all the things people thought necessary to do in order to be fulfilled or entertained or productive.

Rose's lamp glowed softly nearby, and her sofa cushions enveloped them as if they were accustomed to welcoming two bodies joined so closely together. Outside, azalea and oleander bushes whispered against the window, telling secrets of the night.

Bentley padded into the room and tried to stir up some interest by wagging his tail and panting. Being soundly ignored, he stalked off toward the nursery, where he would have a more receptive audience. He was so mad, he forgot to chew up a chair leg.

The minutes stretched out like beads strung together until they made a shining rope of time that bound Lily and Zach to each other. Content, Zach's chest rose and fell with the regular rhythm of his breathing. Lulled, Lily almost fell asleep with her cheek resting against his heart.

Then he began to trace the delicate curve of her inner arm. His hand was large and dark against her fair skin. Lily watched in fascination as his hand moved back and forth, back and forth. His breathing became harsh, and hers became erratic.

A little while longer, she told herself.

Just a small touch, he told himself.

But a small touch was not enough. His body began to respond and he wanted more. Lily tensed, but it was not the stiffness of rejection he felt, it was the tight readying of the body to make love.

There was a sound, a half moan. Neither of them knew who had made it, but it served to make them both vividly attuned to the moment.

She glanced up at him. His face was tight and his eyes were hooded. As for other parts of his body... She was only too well aware of their condition.

"I'm fine now, Zach." Her voice was husky. She cleared her throat and sat up. The small movement was a mistake. It positioned her squarely on his growing arousal. "Really, I am," she added as she hastily departed his lap.

"That's good, Lily."

He didn't move from the sofa. She wondered if he could. She thought every step she took might be her last. Her legs felt like butter. Finally she made it to a chair.

Now that she was out of his arms, she remembered that there was something very important she wanted to talk to him about.

"Zach..." She swung around to look at him—and forgot what she was going to say. His dark eyes were glowing with an unholy fire. The top buttons of his shirt were open, exposing dark chest hair, and his jeans, molded like sin to his delectable body, revealed exactly how much she had excited him.

She quickly glanced away. "About that gun," she said.

"It's nothing. Just something I carry."

"Nothing?" She faced him again. "I touched you and before I knew what was happening, I had an arm against my throat and a gun at my temple."

"You touched me?"

"Don't change the subject."

"You touched me while I slept, Lily?"

"Well, you needn't look as if I had awarded you the Nobel Prize or anything. I was just picking up the magazine you had dropped."

"I see."

His smile told her he was seeing more than she was telling. She started to explain her actions once more, then realized he was cleverly leading her away from the subject again.

"You didn't explain the presence of that gun to my satisfaction, Zach, nor your ability to use it so well."

He laced his hands behind his head and leaned back as if he were totally relaxed. Lily wasn't fooled. She saw the tension in his shoulders and his jaw.

"Call me the last of a dying breed, Lily. I still believe in a man's right to bear arms."

"Many men do, but not all of them carry their firearms so handily."

"A personal quirk of mine."

His expression became closed and guarded. Lily knew she would get no further explanations from him.

"I don't know whether to feel safe or threatened," she said.

"You're safe, Lily."

They stared at each other, and neither of them could have told whether she was safe from him or because of him.

Chapter 7

"I'll get sheets and a pillow for you," Lily said, standing abruptly. "Unless you would prefer the bed."

He had a quick, bright vision of Lily spread across the bed like an exotic flower. He would definitely prefer the bed...with Lily in it.

"No. The sofa will be fine."

"Good. That's settled."

She left the den, her footsteps brisk and efficient sounding. He turned to admire the view. Her hips were softly rounded and womanly, the kind a man could get his hands around and hang on to. By contrast, her waist was tiny.

He still felt the warmth of where she had sat on his lap. There was a residual arousal that let him know exactly how hard it was going to be to stay in the apartment.

Lily came back with the bedding, and he took it from her silently. She stood in front of him for a moment, hesitant, as if she might offer to help spread the sheets.

Her face was still flushed from their tumble on the floor. Her breasts would be that way, too, rosy and moist looking. They got that way in the heat of passion. She had the fair, delicate skin of redheads.

He had seen Lily's body heat up and flush once, long ago, and he wanted to see it again. Now. He wanted to rip aside her clothes and run his hands over her and watch the subtle rouging of her skin. He wanted to feel the silky texture of her beneath his fingers. He wanted to bury his face against her breasts and feel the hum of her heart.

Her eyes slid downward, and her color got deeper. If she didn't leave soon, he would lose all control.

"Well . . . good night," she finally said, her voice husky.

She left before he could say anything. Which was just as well. If he had opened his mouth, he would have said, "Rescue me, Lily. Let me bury myself in you and stay buried until the rest of the world either vanishes or grows sane."

It was a damned good thing she had gone.

He punched the pillow viciously. Then he stripped off all his clothes. Naked, he spotted his gun. He slid it back into its holster, then stowed it under his pillow.

He sank into the soft sofa cushions, and his eyes closed before his head hit the pillow. He thought of Lily, in Rose and George's bed. Was she wearing the black silk gown he'd seen?

John Henry was down the hall, probably getting ready to wake up and cry at any minute.

"Dammit." Zach sat up and reached for his shorts. No sense being unprepared.

In Rose's bed, Lily lay with her arms stiffly at her sides, her back rigid. She was proud of her control. She was so damned controlled, her jaw was clenched. In the morning her teeth would probably ache.

What was Zach doing? Probably sound asleep by now. After all, he was accustomed to having women loll around in his lap and practically drool at his feet. Or was he?

Lily stared into the darkness. If there was anything she had learned in the past few days, it was that Zach Taylor was not what he appeared to be. How much of the rumors she had heard were exactly that—rumors? And how much was the truth?

For that matter, was she what she appeared to be? In her practical suits and with her hair all pinned up, she gave the appearance of a successful businesswoman, as efficient as a machine. Who would have guessed that underneath it all was a wanton woman waiting to be released? Even more telling than that, who would have guessed there was a woman who longed for the things her sister had—home, husband and children?

She had enough to worry about, Lily decided. Life was complicated enough with taking care of a dog determined to drive her crazy and a baby bent on proving her unfit for motherhood. Why look for more trouble?

There had to be a practical solution to all her problems. But before Lily could come up with it, she was sound asleep.

The loud cry brought Lily and Zach out of their beds. Fully alert, Zach hurried toward the nursery, while Lily fumbled her way to her door.

They crashed into each other in the hall. They stayed tangled for a small eternity, her silk gown wrapped around his legs, his bare chest pressing against her breasts, his hand flattened on the small of her back, hers clutching his upper arm.

John Henry cried on. He might have been on the moon for all they knew.

Zach heard the sound of his own blood rushing in his ears. Lily heard her nerve endings snap, one by one. He drew a deep breath and almost drowned in the sweet woman scent of her. She tried to breathe and thought she couldn't.

But she did. Finally. Backing away, she said, ''Excuse me.''

"Certainly."

He wouldn't have given a fig for his chances of surviving this nocturnal encounter with her.

It was Bentley who saved the day—for both of them. He came roaring out of the nursery, his claws scrabbling on the floor, barking for all he was worth. Didn't these people know his baby was crying?

"Go back to bed, Lily. I'll take this feeding."

"Let me, Zach. You're tired."

He was. More than a little.

"Thanks, Lily. Call me if you need me."

She stood in the hallway until he had disappeared. They were always saying that to each other. *Call me if you need me.*

Well, she wasn't going to need him even if hell froze over. She had needed him once and look what had happened. The sweet feeling of being in his arms swept over her. She amended her resolution. She might need Zach, but she wasn't going to admit that to him.

John Henry's cries sent her into motion. Bucking up her courage, she entered the nursery—with Bentley right behind her, looking thoroughly miffed and ready for revenge.

"Don't you dare create a ruckus while I'm busy with this baby," Lily told Bentley as she reached for John Henry. "I have my hands full without you making trouble."

There was nothing Bentley loved more than sneaky revenge. He pretended innocence while she changed the baby's diaper. Then, after she had settled the baby in bed and gone back to her room, he stole out to teach Lily a lesson or two about talking down to a very fine watchdog.

Next morning, the doorbell brought them all out of bed. Zach swung his legs over the sofa and reached for his pants. Lily grabbed her robe and headed for the door. John Henry opened his eyes and wondered what that new sound was and what he should do about it. Bentley sat on his haunches in the hallway, hoping the caller was somebody he wanted to bite.

Lily rounded the corner to the den and came to an abrupt halt. Zach stood beside the sofa, shirtless and yawning. He was a view worth admiring if he hadn't had so much competition.

"Bentley," she whispered, looking at his handiwork. Magazines were pulled out of the basket, their covers torn to shreds; every toy he owned was strewed across the floor, and one of George's old boots decorated a chair cushion. In the midst of all that splendor was an empty carton of milk that obviously had been dredged out of the garbage can in the kitchen.

The doorbell pinged again. "Is anybody home?"

"Mrs. McGruder," Lily whispered.

"I thought she wasn't supposed to visit until next week," Zach said, reaching for his shirt.

"Just a minute," Lily yelled as she rushed toward the den and grabbed George's boot off the chair. "Quick. Help with this mess."

She and Zach went into action.

"The very idea," Lily fumed. "Why Rose keeps such a dog is beyond me."

"Every boy needs a dog... but maybe not one like Bentley." Zach turned to her with his arms full of shredded magazines. "What shall I do with all this?"

"Stuff it into the closet," Lily instructed as she stuffed dog toys under the sofa.

Mrs. McGruder rang the bell again, then followed with a tapping on the door.

"Might as well face the music." Lily passed Bentley as she hurried to the door. "I'll deal with you later, you little devil."

Bentley flattened his ears for his attack on the caller. Zach collared him just as Lily opened the door.

"Mrs. McGruder," Lily said, smiling as if entertaining in her robe without prior notice was something she did every day. "Do come in."

"Hello, Mrs. McGruder." Zach extended one hand while holding on to Bentley with the other. "This is Rose and George's dog, Bentley."

"What a nice little doggie." Opalene McGruder rubbed Bentley's head, and he acted as if he had never intended to take a nip at her plump legs. Then she adjusted her hat and fidgeted with her purse handle. "Well . . . How is little John Henry doing?"

"Great," Zach said.

"Just marvelous," Lily chimed in.

Opalene's eyes, close set like two dried up raisins in her face, darted from one to the other. Her smile was fixed.

Zach was an expert at reading expressions and body language. What he saw made him vaguely uncomfortable. *Something is wrong,* he told himself. *Don't go jumping to conclusions.*

"Come into the den and sit down, Mrs. McGruder." Lily led the way. "Can I get you anything? Coffee?"

"No. . . ." Opalene sank into the chair that had recently held George's boot. "Well . . . yes. Coffee would be good. Black. No sugar."

Zach watched Lily leave the den. She was performing like a thoroughbred under pressure. He was prouder of her than he had any right to be.

Opalene crossed her legs and tugged at her skirt. Then she started fiddling again with her hat that had never needed attention in the first place. Her eyes darted around the room, finally settling on Zach.

"I don't usually drop by like this with no notice," she said.

"Your visit is unexpected, but certainly welcome."

"I guess you're wondering why I came."

Zach didn't like the sound of that. The obvious reason for her visit was John Henry.

"No," he said smoothly. "I'm sure its customary for you to check on the well-being of the babies your agency places. I appreciate that kind of thoroughness. Children are too precious to be left to fate."

"How is he doing?"

She had already asked that once. Zach tensed with apprehension.

"He's eating and sleeping well, and he smiles and blows bubbles a lot. We love him, and I think he loves us." He settled back against the sofa cushions and tried to look relaxed. "Family is very important to the Taylors, Mrs. McGruder. John Henry is part of the Taylor family now, and I will devote my time to his welfare until my brother returns. Lily, too, of course. She's crazy about her sister's baby."

Opalene pursed her small mouth and looked at a spot on the wall above Zach's head. His uneasiness tripled.

"Here's your coffee," Lily said, entering the den carrying a tray. "The way you like it, I hope."

She had changed into slacks, but her hair was still loose. Normally Zach would have taken time to appreciate it. Now he focused all his energies on studying Opalene McGruder.

Lily handed Opalene a cup of steaming coffee, then offered one to Zach. He took it, glad for the quick jolt of energy caffeine would give him.

They all sipped coffee and watched each other over the rims of their cups. Opalene's hand trembled, and Lily's back didn't touch her chair anywhere. She looked as tense as Zach felt.

Lily opened her mouth as if she might say something, then snapped it shut. Zach waited, gauging the situation before he would commit himself to further conversation. Only the tiny slurping sound Opalene made as she sipped her coffee relieved the heavy quiet.

Finally Lily could stand the silence no longer. She set her cup down and folded her hands across her lap.

"I'll take you to the nursery if you want to see John Henry." Opalene gave her a pained looked. "Or I can bring him here, if you prefer," Lily added.

"No. Actually I didn't come to see the baby." Opalene put her own coffee cup on a nearby table. "But I did come about him."

Lily put her hand over her throat, and Zach waited. Opalene caught the hem of her skirt and began to pleat it between her fingers.

"I had visitors late yesterday afternoon, a Mr. and Mrs. Bemus Rockman." She paused, gathering courage. Zach knew the name—Bemus Rockman, sugar magnate, pillar of the community, influential civic leader. Zach had had him under investigation for years, but had never been able to prove any connection between Rockman and the drug underworld.

"I tried to call here after they left, but I got no answer." She folded and refolded her skirt. "So I just decided to wait until this morning."

"We were at the zoo." Lily looked at Zach, her eyes wide and questioning.

He gave her a reassuring wink. "I know the Rockman name, Mrs. McGruder. What do they have to do with John Henry?"

"They think he is their grandson."

"No." Lily half rose from her chair, then sank back down, her face pale.

"I'm sorry, I'm sorry. I didn't mean to blurt it out like that."

The fear that had been growing in Zach hardened to a heavy mass. He wanted to hit something. Instead, he sought to bring a sense of order to the situation.

"Obviously they are mistaken," he said. "You would certainly not have released John Henry for adoption if there had been any legitimate claims to him."

Opalene looked relieved. "Well, of course they're mistaken. I told them that." She released her skirt and tried to smooth out the wrinkles. "But they were most insistent."

"I don't understand any of this," Lily said.

"Why don't you tell us everything, Mrs. McGruder." Zach moved to stand behind Lily's chair and put his hand on her shoulder. She looked as if she needed him, and for some reason, he needed her. More than that, he wanted Opalene to see that they presented a united front.

"Their daughter, Glenda, was a runaway. Many of our girls are." She paused, her pupils dilated. Zach nodded his encouragement. "Anyway...she was at the home the same time as John Henry's mother. Their babies, both boys, were born on the same day. Both of them signed release papers after the waiting period, all according to the law."

Opalene passed a trembling hand over her forehead. "Oh, dear. This is so disturbing."

"I'll get you a glass of water." Lily was glad to have something constructive to do. From the time Opalene had announced the Rockman's claim to John Henry, she had thought she might faint.

"Thank you, dear."

On her way to the kitchen, Lily passed by the nursery. The baby was sleeping, curled into a fat little ball with his rump saluting the breeze.

Lily had to touch him to reassure herself that Rose's baby had not been spirited away by Mrs. McGruder's words. She gently rubbed his silky hair, then pulled a light receiving blanket over his legs.

"Can't have you catching a cold," she whispered, although a cold was mild compared to the terrible problem facing them now. The Rockmans. John Henry's biological grandparents. It couldn't be. She wouldn't let it be. Rose would never get over the loss. And Lily could never live with herself if she lost her sister's baby—no matter that it wasn't her fault.

She wanted to gather John Henry into her arms and run as far away from Opalene McGruder and the Rockmans as she could go. She wanted to run and run until it was safe to stop, until no one besides Rose and George could say, "John Henry is mine."

She gave the baby one last pat, then went to the kitchen to get the water. Ice clinked against the glass as she carried it back to the den.

Opalene took a sip, then pressed the cool glass to her temple.

"I can't tell you how sorry I am about all this," she said.

"We don't fault you, Mrs. McGruder. Please tell us the rest of the story." When she looked blankly at him, Zach prompted her. "Both the girls signed papers . . ."

"Yes. And then they left the home. The Lord only knows where they went. Anyhow…a few days later, Glenda's baby died."

"You're certain it was Glenda's baby? There could have been no mistake?"

Zach's legal training came through. Furthermore, there was a hard edge in his voice that said in no uncertain terms that he would fight to the end for his brother's child. Lily was glad that she was not alone—and that Zach was the one with her. He was tough, even deadly, if his gun was any evidence. He was also fiercely loyal to his family. He had said so long ago, at her sister's engagement party. *The only thing that means anything to me is family.*

He would not let John Henry go. Lily leaned back in her chair. He put his hand on her shoulder, and its steady heat flowed through her, giving her courage.

"There was no mistake, Mr. Taylor. John Henry is not Glenda's baby."

Lily was beginning to relax when Zach posed his next question.

"Why did the Rockmans come to you laying claims to John Henry?"

"Two reasons. They had a letter from Glenda telling about the birth of her son and how she had signed papers and put him up for adoption with our agency." Opalene paused, then drank from her glass like a starving woman.

"And the second reason?"

"Glenda has a record of mental illness. We didn't know that, of course."

"What does that mean?" Lily asked.

"It means that any papers she signed would be highly suspect and probably ruled illegal if her mental incompetence at the time of the signing could be proved," Zach explained.

"But since Glenda's baby died, what's the problem?" Lily didn't give either of them time to answer. "Obviously John Henry legally belongs to Rose and George, and there is nothing the Rockmans can do about it."

Mrs. McGruder looked pained. "Well . . . we *did* have a little mix-up with the records once, long ago. . . . Mr. Rockman knew about it. He knew you had John Henry. In fact, he knew a lot of things he shouldn't have known."

Rockman has hired a private investigator, Zach decided. A man with money and influence could find out anything he wanted to know. Obviously he was determined to have his grandson.

"Have the Rockmans filed suit?" he asked.

"No. But they do want to meet with you."

"No." Lily looked up at Zach. "No," she whispered again.

"It's all right." Zach squeezed her shoulder.

"Well . . ." Opalene stood to go. "I'll tell them the answer is no."

"The answer is *yes*." Zach's voice stopped the woman as efficiently as a thrown javelin. He strode across the room until he was towering in front of Opalene McGruder. "I'll meet with them—alone. Set it up, please, and let me know the time and place."

"As you wish." Opalene shook Zach's hand, and then he escorted her to the door.

Lily sat in her chair as if she had taken root and grown there. When Zach came back to the den, she stood up to face him.

"Why? Why would you possibly agree to see these people?"

"Make no mistake about it, Lily. They don't want to talk, they want John Henry." His expression became so fierce, she took a step backward. "When I fight, I always make it a practice to know my opponent."

Chapter 8

After Opalene McGruder left, Zach and Lily hurried to the nursery. John Henry·was still sound asleep, but neither of them wanted to leave. Lily perched on the edge of the rocking chair, watching him breathe, and Zach paced the floor, stopping every now and then to put his hand on the baby so he could *feel* him breathe.

"This is silly," Lily finally said. "We should go and let him sleep."

"You go if you like. I'm staying."

It was almost as if they both felt their presence would take away any threat to John Henry, as if by staying, they could reverse everything Mrs. McGruder had said and make it not true.

When he woke up, yawning and stretching his legs, they nearly knocked each other over getting to the crib.

"I'll feed him," Lily said.

"I think it's my turn."

John Henry regarded them with his blue eyes. What new turn of events was this? He was getting all this attention without even trying. He thought he was going to like it.

Lily and Zach stared at each other until they both began to feel sheepish.

. "We might as well both feed him, Lily," Zach finally said. "After Mrs. McGruder's visit, I don't think either one of us plans to leave him for longer than it takes to go to the bathroom."

"That's about the size of it." Lily was relieved that Zach understood her feelings about this matter. But more than that, she was impressed that he felt the same way.

"You really love this baby, don't you, Zach?"

"Yes."

"Is it because he is your brother's child, or because he's such an enchanting little scamp?"

"Both, I think. I loved him first because of the family connection, but then he got under my skin." He ruffled the baby's fine hair. "Didn't you, little tiger? Didn't you get under your Uncle Zach's skin?"

John Henry squinched his eyes tight, as if he were concentrating hard on the question. When he opened them, he cooed.

"My little man." Zach picked him and carried him around the nursery, riding high in his arms, wet diaper and all.

Watching him, Lily was overcome with curiosity. For a man who loved family and children, he certainly led a strange life-style. Zach Taylor was a paradox.

Over the past few days, she had seen unexpected glimpses of a different Zach. Was he playing a role at his ritzy mansion in the Garden District, or was he playing a role here, in her sister's apartment? She would almost swear that the man she had seen here was the *real* Zach Taylor. For reasons that eluded her—or that she preferred not to think about—she wanted to know.

"Why aren't you married with children?"

Zach halted in the midst of putting John Henry into the crib. John Henry, thinking that being suspended was a new game, began to bat the air with his arms and legs. Zach held him squirming for a moment, then put him down and began to change his diaper. It gave him reason to avoid Lily's question.

He could feel her expectancy as she watched him. He might postpone answering her for a while, but not indefinitely. He had learned enough about Lily to understand that she was not one to be put off.

Obviously he couldn't tell her the truth. His only solution was to lie. He'd had enough practice that it shouldn't bother him. But it did.

He didn't even want to think about that. Right now, he had to concentrate totally on John Henry. If it were in his power, he would clear up this whole mess of the child's parentage before George got home.

He put the finishing touch on John Henry's diaper, then turned to Lily with his most practiced smile. He hoped he looked more debonair than he felt.

"I would love to have children, Lily, but having children means having a wife—at least, if you want to be respectable. Quite frankly, I'm not ready to settle down with just one woman."

Lily wasn't good at hiding her emotions. For a split second she looked as if she had been slapped. Then she gathered her composure. She threw her shoulders back, lifted her chin and stiffened her spine. Her mouth lost all the softness he had come to admire...and secretly covet. "I see," she said.

No, you don't. And I can't allow you to see. His thoughts were so raucous, Zach wondered that she couldn't hear them.

She couldn't, of course. She turned to leave the nursery. At the door she paused and spoke over her shoulder. "I need to get his bottle ready."

"Good."

She closed the door as carefully as if it were attached to explosives. He was glad he couldn't see her stiff march toward the kitchen. He had hurt women often . . . and sometimes hard . . . in his hell-bent efforts to keep his distance, as well as keep his cover intact. But no matter how often he did it, he always felt soiled afterward.

"Take your time growing up, John Henry. Being adult is not all it's cracked up to be."

Zach and Lily were careful around each other the rest of the day—careful and elaborately polite. And neither of them got very far from John Henry's side.

John Henry basked in the attention. Since he wasn't having to cry for it, he figured all the fawning his uncle and aunt were doing was due to his considerable charms.

Bentley was soundly ignored—except for being fed on time and carried out for a quick run. Any other time he would have taken exception, but since he was also being let off the hook for his shenanigans in the den, he decided not to make a fuss. Let sleeping people lie was his new philosophy.

The strain took its toll. By the time four o'clock came, Lily was having to remind herself not to clench her teeth, and Zach found himself frequently ramming a balled fist into his pockets.

When the phone rang, they both rushed toward it. Zach got there first.

"I've been waiting for your call," he said after greeting the caller.

There was only one caller they had been waiting for— Mrs. McGruder. Lily stood as close as she could to him without touching, trying to hear both ends of the conversation.

"Yes. Eleven o'clock is fine," Zach said. "No... Yes."

Lily couldn't hear a darned thing Mrs. McGruder said except a faint mumble, like an old 78-rpm record played softly at 45-rpm.

"Well?" she said after Zach hung up.

"It's all set. Eleven o'clock."

"I already know that. You said it on the telephone. What I want to know is where the meeting will be and whether there are any new developments."

"Nothing new. The meeting will be at the Rockman estate."

"The Rockmans'!" Zach didn't say anything. Lily couldn't believe he would agree to anything so ridiculous. "You're going to meet at their house, on their turf? Doesn't that put you at a disadvantage?"

"Nothing puts me at a disadvantage, Lily."

That was the kind of thing the old Zach Taylor would say—Zach Taylor the rake, Zach Taylor the debaucher of women. But the man she had come to know in the past few days would have given her a more thoughtful answer. The new Zach— She shut the door on that kind of thinking. There was no new Zach. There was only the complex man standing before her, the man she was discovering she didn't know at all.

She turned to leave, and Zach put a hand on her shoulder.

"Lily." That was all he said. Just her name. But it was the way he said it that made her face him.

He released her, and a softer expression came into his face.

"Don't worry, Lily. I know what I'm doing."

"Do you?" she whispered.

"Yes. And I can promise you that nobody is going to take John Henry away from us."

Could she believe the promises of a man like Zach Taylor?

He seemed to read her thoughts. "Trust me, Lily."

She studied him awhile, then came to the only logical conclusion. "I have to trust you, Zach.... On this matter, I have no other choice."

Later that night, while Lily and John Henry slept, Zach left the apartment. Under cover of darkness he drove to his house and roused his butler.

Sam came instantly awake. He ran a hand through his red hair, pulled on his pants and joined Zach in his study.

"What's up, Zach?"

"Plenty, Sam. And none of it good." He recapped the events of the past two days.

"There are two things you have to do, Sam.. Find out everything we don't already know about Rockman before my eleven o'clock meeting tomorrow morning, and keep an eye on the 13 Royal Street Apartments without Lily knowing it. I don't expect trouble, but I'm not taking any chances."

"Hell, you don't ask much, do you?"

"Only what I know you can deliver."

The two men clasped hands, old friends and comrades in danger.

"I have to get back now," Zach said. "Lily might wake up and need me."

"What will you do if she's awake when you get back?"

Zach rumpled his hair and jerked the front of his shirt so a button tore loose. Then he assumed an unsteady gait as he walked toward the door.

"A man can't stay trapped in a small apartment forever—especially when there are good women and good wine to be had."

Sam watched Zach leave the room. Then he said softly, "I hope you don't have to put on that act, my friend."

Lily was not awake when Zach returned. Neither was John Henry. Zach gave thanks for whatever kind fate was watching over him, then climbed into his sofa bed for a few hours' sleep. Morning would come quickly.

Bemus Rockman's estate was vast, impressive and tightly guarded. As well it should be, Zach decided as he stopped at the security gate. The information Sam had collected on Rockman was not pretty. For all his squeaky-clean facade, he was a man with secrets. Rockman had been implicated in illegal cockfighting ten years earlier, but no charges were ever brought. There was also one incident of bribery of a public official, but charges were dropped. It wasn't much, but it was enough to give Zach a better idea of the kind of man he was dealing with.

Rockman had a wife—the former Dora Beauchamps, whose claim to glory rested solely on her marriage to Bemus and her title to beauty, Miss Sugarcane of 1955—and one child, Glenda, whose history of misconduct went all the way back to seventh grade. In her short lifetime of nineteen years, Glenda had seen three child psychologists, four school counselors and two psychiatrists. Miss Glenda Rockman, who had been a model student until she was twelve years old, definitely had problems.

There were no sons in the Rockman family, no nephews, no cousins, no one to carry on the family name and the family tradition. No wonder old Bemus wanted John Henry.

Zach parked his car outside a four-car garage, then went to meet his opponent.

Bemus Rockman had the sleek look of a man who had everything money can buy—tailors, hairstylists, body trainers. He was fit and tanned and jovial. Too jovial. It rang false. Only the hint of a bulge over his belt showed that he was getting on in years.

Zach was glad to note the flaw. Nature was one opponent who couldn't be fooled or bought off or conquered.

"Welcome to my humble home." Rockman extended his hand.

"Mr. Rockman." Zach shook hands. "Zach Taylor."

"Call me Bemus." He waved Zach toward a chair, then sat opposite him on a leather sofa. "As Mrs. McGruder told you, I want to keep this meeting real casual, real friendly. Just talk between friends."

Zach was accustomed to acting. If Bemus wanted *friendly,* that's what Zach would be. Let the man think it was going to be easy to get what he wanted. That way, he would be off guard. "She told me. Naturally, I want to keep this discussion friendly, as well."

"That's good." Bemus smiled. "Taylor... Haven't I heard that name? Oil, right?"

"That's right." It was Zach's turn to smile. "And your name is synonymous with sugarcane."

"When a man works as hard as I have at his job, it's nice to know people have heard about it."

Bemus made a careful steeple of his fingers and studied Zach. Deliberately keeping his body relaxed and his expression neutral, Zach returned his steady stare.

"What do you do, Zach?"

The seemingly casual question could be loaded. Since Bemus had apparently hired an investigator to find out about John Henry, chances were he also knew about Zach.

"I practiced law for a while, but I've taken the last few years off to regroup."

"That's wise. A man can always benefit from reassessing his life. Take me, for instance. To all appearances I'm a man who has everything—a fine wife, a comfortable home, a good living."

"It does look that way. We both know, of course, that appearances can be deceiving."

"Ahh..." Bemus smiled. "I should have known I couldn't get anything by a lawyer."

Zach acknowledged the compliment with a smile. It was obvious what Rockman was leading up to. Zach waited.

"Yes." Bemus looked at Zach over his steepled hands. "I have everything a man needs...right here on the estate...everything except a grandchild."

"Mrs. McGruder told me about the death of your daughter's baby. I'm sorry."

"The death of a child is always cause for grief and regret." Bemus paused. An ordinary observer might not have noticed the narrowing of his eyes, but Zach was no ordinary observer. "Tell me about the baby in your care. John Henry, I believe you call him."

"He's adjusted well to his new home. He's robust, usually cheerful and very strong willed. He's going to make a hell of a Taylor."

"Blue eyes, blond hair?"

"Yes." Only long years of practice enabled Zach to appear relaxed. If Bemus Rockman knew the color of John Henry's hair and eyes, he had seen the child. Or someone else had seen and reported.

"That's a Rockman family trait." Bemus picked up a color photograph of his daughter and turned it for Zach to see. "Blue eyes and blond hair have been handed down for generations—from my grandfather to my father to me to my daughter. And finally, to my grandson."

"I understand your position, Bemus. If I had a beautiful daughter like yours who had given birth, I would be anxious to find the child, as well."

"I've found him, Zach." Bemus laid the picture aside. "He's in your care. I might add that I'm pleased you seem to have taken such good care of him."

"Obviously you don't believe your daughter's baby died."

"No. She described him perfectly in her letter to us."

"There are many blond-haired, blue-eyed babies."

"There are only two babies that concern me—the two at Sweet Angels Adoption Agency. One died, but my daughter's survived."

"You have proof, I suppose."

"Not absolute, if that's what you're looking for. But enough to create reasonable doubt about just who John Henry's real mother is. Enough to make a judge strongly consider returning a child to blood relatives who want him, who love him and who can provide him with the best of everything."

"Sweet Angels has a sterling reputation. It will be very difficult for you to discredit Mrs. McGruder and her staff."

"Difficult, but not impossible. And then, of course, there's the problem of my daughter's sanity. She was not mentally competent to sign away rights to her baby." Suddenly Bemus leaned forward, his face intense. "Why don't we make this easy, Zach? Let me get my lawyer to handle the necessary papers, and you turn this baby over to his rightful grandfather.... His grandmother, too. Lord, you don't know how Dora has grieved over the loss of this child."

"My answer is no."

"Talk it over with your brother. I understand he's out of town. I'm sure he wouldn't want a child that belonged to somebody else. He can get another one. There's always a child to adopt...but there's not always a grandson born to a man who has lived all his life for the moment he would hold his heir in his arms."

If Bemus Rockman was acting, he was doing a damned fine job. He would present a very sympathetic figure in court.

"I don't need to talk this over with my brother. I know him. He would never give up his child."

"We could save a lot of heartache. Think of the women. Think of Dora, pining her heart out. Think of your sister-in-law, looking at that baby and wondering if she's deprived his grandparents of him.... Think of the baby. Do you want him to be shuttled around like a sack of mail until this thing is settled?"

"Nothing will be different for him. In his best interests, he'll be left in his present home until this matter reaches its right and proper conclusion—that he is legally a Taylor." Zach stood up. "John Henry will always be a Taylor."

There was no longer a need for manners and pretense. Each knew where the other stood. They were enemies. Their battlefield would be the courtroom.

After Zach left, Bemus picked up the telephone.

"Smothers, get over here."

He poured himself a glass of whiskey while he waited. It settled his nerves. And he needed them settled after his encounter with Zach Taylor. Now, there was a cool one. From all he'd heard, Taylor was a playboy, a useless man living on family money. He had thought it would be easy to get a man like that to come around to his way of thinking.

Taylor? Taylor? Why did that name give him such an uneasy feeling, as if there was something he knew but couldn't quite remember?

Hell. If Smothers was so damned misinformed about Zach Taylor, maybe he had made a mistake about the baby, as well.

Smothers came in the back way, still stuffing his shirt into his jeans. His bald head was perspiring, and his mouth was twitching. Smothers always twitched around Bemus. That was one of the reasons Rockman kept him on the payroll. He liked to have people just a little nervous around him. It made them eager to do what he wanted.

"What kind of a damned investigator are you, anyway?" Bemus eyed Glen Smothers over the top of his whiskey. "Zach Taylor was nothing like you described him."

"He lives from one party to the next. That's what everybody says."

"Then how come party boy sat in that chair over there as tough as nails? How come I have the uneasy feeling that I've heard something about Taylor besides oil?"

"I don't know, Mr. Rockman."

"I pay you to know. Check him out again. Thoroughly this time." Bemus set his glass on the table and picked up the picture of his daughter. He studied it for a long time, then turned it to face Smothers. "See this? This is my daughter. Remember? And you said John Henry is her son."

"That's right."

"Could you be wrong?"

"There's always a possibility of error when dealing with witnesses."

"Would your witness have any reason to lie?"

"No. She was most eager to help me, especially when she saw that I . . . what you . . . what I was willing to pay."

"That's right, Smothers. *You* paid her. Not me."

"Well, she was very old. It could be that her mind is not as sharp as it once was. But, no, she didn't strike me as the kind of woman who would deliberately lie."

"Refresh my memory. What exactly did she say about the two babies?"

"A lot was going on when those babies were born. Sweet Angels had two new workers in the nursery and one new file clerk. The kids were green, nervous, trying to learn the ropes. Plus there was a fire in the kitchen . . . a small one. Turned out to be nothing more than a rag left too close to a hot stove, but it set off the alarm anyhow." Pausing, Smothers looked at Bemus to see how he was doing so far.

Bemus nodded his encouragement. "Go on."

"Well, my source, Miss Clara Justice, said the new kids panicked, put the wrong baby in the wrong crib when all the excitement died down. Said they got the records all mixed-up and everything."

"She's sure about that?"

"Not a hundred percent. I guess under those circumstances, nobody can be a hundred percent. But she's sure enough to swear it in court."

Bemus looked off into the distance a long time. His mouth turned up in a secret smile, as if he were seeing visions that no one else could see. Finally he focused his attention back on Smothers.

"That's good enough for me, and we'll make damned sure it's good enough for a judge." He clapped Smothers on the shoulder. "I'll have to change the baby's name, though. How does Bemus II strike you?"

Lily understood the agony of waiting. While Zach was at the Rockman estate, she roamed around the small apartment, looking for things to do. She straightened the kitchen three times. She dusted the furniture twice. She called her secretary at the bank. She stacked magazines that were perfectly aligned, straightened cushions that weren't crooked, tightened toothpaste caps that weren't loose.

Both John Henry and Bentley were being angels. For once she wished they would misbehave. At least it would keep her mind occupied.

She created a dozen horror stories about Zach's meeting. Rockman would have proof John Henry was his grandson. Zach would feel guilty about taking the man's grandchild. He would agree to give John Henry up. Or...Rockman was a monster parading as a grandfather. He wasn't really after the baby: he was after Zach. Having lured him to his house, he would murder him...for having played a Rockman daughter false.

She was being silly. She was bordering on paranoid. She was going to start ripping copies of *Vanity Fair* to shreds if he didn't come back soon. She might even take to hiding behind the door to growl and bite legs. The idea had a certain appeal.

When Zach came back, she rushed toward him, stopping just short of grabbing his arms. His face told her nothing.

"How did it go?"

"Pretty much the way I expected. He believes John Henry is his grandson. He'll file suit."

"Can he win?"

"I intend to do everything in my power to see that he doesn't."

"What can you do?"

"Build a case, Lily—and hope its airtight."

"How?"

"For one thing, I have to locate Glenda Rockman and find out who fathered her baby."

"Of course! DNA testing. Why didn't I think of that?"

By taking blood samples from mother, father and baby, then matching genetically transferred chromosomes, they could prove one hundred percent who was *not* the mother. Indisputable evidence. One mismatched chromosome would be enough.

Here was something Lily was familiar with—facts and figures. Or in this case, blood types. Finding Glenda and getting her to talk was crucial. Proof of parentage required the blood types of all three: mother, father and baby.

Given something concrete to work with, she felt better about the Rockman situation than she had felt in two days.

"If we can locate Glenda," she continued, "and if she's willing to name her partner, and if we can get the boy's blood type..." The enormity of the task began to sink in. "That's a lot of ifs, Zach."

"I'll handle everything."

"You will not. I have as much at stake here as you do. John Henry is my nephew, too, you know."

"Of course he is. And I'm sure you're quite capable, but this is my area of expertise."

He put his hand on her shoulder. The same gesture had been soothing during Mrs. McGruder's visit, but now Lily found it irritating. She shook it off and glared at him.

"And don't try to treat me as if I'm some bimbo."

Zach fought a losing battle to hide his smile. After playing a cat-and-mouse game with Rockman, it was good to be with a lively redhead who didn't hesitate to show her feelings. He realized that was one of the things he liked most about Lily: she let her emotions show. He'd be willing to bet that she thought she was all business, efficient and inscrutable. In fact, that was one of the things she had revealed to him so many years ago when she came out among the Mardi Gras revelers. She had needed an affirmation that she was a *real* woman, not just a machine.

"I would never mistake you for a bimbo."

"And don't talk down to me, either."

"Never."

"And wipe that smile off your face."

He made a swiping motion. "It's done."

"Good."

Lily glared at him, then crumpled. To her mortification, she felt hot tears in her eyes. She blinked hard, desperately trying to keep them from spilling over. They escaped anyway and came rolling down her cheeks. She swiped at them.

"Damn. I'm getting worse than Rose." She sniffled, then swiped some more.

"It's all right to cry, Lily."

"It's not. I have to be strong."

"Not all the time." Zach pulled her into his arms and pressed her head onto his shoulder.

She thought about resisting, but his shoulder was so broad and it felt so good to have somebody to lean on for a change that she allowed herself one moment of weakness.

Zach patted her shoulder in a brotherly manner. "Hey," he said, leaning back to look at her. "How about a long, cool glass of lemonade? I'll make it."

"Well . . . all right."

He took her hand and led her into the kitchen. Her tears were gone, and so was the need to cry. Lily was amazed that such a small gesture could provide such great comfort. All he had done was hug her. She wished she could bottle up his hugs and save them for days when things went wrong. Days when her secretary misplaced the *Blue List* and a bad market didn't rally and a big investor ranted about low yield on investments and blamed her. If she had a bottle of hugs, she could take them out one by one, like Carter's Little Liver Pills, and use them for whatever ailed her.

Her spirits somewhat restored, she perched on a kitchen stool while Zach squeezed lemons into a large pitcher. He was at ease in the kitchen. That surprised her. All these years she had thought of him as a man at ease only in the bedroom.

He glanced up at her and smiled. "Everything's going to be all right, Lily. I was a very good lawyer, and I'll put everything I've got into keeping John Henry. There will be times when you can help. I appreciate your intelligence."

"Thank you for that."

"You're more than welcome."

He turned back to his task, but not before he had favored her with one of the most intense scrutinies she'd ever endured. He had the sexiest eyes of any man she'd ever met. And the sexiest mouth. The bottom lip was full and sensual. She didn't want to remember how it felt, how it tasted—but she did anyhow. Which just went to show what a state she was in. Tension was taking its toll. When all her energies should be focused on John Henry, she was caught up in a web of magic that Zach Taylor wove so well.

He added water to the lemon juice and poured in sugar. As if he needed it. All he had to do was stick his finger in the pitcher and the whole shebang would be sweet, as sweet as the hugs he gave, as sweet as— *Stop it right now,* Lily told herself.

GET 4 BOOKS

Return this card, and we'll send you 4 brand-new Silhouette Intimate Moments® novels, absolutely FREE! We'll even pay the postage both ways!

We're making you this offer to introduce you to the benefits of the Silhouette Reader Service™: convenient home delivery of brand-new romance novels, months before they're available in stores, AND at a saving of 43¢ apiece compared to the cover price!

Accepting these 4 free books places you under no obligation to buy. You may cancel at any time, even just after receiving your free shipment. If you do not cancel, every month, we'll send 6 more Silhouette Intimate Moments® novels and bill you just $2.96* apiece plus 69¢ delivery for the entire shipment!

Yes! Please send me my 4 free Silhouette Intimate Moments® novels, as explained above.

Name

Address   Apt.

City   Prov.   Postal Code

345 CIS AGL7

DETACH ALONG DOTTED LINE AND MAIL TODAY! – DETACH ALONG DOTTED LINE AND MAIL TODAY! – DETACH ALONG DOTTED LINE AND MAIL TODAY! – DETACH ALONG DOTTED LINE AND MAIL TODAY!

Get 4 Books FREE

SEE BACK OF CARD FOR DETAILS

Ice tinkled against the glass. Lemonade rushed over the cubes, leaving bits of pulp caught in the crevices.

"We'll drink to our success, Lily."

When he handed her the glass, Zach's hand touched hers. She wanted to grab hold and hang on.

What was happening to her? She took a long drink of lemonade. Forced confinement. That was her problem. Plus taking care of a baby and a dog. She was not used to the domestic scene. The bank was her natural habitat, the efficient, organized, cool, sterile bank. Everything she needed to know could be learned by studying the latest reports, the latest figures, the most up-to-date manuals.

No wonder Rose went around in a merry fog. If Lily had to live like this, she might get to be just like her twin sister.

Lily took another long drink of lemonade. Viewed through ice crystals and the side of her glass, Zach looked no less appealing. A tiny piece of lemon pulp was caught on his upper lip. She wanted to walk over to him—no, she wanted to *slink* over to him, put her arms around his neck and kiss that tiny piece of pulp away.

The whole idea was perfectly ridiculous, of course. She would never be having outrageous notions if she weren't in Rose's kitchen where the sugar was kept in the flour canister and the flour was where the cornmeal ought to be and Lord only knew where the cornmeal was.

Lily needed to get back to her job. Soon.

"Did Rose and George call while I was gone?"

Zach was asking a perfectly sane question. It got Lily's mind off his lips. Nearly. "No. Thank goodness." She emptied her glass. "I don't know what to tell them when they ask about John Henry."

"The truth, of course."

"The truth? You mean about Bemus Rockman? About the possibility of a lawsuit? About the possibility of losing John Henry?"

"Yes. Everything." Zach put his glass in the dishwasher and stood facing Lily. "They deserve to know."

"I can't tell Rose. She'll cry her eyes out."

"Rose loves to cry. It's not a sign of weakness. It's merely her way of coping."

"You don't understand, Zach. I've always protected Rose. There's no need to upset her about something that might never happen, something that will probably be settled before they get back from Spain."

"It won't be over before then. And hiding the truth is not good for anybody. It creates mistrust. One lie calls for another, then another, until there's a whole snowball of lies, rolling down the hill out of control."

Since when had he been adverse to hiding the truth? she wondered. He was so damned good at hiding the truth that he had lived a lie for four years, acting as if that night in the Monteleone never happened.

Lily was sorely tempted to point all that out to him, but she refrained. There was much more at issue here than ancient grudges.

"But what good is it to worry them . . . perhaps needlessly?"

"This decision is not negotiable, Lily."

"Dammit, Zach. This is not a court of law. This is my *sister* we're talking about."

"And it's my brother."

They faced each other across the kitchen table like two Roman gladiators, prepared to fight to the death. If air could snap and crackle like Lily's favorite cereal, it did. She kept eye contact, hoping she could back him down . . . and knowing she couldn't. At last she sighed.

"Look, Zach . . . would you be willing to compromise?"

"I never agree to a compromise until I know what it is, but, yes, I'm willing to listen."

"Tell George, if you must, but please ask him not to tell Rose."

"Fair enough. I'll ask him, but I think it must be his decision. I've heard him say time and again that keeping secrets is bad for a marriage."

"Keeping secrets is bad for any relationship," Lily said, watching Zach for a reaction. She got nothing...which was about what she had expected. It would take more than a well-turned phrase to crack the armor Zach Taylor wore. And she didn't want to crack it anyhow, not on a permanent basis.

But every now and then when life crowded in on her and made her feel vulnerable and out of control, she did wish he would say just once, "Lily, I remember that night."

Chapter 9

"What you need is something to take your mind off all this." Zach gestured toward the baby bottles and cans of formula and boxes of pablum. "What we both need is a break."

Lily thought, with a certain longing, of days when she had come home from work to nothing more stressful than mixing herself a mint julep and sitting on her balcony listening to the strains of jazz drifting up from the streets. Of course, then she didn't have John Henry to love. And she wouldn't trade her time with him for all the quiet, uneventful days of her life.

"I hardly see how that's possible," she said. "I think John Henry is a little too young to go out on the town."

"Never underestimate a Taylor," Zach said, laughing.

"I wouldn't dream of it." Lily stared at him in a manner that wasn't meant to be bold, but to her chagrin, it turned out that way. She was remembering, and those memories made her cheeks hot. The one and only time she had gone out on the town with Zach, she had ended up in his bed.

"Actually, Lily, what I have in mind is far tamer than going out on the town. I thought I'd arrange a little entertainment for us here at the apartment."

Here at the apartment? Candlelight and wine and temptation. The bed just down the hall. And nobody to know. Except her. She would know.

All her speculation was silly, of course. Zach was here merely for the sake of John Henry. She was no more to him than somebody to take turns changing dirty diapers. Except once. That night in the den. And it would never happen again.

"You go ahead without me, Zach. I'll take care of the baby, and you go wherever you need to go. Do whatever you need to do to take your mind off everything." He watched her without saying anything. She considered herself pretty good at judging a person's reactions by studying expressions. Zach's told her nothing. "Look, I know you're used to quite a—a flamboyant life-style. And being confined here must be very hard for you."

She paused, watching him. Still he said nothing.

"In fact, why don't you move back to your house? You can start working on the case. I can take care of John Henry by myself. That's what I intended to do from the very beginning...." His eyes were terrible. She had to keep talking to keep from shivering. "Not that I'm not grateful for all you've done. In fact—"

"Stop it, Lily."

"Stop what? I'm not doing anything except making a generous gesture."

"You know damned well what you're doing. You're shutting me out."

Zach was surprised at how much it hurt. He was surprised at how much he had wanted to escape reality with Lily one more time. Not that he had planned to take her to bed again. He didn't like playing with that kind of fire more than once.

What he had planned was a take-out meal in the apartment, maybe Chinese, with good wine and candlelight and music on the stereo and maybe Sam or somebody he trusted sitting in the nursery watching John Henry. Nothing elaborate.

"I'm not. I *said* I was grateful to you."

"I don't want your gratitude. I want your kindness. I want one evening with you, one hour when I can believe that life is good. I need to feel ordinary, Lily."

Too late, Zach realized the enormity of his confession. But he couldn't take the words back. They pulsed in the air as if they had a life of their own. Too many years of sacrificing even the simplest pleasures had made him vulnerable. He saw exactly how vulnerable as he watched Lily's face.

"Zach, I'm sorry," she whispered as she put her hand on his arm. "I didn't mean to hurt you."

Her mouth was soft looking, and her eyes were bright with a hint of tears. He would have given everything he owned for the freedom to kiss her—kiss her without regret, kiss her without worrying about danger, kiss her without thinking about tomorrow.

His muscles ached with the tension of holding back. His heart hurt with the effort of denial. And his spirit took another battering from the knowledge that he had to keep living a lie.

Calling forth a nonchalant smile, he patted her hand.

"You didn't hurt me, Lily. How can you hurt a man who has no heart?"

She pulled her hand back as if it had been burned. "Of course. How could I forget?"

Leave, his mind screamed. *Leave now before you start a list of confessions that won't stop.*

"What you did, Lily, was make some suggestions that are very sound. I do need to start preparing a case. I have an idea that Bemus Rockman won't wait long before filing suit."

"You're leaving, then?" Lily was surprised. Even though she had suggested it, she guessed she'd wanted him to insist on staying. She was so confused, she didn't know her own mind anymore.

"Yes, I'm leaving. But I'll be back."

"Well, sure. Anytime. You're always welcome to visit John Henry. And there will be times we need to talk about the case."

"I'll be back *tonight,* Lily. And not for a visit. To stay."

"But I thought . . ."

"Until George and Rose come back, I'll be here."

She tried not to let her quick rush of gladness show, but she could feel her face getting flushed. Her only salvation was a hasty exit.

"You do what you must, and I'll do what I must," she said over her shoulder.

After she had gone, Zach stood in the kitchen, trying to figure out how he had let the situation with Lily get so out of hand. And at a time when he needed to be spending all his energy on the problem of proving Bemus Rockman wrong about John Henry.

The silence reminded him just how much he missed Lily's presence, how much he had come to depend on it. He picked up her empty lemonade glass and ran his finger around the rim.

There was a tiny lipstick smudge. Peach colored. Like her skin. Like the blouse she had worn. Like the soft, inner folds of her body. Peaches and honey. A heady sweetness that even now he could taste merely by closing his eyes and remembering.

He pressed his lips to the glass over the spot where her lips had touched. Her name whispered through his mind like a song.

He tried to shut it out with practical matters. *I have to go. There are so many things to do.* But her name kept singing through him. *Lily, Lily.* More delectable than ripe summer peaches. Sweeter than clover honey.

He put the glass in the dishwasher. For the first time in seven long years of living on the edge, he began to feel burnout. It was a feeling he couldn't afford to have.

Calling up the discipline he had depended on for so many years, he left the apartment and headed for his house on St. Charles Avenue.

Sitting in the rocking chair beside John Henry's crib, Lily heard Zach leave. She wasn't hiding, she told herself as she watched the sleeping baby. She was merely getting out of Zach's way.

John Henry sighed and Lily reached over to smooth back his hair. It was slightly damp from the healthy moisture sleeping babies exuded. Or so the baby book said.

Leaning back, she set the rocking chair into motion. A group of sparrows collected on the sill outside the nursery window and set up the commotion birds often indulge in for no apparent reason other than the fact that the sun was shining. Lily rocked and listened to the twittering. Far down the street, a jazz musician took up an alto sax and added a blues note to the birds' song.

The sound of the sax was mournful. It suited Lily's mood.

What would have been so bad about agreeing to an evening with Zach? Was she so petty she couldn't let go of something that had happened four years ago? When did self-protection become grudge holding?

All he had wanted was kindness. Listening to the mournful sax, Lily's heart broke. How well she understood the need for kindness, just a simple moment when people would look at her and say, "Lily, you don't have to be the brightest and the best. You don't have to be the torch bearer for the Cooper family in the arena of success. Why don't you kick your feet up and let your hair down and allow yourself to be ordinary?''

That's what she wished somebody would say. And she guessed Rose had said it to her in a dozen different ways, but Rose was her sister. No matter what she said, she still depended on Lily to be the strongest, the brightest and best, the sensible twin.

Lily stood up. "Call me foolish, John Henry. Call me softhearted. Call me a silly romantic, even. But I'm going to give Zach a night of kindness."

As she smoothed the blanket over John Henry's plump bottom, she thought of all the small kindnesses Zach had given her—the small hugs, the simple assurances that everything would be all right, the smiles when she was crying, the rescues when Bentley was on a tear and John Henry was doing his best to make himself heard across the river. It was time to put the past behind her. Not completely, of course. She was wise enough not to forget the lessons of the past. But she was also generous enough not to use them as a barrier against a man who had a heart, after all, who had probably had a heart all along.

In the den, she made her telephone calls. First she checked in with her secretary at the bank. Assured that the stock market hadn't crashed during her absence and wasn't likely to, she called Impastato's and ordered Sicilian food. After much cajoling and a promise to pay a handsome sum, Lily talked them into delivering. Next she called her favorite grocer and gave him a list of things she needed.

Then she sat down to await the delivery boy's arrival. She even kicked her shoes off. It felt wonderful.

"Sam, we have a lot to do, and we're going to need help."

Sitting in Zach's home office behind closed doors, the two men discussed Bemus Rockman's intent to gain custody of John Henry and what they could do to stop him.

"Keep digging into his background, Sam. I'm hoping that when we find Glenda, we'll prove beyond a shadow of a doubt that John Henry is not her child. If that fails, if we can't find her, or in a worst-case scenario, if the adoption agency made a mistake and she *is* the mother, then we have to be prepared to attack Bemus from another side."

"Prove him unfit for custody."

"Exactly. The judge's main consideration will be the baby's best interests."

"I'll keep looking. There are sources I haven't tapped yet."

"Good. In the meantime, I'll organize a search for Glenda." Zach rubbed his hand across his eyes. "Damn. I wish I could conduct this search personally."

"You can't do everything, Zach. You're not Superman . . . though sometimes I think you try to be."

"You could be right, Sam." Zach picked up the phone, and Sam went back to the computer room. For two hours there were no sounds in the mansion on St. Charles Avenue except the electronic whir of machines and the quiet hum of male voices as the two men set their plan into motion.

After Zach was satisfied that he had done everything he could, at least for a while, he headed to the river. In times of stress, he often found comfort and peace in watching the unhurried journey of the deep waters as they made their inexorable way toward the Gulf of Mexico. Through time unknown the river had held its course.

It hadn't always been a gentle course. Sometimes the water rose angrily over the banks, defying the petty efforts of men to control it. The river gobbled up trees and buildings and cars, carrying them on its angry rush toward its destination.

But always after a rampage, the river settled inside its banks and took up its steady course once more, defying men to tame it, defying men to change it.

For seven years Zach had been on a steady course. Only once had he deviated—four years ago when he took Lily to his bed. And now she was in his life again. And he was tempted to deviate once more. Could he overflow his boundaries and hope to get back on course?

He gazed out over the Mississippi. Sunlight sparkled on waves, making the river look deceptively mild. But Zach knew better. The waters were full of dangerous currents. Just as he was. Dangerous currents of passion and need were tugging at him. Could he give in to them and not drown in the undertow?

He had to give in. If he didn't, he feared his battle-weary spirit might shrivel and die. And then he would be in no shape to help anybody.

He picked up a stone and skipped it across the river, then watched it sink in the deep, blue water. He knew he was being hopelessly romantic, but he viewed that small act as symbolic. Tonight he was going to lift a few burdens off his soul and watch them sink under a large dose of kindness.

He had no illusions. Nothing in his life would change permanently because of tonight. He wouldn't suddenly become free to live an ordinary life. He wouldn't miraculously put the past behind and take up a different future.

What he would do was give a little kindness, and hope he got some in return. But first, he had things to do. When he left the river, he was whistling.

Lily didn't know what had possessed her to bake a cake. Wasn't it enough that a great Sicilian dinner was going to be delivered at precisely eight o'clock? Wasn't it enough that she had searched out every candle Rose possessed and put them on the dining-room table where they awaited the touch of a match? Wasn't it enough that gardenias from the courtyard were sending their sweet fragrance throughout the apartment?

No. She had to do something extra special, something with her own two hands to prove her sincerity. Flour decorated her face and the front of her blouse. Bits of sugar clung to her arms. Cake dough that had failed to rise rested in abandoned pans on the countertops. Icing that was too thick to spread hardened in the mixing bowl.

If she got any more sincere, she'd never be able to clean up the mess.

John Henry watched from his vantage point in the portable playpen. Lying on his stomach, surrounded by toys, he found his Aunt Lily a much more fascinating object. When she had brought him into the kitchen, she was smiling and humming a nice tune. That had been fun, but he was having even more fun now. He loved all the racket she made banging pots into the sink. He liked the clickety clack her shoes made when she stomped across the floor. But most of all, he loved that word she said every now and then under her breath. When he got a little bigger, he thought he might try it.

Lily opened the oven door one last time and shoved her pans inside. "Now rise, dammit," she muttered. Too late she remembered her small audience. He'd been such an angel all afternoon that she'd almost forgotten him. She guessed the first word he would utter would be *damn*.

"Well, now, John Henry, was this fun?" Lily went over to the playpen, leaned in and patted the baby's bottom while he smiled. "You're getting to like your Aunt Lily, aren't you? Yes, you are. Yes, you are, you little angel."

Bentley bumped against Lily's legs, demanding his share of attention. Feeling generous now that she was getting the hang of domesticity, she patted his head.

"Even Bentley has been a good boy. Yes, you have."

Bentley wagged his tail so hard, he thought it might come off.

The good smells of baking began to fill the air. Lily peered through the glass door of the oven. The cake batter was rising as if it had been mixed by an expert. There was nothing like success to restore a woman's spirits.

Humming, Lily went to the sink to tackle the dirty dishes. While she rinsed and stacked them in the dishwasher, John Henry decided it was time for his meal. Without preamble, he told his Aunt Lily so in a wailing soprano he'd been practicing.

"Just a minute, sweetheart." She abandoned the dishes and heated his bottle.

John Henry knew his food was coming, but he liked the racket he was making, so he kept on crying. Bentley took that as a signal to add his own voice to the tune.

Lily's nerves began to fray, but she staunchly refused to give in to the tension.

"All right now. All right." With the bottle in one hand, she surveyed the kitchen. "Cake's baking. Dishes are nearly finished. This is all going to work out."

She picked up John Henry and started feeding him. Things were going fine for the first ounce or two. Then she forgot to burp him. That was okay with him until his stomach started feeling tight. The only thing he knew to do about it was to spit up. He spit a little more than he meant to, and then Aunt Lily got nervous.

"Oh, dear." Lily cleaned John Henry's mouth, then belatedly put him on her shoulder to burp. From the oven came the smells of burning cake. The stack of pots in the sink tilted and fell over with a crash. A mixing spoon toppled to the floor. Bentley attacked it, barking in his best dog-of-the-house manner.

All Lily's careful plans began to go up in smoke, almost literally, judging by the smell coming from the oven. Torn between upsetting John Henry by taking away his bottle and getting the cake out of the oven, Lily decided on the cake. It wouldn't matter about a bottle if the house caught on fire.

A fine mess she was in. And all because she had set out to impress a man. So there, she'd finally admitted it. Kindness had certainly been a motive, but she had another, far less lofty one. Deep down she was still trying to gain validation as a woman. *See,* she wanted to say, not only to Zach, but to the male population at large, *being bright and successful doesn't mean I'm lacking in natural feminine wiles and traditional feminine skills. Howard was wrong.*

"I've got to take your bottle away and get you into the nursery, John Henry." Hurrying along with Bentley barking at her heels, she decided that she didn't care much for self-discovery.

She could just hear what Rose would say. "You're being too hard on yourself, Lily. You're always too hard on yourself."

Maybe Rose was right. Maybe she should forget about *why* she was doing something and just go ahead and do it because it felt right.

"Here we are, sweetheart. Aunt Lily will be back in a second." She put John Henry in his bed, then hurried to the kitchen and took the cake out of the oven. It was as black as an old leather shoe.

"I can't worry about that now."

Lily set to work solving her problems, one by one. First John Henry, then the dishes, then the cake. By some miracle, she was sitting on the sofa, bathed and dressed and looking fairly normal—she hoped—when Zach came through the door.

He had an enormous bouquet in one hand and a bottle of wine in the other.

"Peace offering," he said, holding out the roses.

"Thank you, Zach. They are lovely." She was smiling when she took the flowers. "I'll get something to put them in."

She left a trail of fragrance in her wake. Zach didn't go straight to the sofa, as comfortable and inviting as it looked after his long, hard day. He merely stood in the den, soaking up the sights and smells of his temporary home. Gardenias spilled over the side of a crystal bowl on the coffee table, their creamy petals giving off a sweet scent that blended with Lily's more exotic fragrance. An arrangement of glowing candles cast soft shadows on the walls. There was even music. Lily had selected blues tunes, and the haunting melodies drifted around him.

Zach sank onto the sofa so he could watch Lily's entrance into the room.

"Aren't they beautiful?" she said when she came back. She placed the arrangement on a marble-topped table beside George's favorite chair.

"Not nearly as beautiful as you." Lily's hair was down. It made a glorious, shining frame for her heart-shaped face. Her dress was green, like her eyes, and silky enough to swirl around her legs when she walked.

"Thank you." Lily graciously accepted his compliment, then sat beside him on the sofa. "Zach, I said some things I shouldn't have this afternoon."

"So did I, Lily. We all do at one time or another." Zach reached for her hand. "Stress, Lily, makes us say and do things foreign to our natures."

"That's kind of you. But don't pin any medals on me. I'm learning that my nature is pretty volatile."

"You'll never be dull."

"My ex-husband thought I was."

"He was a fool."

Lily drew a sharp breath and put her free hand against her throat. Their gazes met and held for so long that all eternity seemed to be gathered in the small apartment at 13 Royal Street.

Lily didn't speak. She didn't dare. She barely dared breathe.

"I remember, Lily. I've always remembered." Zach lifted her hand to his lips and pressed a lingering kiss in her palm. She could feel its impact all the way down to her toes.

"I thought I had good reasons for denying that I was the masked man who took you to the Monteleone, that I was the one who took you to that silk-draped bed."

Color blazed in her cheeks. Heat coursed through her body. After all these years, Zach was finally telling the truth. She had thought she would feel vindicated. But that was the smallest part of what she was feeling. Gratitude, relief, need, desire all clamored through her.

"I was wrong, Lily. By denying that night, I lost your respect, and I've discovered lately that you're one of the few people whose opinion really matters to me."

"I've waited a long time to hear you say that, Zach. All these years I thought... I don't know what I thought. I guess that Howard was right, that I'm not very good at being a woman."

"You're a wonderful woman. You're intelligent, complex, warm, spontaneous and very spunky."

"You really believe all those things?"

"Yes. They're true, Lily. Your ex-husband did you a grave injustice in telling you otherwise."

"It wasn't just him. All my life I've had trouble with men."

"Then they've all been blind."

Their fingers were still laced together. She felt his strength, his steadfastness, even his sincerity.

"Zach, if I hadn't seen another side of you over the last few days, I would be wondering about your motives."

"As well you might, considering my life-style."

"Rose says you have good reason for living the way you do."

Zach smiled. "She's defended me, has she?"

"Yes. She had to. Over the years I've called you every name in the book—rake, scoundrel, womanizer, party boy. I've thought some terrible things about you."

"I wanted you to, Lily."

"Why?"

Zach didn't answer. Instead, he kissed her hand once more, gazing steadily into her eyes as if he was trying to see her soul. Until that moment Lily hadn't known it was possible to feel apprehension and passion at the same time. What would he say? Would his confessions last long enough for her to know the real Zach Taylor? What would he do? Would he take her into his arms, into his bed? Would she let him?

At last Zach left the sofa. He stood in front of the dark window, looking out. What was he seeing? The French Quarter, lit with neon and decorated with bars, laid out like a bawdy woman awaiting her lover? Or was he looking inward? Today seemed to be the day for introspection.

When he turned from the window, she saw his inner struggle reflected on his face. He looked lonely and vulnerable and as sad as the mask with the single teardrop diamond. A part of her heart went out to him and became his forever.

On that night so long ago, she had not been wrong about him. She'd sensed his loneliness, his pain. But over the years she had forgotten that side of him and remembered only that he had rejected her.

"I can't tell you why, Lily. You'll have to take my word that I had—and still have—very good reasons for discouraging close connections with people."

"I understand." She wasn't sure she did. All she saw was a man who was lonely, a man who chose to reveal a small part of himself in order to have an evening of kindness.

She went to him and put her arms around him. He gathered her close, leaning down so his cheek touched hers. He smelled faintly of after-shave mingled with the distinctive scents of outdoors—sunshine and Spanish moss and river.

They stood that way for a long while, gently rocking as if the rhythm of blues music were caught inside them. Lily was glad. She was glad about the Sicilian food that would be coming. She was glad about the gardenias and the candles.

She was glad about the reconstructed cake. But most of all, she was glad to be in his arms, so close that their heartbeats blended as one.

"I really do understand, Zach," she whispered. His arms tightened around her. "You're lonely and I'm lonely. There's no reason we can't be kind to one another."

"For as long as I'm here . . . in my brother's apartment, watching over my brother's baby."

Without asking, Lily knew what he was saying. As soon as George came back from Spain, Zach would be out of her life again, just as surely as he had disappeared from her life four years ago.

Chapter 10

Still holding Lily in his arms, Zach tangled his hand in her hair. It felt silky and alive.

"You have beautiful hair, Lily. I'm glad you wore it down."

"I don't usually."

"I know."

"Tonight I got the feeling of...I don't know...freedom, I guess. I gave myself permission to do whatever I want as long as nobody else is hurt," Lily told him softly.

"I'm glad that permission included hugging a former rake."

"Former?"

"For the next few days."

They laughed together, then drew apart. Without the least bit of self-consciousness, they linked hands and went back to the sofa. Zach stretched his long legs and leaned his head back, sighing.

"Sometimes I envy George."

"Sometimes I envy Rose."

Zach turned to look at her. "If I were George and you were Rose, I would kiss you."

"If I were Rose and you were George, I'd let you."

"Would you let *me,* Lily?"

Lily decided that the moment had come when zebras should fly and the sun should rise in the west. Zach, who was known for taking what he wanted, was asking permission to kiss her.

As if he guessed her thoughts, he smiled. "Would you let me," he added softly, "knowing that nothing permanent could ever come of it?" He put his hand on her cheek. "I have to know, because I don't ever intend to hurt you again."

"Sometimes hurts come unintentionally." She covered his hand with hers and pressed it closer to her cheek. "I'm willing to take the risk."

Zach cupped her face, tipping it up so her mouth was only inches from his. "I've been wanting to do this for a very long time."

"And I've been wanting you to."

He drew her face closer, so close, his lips barely grazed hers. "Think of the time we've wasted," he murmured just before he claimed her mouth.

It was the most exquisitely tender kiss Lily had ever known. She knew Zach was a passionate man, for once she had been partner to his passion. She knew he was full of fire and hard edges and iron control. But there was nothing hard or controlled about the kiss. It was as spontaneous as sunrise, as gentle as summer dew, as refreshing as spring rain.

He fitted her close to his body so that his chest felt like an extension of hers. It was a broad, solid chest, blatantly male and infinitely reassuring. Lily felt as if she had lived all her life for that moment. She had been kissed before. She had even been kissed by Zach. But never had such a foundation been laid. They had come together out of a mutual need for kindness, with a full understanding of what lay ahead.

Lily sighed against his lips, and he eased back for air.

"I might not get enough of this, Lily."

"Nor I." She smiled. "I always surprise myself around you."

"How's that?"

"By doing things I don't ordinarily do...like crying over little problems and making too much of hugs and wanting to be things I'm not. I don't know if you bring out the best in me or the worst."

"The best, Lily." He tangled his hands in her hair and watched the silken strands drift through his fingers. "And you bring out the best in me...." He leaned closer. "The very best," he murmured as he took possession of her lips once more.

She was easy to kiss, a naturally passionate woman who kissed with her body, her soul. She settled closer to him in subtle, delicious ways so that he felt her body changing, responding to him. Through the silky fabric of her dress, he felt her skin heat up. Without any urging, her mouth opened for the thrust of his tongue.

Desire spiraled through him, bright and hot and so intense, he almost lost control. The need for kindness became a need for release. A simple kiss became a prelude to love.

They began to sway to the beat of the music that swirled around them. Or perhaps they were swaying to the beat of the passion that swept through them. Zach didn't know. And he was too far gone to tell whether he was being controlled by internal or external influences.

Lily was ripe and lush, yearning for his kiss. Her breasts were heavy with passion, their nipples hardened and peaked against his hand. And the sweet, heady smell of gardenias mixed with the exotic scent of Lily's perfume.

It was enough to make any man lose his sanity. But he was not just any man, and she was not just any woman. A part of him was beast, ready to devour; but another part of him was reluctant hero. It astonished him that he hesitated to take what he so desperately wanted, what he so desperately needed, because in doing so he might inflict pain.

He had asked for a kiss...but he wanted more, so very much more. Groaning, he gathered her closer, not ready to let her go. Was he trying to lose himself in her, or was he trying to find himself? He didn't know. All he knew was that he had to hold on to her just a bit longer.

He kissed her, knowing that kissing was not enough, but understanding that it would have to suffice. And when at last they were both breathless, he drew back.

Passion flushed Lily's cheeks and made her eyes bright. He traced the love-pouted lines of her lips.

"You're a tempting woman, Lily."

She closed her eyes and leaned her cheek into his hand. The gesture was completely artless and totally feminine.

"I should have had to fight a dozen men to get to your door tonight."

"No wonder you're such a successful rake. You know exactly what to say to turn a woman's head."

They laughed together. Bentley strolled in to see what all the commotion was about and after finding nothing to interest him, strolled back to the nursery to take up guard beside the crib.

The doorbell rang. Lily and Zach both started off the sofa.

"That will be the food," Zach said.

"How did you know?"

"I ordered Chinese."

"I ordered Sicilian."

They began to laugh, and might have gone on laughing for quite a while if the doorbell hadn't pinged again.

It turned out to be the food Lily had ordered. She carried the steaming dishes into the dining room and set them on the table. Candlelight flickered over the tinfoil covers, and gardenias perfumed the air.

"You did all this for me, Lily?"

"Just for you, Zach."

The doorbell rang again.

"*That's* the Chinese food," he said, and they both started laughing again.

"I hope you're really hungry, Lily," he told her later as he placed his order on the table alongside hers.

"I'm ravenous."

They gave each other a quick glance that caught and held.

As they sat down at the table, Lily realized that the thing she found most attractive about Zach was his intelligence. Forget that he was heart-stoppingly gorgeous. Forget that he could kiss as if he had invented it. None of that would have mattered to her if he hadn't had the kind of mind that challenged her at every turn. She felt stimulated, revitalized.

Zach poured the wine, and they ate with the gusto of healthy people enjoying life. Between the Chinese and the Sicilian courses, they talked about everything from Hawthorne to Hemingway, from Renoir to Warhol, from Jefferson to current politics.

John Henry slept like an angel, and even Bentley behaved. He wandered in every now and then and marched around the table with his nose in the air, as if he were on patrol. Then he marched out again, canine master of the apartment.

The candles burned low and the wine bottle grew empty. Replete with good food and good conversation, Zach and Lily sat across the table, studying each other. Both liked what they saw.

"Thank you for a wonderful evening, Lily."

"Thank *you*, Zach."

"I'm beginning to understand my brother's contentment."

"And I'm beginning to understand Rose's."

They considered each other awhile longer as soft music and seductive scents drifted around them. Zach noted that Lily looked as vulnerable and feminine as she had that long-ago night during Mardi Gras, when magic had been at work and miracles had seemed possible.

"I baked you a cake," she confessed, leaning across the table, her voice a husky whisper.

"What?" he asked, not paying attention to anything except the curl that lay against her cheek like the petal of a bright flower.

"I wanted to do something special, something with my own hands, to let you know that I'm sincere about..." She paused, biting her lower lip in a manner as beguiling as it was uncharacteristic.

"About new beginnings...?"

"Yes. A new beginning." She leaned her elbows on the table and propped her chin in her hand. "It's not much of a cake, but then, I'm not used to baking."

"I'm touched, Lily."

The candlelight picked up bright sparkles in the centers of her eyes as she leaned closer. Zach had a hard time keeping his mind on the conversation.

"You don't have to eat it if you don't want to."

"Not eat it? This very special cake you baked?" He leaned back and laced his hands behind his head. "I'll eat every morsel...."

"Don't make any rash promises till you see the cake."

"Well? Are you going to keep me in suspense all evening, or do you plan to unveil this uncommon cake?"

"I'll be right back."

She left in a swish of silk skirts and a swirl of sweet fragrance. Zach closed his eyes and longed for the right to take what he wanted. He longed for the freedom to enjoy other such evenings of candlelight and wine and gardenias. But most of all, he longed for the freedom to drop his mask forever, to leave his other life behind as surely as he had left his diamond-studded mask on Lily's pillow so very long ago.

"Ta-dah!" Holding the cake high, Lily entered the room. Her cheeks were flushed with wine and accomplishment. The cake was sitting lopsided on a silver platter with gobs of chocolate icing holding it together and a circle of strawberries trying to camouflage the fact that its rim was jagged.

She set the cake in front of him, and even with its sides shored up by icing, he thought it might collapse.

"It's the finest cake I've ever seen," he said.

"You're just saying that." Lily wielded a cake knife, cutting him a generous slice. "But I'm awfully glad you did."

His first bite told him the story of the cake: it had been burned. Lily had probably scraped all the burned parts off, then put the remainder back together with icing. "Mmm," he said, rolling his eyes. "Best cake I ever had."

Lily laughed. "You lie so well."

"It comes from practice."

"Can you taste the burned part?" she asked, cutting her own slice.

"What burned part?" He swallowed the charred lump without blinking an eye.

"I had a little trouble, but nothing I couldn't fix."

"A resourceful woman. Just my kind."

Lily took her first bite. "Oh, my." She tried another. "This is horrible." She laid her fork aside. "Why didn't you tell me?"

"It's not horrible, Lily." Her chin trembled and her eyes got that too-bright look of a woman close to tears. Zach hurried to her side. Leaning down, he put his arms around her. "I could hardly taste the burned part at all because the chocolate icing is so delicious." He dipped his finger into her cake and came up with a gob of icing. "See?" he said, licking the icing. "Mmm." He dipped his finger into the cake again, then offered it to her. "Try it, Lily."

Holding on to his hand, she popped his finger between her lips. Moist and soft and warm, her mouth closed around him. Too late he realized exactly what kind of fire he was playing with.

Lily did, too. She regarded him with eyes suddenly gone wide. For a breathless moment they stared at each other, and then her mouth began to move. She sucked at the icing, using her tongue to lick it off his finger. Desire jolted him so hard, he almost cried out.

Lily's head was tilted back so that her hair brushed against the front of his shirt. He couldn't actually feel her hair through his shirt, but he imagined that he could. He imagined the silky strands spread across his chest, red curls weaving among dark, fire and smoke. Heat coursed through Zach, and he was so close to the edge of control he had to clamp his teeth together. He could feel his tight muscles ticking in his jaw.

Time telescoped, holding the moment bright and shimmering. Zach memorized the golden sunbursts in the centers of Lily's eyes. He memorized the delicate bloom of color on her cheeks. He cataloged the sensual, pouty shape of her mouth surrounding his finger. But most of all, he stored away the memory of the currents flowing between them, sexual currents made stronger because of the tenderness and kindness they felt for each other.

He knew the moment wouldn't last, *couldn't* last. Like a man too-long lost in the desert, he drank hungrily while he was at the fountain.

Self-conscious, Lily released his finger with a soft popping sound. Zach wanted to linger, but decided that distance was his best defense. With the table between them once more, he tried to reestablish the easy camaraderie they'd enjoyed during the meal. But erotic visions kept getting in the way.

He was almost relieved when John Henry woke, demanding attention.

"I'll get him," he said. "I haven't seen him since early morning."

"Fine. I'll clean up."

"It was a lovely party, Lily. Thanks."

"It was my pleasure."

After he had gone, it seemed to Lily that he still lingered. The air was charged with the vitality he always wore like a cloak. His outline, large and solid and reassuring, still seemed to hover over his chair.

She ran her hands over the carved wooden chair back as if she could capture Zach's essence that way. There was something magical in the room, in the apartment, that Lily wanted to hold on to. She felt like a child who had suddenly discovered that there was a world outside the nursery, a world full of bright adventures and wonderful possibilities.

She stood beside Zach's chair, daydreaming, until Bentley passed through, reminding her that the *real* world waited.

Faint sounds of a New Orleans night drifted through Lily's window—the heavy clop of horses' hooves on pavement as carriages wound their way through the French Quarter; the muted sound of a jazz saxophone; the bright, high-pitched call of a Creole selling his wares. Restless, Lily got out of bed and stood with her forehead pressing against the windowpane.

Here she was in Rose's bedroom once again, with Zach sleeping on the sofa. That didn't seem right. Especially after the wine and roses, after the chocolate icing and the wonderful feeling of camaraderie that had developed between them earlier in the evening.

Camaraderie? Who was she kidding? What she was feeling was far more erotic than friendship. How had it happened that they had gone to separate beds, anyhow?

Lily knew exactly how it had happened. After the dishes were put away and John Henry was tucked back into his crib for the night, a restraint had come over them. There seemed to be nothing that was right to say, and they had finally parted in the hallway with a stiff good-night.

Lily walked to her door and opened it a crack. Then she stood listening, trying to hear Zach down the hall. There was no rustling of bedclothes, no snoring, no pacing. Nothing except a silence so ripe, it might burst open at any moment.

"Soon he'll be gone," she whispered, pressing her hand over her heart. George would be dismissed from the Spanish hospital, then he and Rose would come back to take up their life in the apartment with John Henry. Lily would be back at the bank, far away from a pair of piercing black eyes and a smile that made her heart turn upside down.

She put her hand on the doorknob, then drew back. What was she doing? Was she mad, asking for the same kind of trouble twice? *Not the same,* she reminded herself. She knew Zach now, at least the part of him he had chosen to reveal.

She took a deep breath and put her hand on the doorknob once more. All her life she had been careful. All her life she had been sensible. Except that night she had gone to the Mardi Gras. And it had been one of the most memorable nights of her life.

She had to take a risk. If she didn't take it, something inside her might shrivel and die forever.

Boldly now, she pushed open the door. Her bare feet padded on the carpet, hardly making a sound. When she approached the den, she began to tiptoe. Zach might be asleep. If he was, she wouldn't wake him. She would go back to her bedroom and shut the door and try to forget about the madness that drove her.

It was completely dark in the den. Lily stood in the doorway, letting her eyes adjust. Finally she was able to make out a dark shape at the window.

Zach was wearing nothing but shorts. Feeling almost like a thief, Lily observed him unnoticed. He was an imposing man. In the dark he looked as remote and majestic and intimidating as a mountain in Alaska.

What if he turned her down? That thought hadn't occurred to her. *Leave while there's still time,* she told herself. Her gown whispered around her legs as she turned to go.

"Lily?" Zach spun from the window.

She pressed one hand to her throat and faced him. "I couldn't sleep."

"Neither could I."

"Because of Bemus Rockman?"

"No...." They watched each other across the dark distance. The air crackled and sizzled between them. "Because of you, Lily." She drew in a sharp breath. "I was standing at the window, thinking of how you would look in the dark with your hair spread across the pillow."

"I wasn't in bed. I've been at my window, too."

A long silence thundered around them. Lily took a step into the room.

"Because of you, Zach...." She took another step. "I was at my window because of you."

"Lily." He crossed the room in three long strides. He didn't pull her into his arms when he reached her, but stood with his great body emanating sensual heat.

She wet her lips with her tongue, waiting. Zach put one hand on her face and began to trace its lines.

"Your face is shaped like a heart." With one finger he dipped the moisture off her lips and pressed it to his own.

His nearness, his body heat, his touch upon her skin...all made Lily a little crazy. She didn't care if she had only one night with him. She didn't care if he walked away tomorrow and never came back. She didn't care that they lived in separate worlds. All she cared about was the moment.

"Zach..." She moved toward him and found herself wrapped in his embrace.

With his face pressed into her hair, he whispered, "If you don't want to be here, turn back now, Lily." His heart hammered against hers. "Turn back now before its too late."

"I don't want to turn back."

Zach tipped her face up to his. "Then kiss me, Lily. Kiss me with your soul."

And she did. It was so easy with him. Her emotions overflowed as naturally as spring water. She felt the wonder and the beauty of his lips upon hers, but more than that, she felt the joy of knowing that the kiss was more than just physical. It was a joining of spirits, a blending of souls, a meeting of hearts.

Zach lifted her and carried her down the hall to the bed. He kicked the door softly shut behind them.

Moonlight streamed through the curtains, making a swath of light upon the floor. It was in that bright path that he set her.

His eyes were very dark as he slid her nightgown straps down, following their descent with his hands.

"Your skin is as soft as gardenias." He bent over her and kissed the hollow of her throat. His tongue flicked against her skin. "Soft and delicious . . ."

Straightening, he drew the gown down over her breasts. "And beautiful," he added. He wet the tip of his finger with his tongue, then traced her nipples until they were hard and erect.

She felt limp and hot and moist. Throwing her head back, she offered herself up to him. He took one breast into his mouth, teasing the tip with his tongue until she thought her legs would buckle. She tangled her hands in his hair and pulled him closer.

Groaning, he began to suckle deeply, thoroughly. Star bursts of pleasure centered in her breast, then radiated outward until Lily felt as if she were a Fourth of July rocket set to go off.

Time became a slow-moving stream, murmuring and whispering through a sunlit meadow so bright, it hurt to think about, let alone look. In the distance, haunting music of the night filtered into the room where the two of them stood, weaving in and around and through them so that they were caught up in its slow, sensuous beat.

"Lily... Lily." Zach murmured her name over and over, moving from one breast to the other, hungry, obsessed.

He couldn't get enough of her. He feasted upon her breasts until her breath was coming in short rasps, catching in her throat so that her voice became husky.

"Please, Zach, oh, please."

Slowly he slid her gown down, following her body shape with his hands, murmuring incoherent words of pleasure. When her gown lay on the carpet in a pool of red silk, Zach knelt before her. With his hands cupping her hips, he brought her forward until she was offered up to him like a night-blooming flower.

"Sweet, so sweet," he whispered.

Pleasure burst through Lily so hard and fast, she had to catch his shoulders in order to stand upright. She opened her mouth to say his name, but nothing came out except a gasp.

From far away, an alto sax mourned love lost, and a clarinet added its plaintive note to the blues. The songs drifted in and out of Lily's consciousness, a sad counterpoint to the joy of Zach's lovemaking.

When she thought she might collapse, screaming and begging for more, Zach lifted her up and carried her to the bed. Bracing one knee on the mattress, he lowered her to the sheets.

"Do you want me, Lily?"

"Yes, more than I thought possible."

"I want you, Lily. I want all of you." He stripped off his shorts, then lay beside her and pulled her into his arms. "I want to know every inch of your body. I want to feel it, taste it."

She closed her eyes, desire trembling through her so fiercely, she could barely think, let alone speak.

"Lily?" he whispered.

"Shh..." She put her hands over his lips. "No more talk."

His eyes blazing with the fire that burned through him, Zach lifted himself over Lily and slid into the satiny, welcoming recesses of her body. At even that moment of complete unity, he felt the sadness of their parting. Soon he would leave her. Soon he would say goodbye. But not yet. Not now. For the rest of the night, he would bask in the glow of her passion, revel in the delights of her body and store away the sweet, hot memories so he could take them out when his life became burdened with crime and fear and loneliness, take them out and remember.... Remember how the music of her sang through him from head to toe, remember how her skin glistened in the moonlight, remember how she whispered love words to him, urging him on....

Years of need could not be assuaged in an hour... for either of them. Time and again they peaked, only to pull back, drawing out the anticipation until it was fairly humming through them.

A fine sheen of sweat covered their bodies. The covers became hopelessly tangled around them until Zach kicked them to the floor. He rolled over, taking Lily with him. She leaned over him, letting her hair fall in a bright curtain across his chest. He lifted a strand of her hair to his lips while her hips took up a rocking cadence that caused the bedsprings to squeak.

Passion bound them together like a bright ribbon, winding tighter and tighter until they were both panting with the need to break out of its hold. Zach surged into her, calling her name. "Lily... Lily... Now!"

She threw her head back, and shudders racked her body as she and Zach found release at the same time. Rigid and straining, they held on until the gentle ebb of passion made them sag.

Her body as liquid as melting honey, Lily stretched across his chest. His breathing was harsh and raspy as he smoothed her damp hair off her forehead.

Words would have been redundant. They lay silently, clinging to each other, touching softly, kissing gently until at last Lily's head dropped onto Zach's shoulder.

When the even rise and fall of her breathing signaled that she slept, Zach gathered her close and arranged her in a tight coil against his body. He knew he wouldn't sleep. This time with her was too precious to waste a minute of it in slumber.

Chapter 11

The harsh ringing of the telephone brought Lily awake. She tried to sit up and found herself pinned to the bed with a large arm across her chest. Memories flooded through her. Her cheeks got hot... but not from embarrassment. If she could go back in time, she wouldn't change a single moment of what had happened last night. The pleasure would burn in her forever.

The telephone continued its insistent ringing. Gently she tried to lift Zach's arm away so she could reach the receiver, but the arm was like a band of steel. She felt like an ant straining at a lion.

"Lily?" Zach came awake quickly, both eyes wide open and alert. "I didn't mean to sleep." He swung his legs over the side of the bed and stood there, wearing nothing more than a smile. "Do you want me to get that?"

"No." Her view was so entrancing, she reached backward for the phone. Naked, with the early morning sunlight gleaming on him, Zach was a magnificent sight. "I will," she added.

Grinning, Zach leaned across her, plucked the receiver out of its cradle and handed it to her.

"My pleasure, sweet," he whispered, dipping his tongue into her ear. Then, grinning wickedly, he went into the bathroom.

"Hello," Lily said, her voice cracking so that she sounded seriously ill.

"Lily? Is that you?"

The caller was Rose. Lily cleared her throat and pulled the sheet over her breasts.

"Yes..." She still sounded like a frog in heat. "Yes," she said again. "It's me."

"You don't sound like yourself. Are you sick?"

"Me? Sick?" That was a laugh. Sick with passion, maybe. But otherwise feeling as if she could fly all over the French Quarter without wings. "No. I'm fine. Just a little sleepy, that's all." She gave a great yawn to convince her sister. "I'm still in bed."

Zach wandered back from the bathroom and climbed into bed. His eyes gleaming, he pulled down the covers and nipped her breast. Lily sucked in a sharp breath and bit her lip to keep back her cry of pleasure.

"Lily? Are you sure everything's all right? Bentley's behaving, isn't he?"

"Bentley's an angel."

Zach winked at her, then drew her onto his lap, sheet, telephone and all.

"And John Henry? How's my little baby?"

"Perfect, Rose. He couldn't be better." *Except that we don't know who he is.* Lily told herself she was lying only a little, and all for a good cause.

"I'm glad to hear that. And Zach? How's he holding out? All this baby-sitting's not too hard on him, is it?"

"No. Zach's fine. It's not too hard at all."

Grinning wickedly, Zach whispered in her ear, "Liar."

"Shush," she whispered.

"Lily? What's going on there?" Planted firmly across Zach's lap, Lily felt a lot going on, but nothing she dared tell Rose. "I swear, you're not making a lick of sense. Go get Zach and let me talk to him."

Lily covered the mouthpiece with her hand. "She wants to talk to you."

"Well, put me on." He took the receiver and began to talk to his sister-in-law, his voice as smooth as cream. "Rose? How are you, sweetheart...? That's good. And how is George...? Umm... Yes... That's good news."

Lily was torn between wanting to know about the good news and wanting to sock Zach for being so controlled in a situation that had her hot and panting. His mind might be functioning like a well-oiled wheel, but with nothing except a thin sheet separating them, she had no doubt whatsoever about the state of his body.

"Let me speak with George, sweetheart."

Lily tensed. She knew what was coming next. Zach's arm tightened around her. Then he began to tell his brother about the dispute over John Henry. "We're doing everything we possibly can, George. Yes, it's crucial that we find Glenda.... I've got the best people in New Orleans on it right now.... Yes... I will.... And George, Lily doesn't think Rose should be told.... That's right. She doesn't want to upset her needlessly.... Try not to worry.... I know you do. Thanks, George."

"Will he tell Rose?" Lily asked after Zach had hung up.

"Not yet. But he will before they come home.... They'll be home in a week, Lily."

"One week?"

They looked at each other, both thinking the same thing. From somewhere in the Quarter a lonely sax began to play "Willow Weep for Me."

"Come here, Lily." Zach pulled her close, and together they sought to hold back time.

* * *

Forgetting. Zach found it so easy to do with Lily.

With the early-morning sun streaming through the window, they made slow, leisurely love. Forgotten was his reason for being in his brother's apartment. Forgotten was his lonely past. Forgotten was the custody battle they all faced. All he knew was the moment. All he knew was the silk of Lily's thighs and the warm satin of her most secret places. He knew the nectar of her kisses and the tenderness of her embrace. He knew the shine in her emerald eyes and the erotic words upon her lips.

But most of all, he knew her soul. He knew she was warm and kind and giving.

They moved together with a languorous rhythm while New Orleans awakened around them. Metal rang against metal as the garbage collectors picked up the previous night's trash. Alley cats sang their last song before slinking back to the restaurants where the smell of fish promised a free meal. Taxis honked and tooted their way through the narrow streets, not because traffic was heavy, but merely to announce the arrival of a new batch of tourists.

Oblivious to everything except finding release, Zach and Lily clung together.

Down the hall, Bentley cocked his ears. With his tail waving and his tongue hanging out, he took up watch beside the little loud person's bed.

John Henry was stirring. He opened his blue eyes quickly so he could see everything in his room at once, the way he liked. He saw the circus mobile floating above him, the streaks of sun on his ceiling and the white railings along the side of his bed. He shaped his mouth into a pink rosebud and yawned. Then he stuck his feet in the air and watched them wiggle. His stomach felt a little rumbly, and that meant it was time to call the grown-ups. But he was having such a good time playing with his feet, he decided he would wait a little while. Besides that, it would be nice if they would come in and discover he was hungry instead of him having to call them. He was tired of having to do all the work.

In the master suite, Lily and Zach came to the end of their leisurely journey and lay in each other arms, stroking and whispering.

"You're an incredible woman, Lily Cooper."

"And you're an incredible man."

"Wait till you see what I do in the shower."

"Is that an offer?"

"Yes. But first I'd better check on our little man."

"I can."

"No, let me. You need your rest for other things." He kissed her cheek softly, then pulled on his shorts and left the bedroom.

Lily stretched and made contented humming noises. She felt pretty and pampered and loved. She knew, of course, that her condition was only temporary. But she intended to enjoy every moment of the time she had left.

One week, Zach had said. George and Rose would be home in one week. She wouldn't think about that now. Thinking about future sadness robbed the present of its pleasure.

She lolled in bed, thinking of what she should do. She should put on her robe and go down the hall to see if Zach needed help with John Henry. Or perhaps she should go into the kitchen and make a logger's breakfast for the two of them. She was getting hungry, and Zach was bound to be.

Or she could take a shower. She fluffed up her pillow, then lay flat on her back and closed her eyes. She would rest just a minute, then decide what to do.

In the nursery, Zach found John Henry wide-awake, playing with his feet.

"Good morning, John Henry. How's my little man this morning?"

John Henry smiled and burbled and wiggled every movable body part, trying to tell his uncle how he was. Uncle Zach changed his diaper, then picked him up and waltzed him around the room, singing a song about bluebirds on his shoulder. The words were funny, something like zipping and dooing and dahing. John Henry liked them. But most of all, he liked his Uncle Zach.

He did the best he could to tell him so.

"You must be ready for breakfast, huh?" John Henry loved the way Uncle Zach could hold him with one arm while fixing the bottle with his other hand. He reckoned that took a baby expert.

After they had settled into the rocking chair with his bottle, Uncle Zach began to talk and rock. "Someday, when you get big, I'm going to take you fishing, John Henry. We'll go out on the river in a boat and sit in the sun with our lines hanging in the water, and we'll talk about all kinds of important things. And I'm going to teach you to play ball and how to make a willow whistle and how to do birdcalls."

The rocking chair squeaked pleasantly, and Bentley sat beside them, thumping his tail on the floor. The early-morning sounds of the city filtered through the window.

Zach understood true contentment. The cozy apartment, the sweet baby, the loving woman. He had it all. But it was only temporary. One week and it would all be gone. He would make the best of the time he had left.

"Let's go see Aunt Lily," he said after John Henry finished his bottle.

They found her still in bed, asleep. Gently Zach placed John Henry beside her, then stood back to admire the picture they made, beautiful woman and bright-eyed baby. He wished they were both his. Then he was ashamed of himself for coveting a child that belonged to his brother—and a woman who would never belong to him.

Lily came awake, laughing to find John Henry in bed with her. Zach sat down beside them, and they spent the next hour playing together. Lily resorted to baby talk, and Zach got carried away inventing silly songs.

"Just listen to us," Lily said. "Weren't we the same people who talked about reading Shakespeare to him?"

"I think he probably prefers, ''Ou widdle sweetie pie.'"

"Did I say that?"

"You did."

"Rose would approve."

At the mention of her sister's name, they both became sober, thinking of the impending court battle.

"Do you think George told her?" Lily asked.

"Probably not yet. They have a week before they come home."

"So little time."

They looked at each other with naked faces, making no pretense to hide their feelings. Zach cupped her cheek.

"I have to see if there's been any progress in finding Glenda." He circled his thumbs over her soft skin. "I'll be back as soon as I can, Lily."

"Take your time. Finding Glenda is more important than..."

"Than us?"

"There is no *us,* is there, Zach? We agreed."

He was silent a long time, wishing he could deny that what she said was true. But his course was set. It had been set seven years ago, and there was no turning back.

"For a week there is the two of us, Lily." He kissed her lightly. "Can you handle things here alone?"

"Yes."

"I'll call and let you know if there's any news."

There was news, and it was good. One of Zach's men had a lead on Glenda.

"The call just came in from Bobby," Sam told him. "They think the girl is staying at a friend's house in Hammond."

"I want to handle the questioning myself. Bobby understood that?"

"Yes. He's waiting for your instructions." Sam handed Zach the telephone number.

First Zach called Bobby, then Lily.

"We think we've found Glenda, Lily. I'm going to drive up. If she tells me the father, and he is somebody local, I'll go ahead and arrange the blood tests."

Lily was ecstatic. "We're nearly there, Zach."

"It's too early to tell. If everything goes well, I should be back sometime tonight. Call my home number if you need anything. My butler will take care of it."

"Most expensive damned butler you're likely to ever have," Sam said after Zach hung up.

"I always go first class." Zach jangled his car keys in his pocket, anxious to get to Hammond. "Sam, do me a favor."

"Sure thing."

"I don't expect Lily to have any trouble, and if she did she might not call you."

"She's stubborn, huh?"

"And then some.... Cruise by the apartment a couple of times, just to make sure there's nobody suspicious hanging around."

"Right. Can't be too careful."

"Thanks, pal."

Zach's mood was jubilant as he drove toward Hammond. He turned on the radio and whistled along with the tune. Then he found himself tapping his fingers to the rhythm. He even found himself noticing how blue the sky was, how majestic the live oaks appeared with their shawls of Spanish moss, how seductive the city looked with its romantic architecture.

He was accustomed to success in his business. Finding Glenda was cause for gratitude, but not cause for the great jubilation he was feeling. *Lily* was the cause of his mood. *Lily and John Henry.* He knew it as surely as if a giant hand had written the truth across the summer sky.

And soon he would lose her...again.

Don't think about that now, he told himself. He needed all his attention focused on the problem at hand. John Henry's future depended on Zach.

Glenda's friend lived in a modest white frame house on a quiet street in one of Hammond's middle-class neighborhoods. Children played in the street, racing tricycles and pitching balls and skipping rope. Two teenage girls stood gossiping at a sagging fence. A stocky woman with her hair tied in a bandanna hung clothes on the line beside a small yellow house.

Zach parked on the street. The children waved and called greetings to him as he walked up the cracked sidewalk. A sign on the mailbox in front of the white frame house said *The Walters* in curlicue letters, painted red.

Two white rockers with fading green cushions sat on the front porch. There was no doorbell, so Zach knocked. A middle-aged woman with brown hair and a wide pleasant face answered the door.

"Mrs. Walter? I'm Zach Taylor from New Orleans."

"Yes?" At the mention of New Orleans, Mrs. Walter's face took on an anxious look.

"I came to talk with your daughter, Angela."

"She's not in any trouble, is she?"

"I can assure you that she's in no trouble. But I do need some information from her."

"What about?"

Zach told her why he had come. Mrs. Walter still hesitated.

"The Rockman girl is no longer here, Mr. Taylor."

Zach was disappointed but not defeated. It had all been too easy. Nothing in life was that easy. Still, there might be something gained from this trip.

"I would like to talk with Angela, Mrs. Walter. It's possible she can tell me something that will help in locating Glenda."

Mrs. Walter wavered a moment, then opened the door for him. "I don't usually like to get mixed up in other folks' business, but I guess it won't hurt this once. You might as well come on in. I'll go see if Angela wants to talk."

Zach went into a small den furnished in Early American furniture, upholstered in a bright pattern of gold and orange favored in the sixties. Knitted afghans were thrown across the chair and the sofa to protect the fabric. Ceramic figurines crowded the tables, and framed needlepoint pictures covered the walls. There was not a spot of dust anywhere, not a scuff mark on the linoleum floor, nor a single nick to mar the polished surface of the tables. The room looked as if it had been preserved for some great future event, perhaps a church social or an afternoon tea party or a wedding reception.

Zach didn't know where to sit, so he stood, waiting, trying not to appear anxious.

He heard footsteps down the hall, the muted sound of voices, then more footsteps. Suddenly Angela stood before him.

"Mr. Taylor, I'm Angela Walter. Mama says you want to talk about Glenda."

Mrs. Walter left them alone, and Zach told Angela why he had come. Briefly he outlined Bemus Rockman's claim, his plan to file a custody suit.

"I don't want to do anything that will hurt Glenda," Angela said.

"I can assure you that I won't do anything to hurt Glenda, but it's imperative that I find her. My brother and his wife could lose the baby if I can't prove that he's not Glenda's son.''

Angela chewed her bottom lip, then finally gave a slight nod. "All right. I'll tell you what I know."

"Do you know where she is?"

"She didn't say where she was going."

"When did she leave?"

"Last night. We had gone to the movies. It was late when we got home. I was in the bathroom brushing my teeth when suddenly Glenda came in and said, 'I'm leaving.' Just like that."

"Did she tell you why?"

"I didn't ask. She's always been like that. Ever since I've known her, and that's a long time. We used to go down to New Orleans a lot in the summer, when we were kids and all. Even back then, Glenda was unpredictable. She'd do things for no reason at all except that she wanted to do them."

"Did she mention anything—any place, any person—that would indicate where she might have gone?"

"No... Not that I can think of." Angela frowned, trying to remember. "I'm sorry, Mr. Taylor. Glenda didn't tell me anything that would help you."

Zach considered himself a good judge of people, and he could tell that Angela was telling the truth. He handed her a card with his number.

"Will you call me if you hear from her?"

"I will." She offered her hand. "Good luck, Mr. Taylor."

"Thank you, Angela."

Outside, the children on the street had abandoned their tricycles and started a game of hopscotch. They hopped on spindly scraped legs, their voices rising like birds on the summer air.

Zach rammed his fists into his pockets and concentrated on the children. Someday John Henry would play with children like that, high-spirited, naturally self-centered little people who didn't yet know the meaning of failure.

Zach couldn't fail. Not this time. A vision of his sister lying in a pool of blood came to him. He hadn't had that vision in a long time, not since the advent of John Henry into his life. The blood spread across his vision, blurring the children's images.

He hurried to his car. The best way to hold memories at bay was to keep busy. Although Angela hadn't been able to help him, there was still much he could do in Hammond.

Glenda had been there. Somebody, somewhere might have seen her, talked to her. Somebody might know where she was.

He had to find out.

He spent the rest of the day in futile efforts to get a lead on Glenda Rockman. The girl was either clever or lucky. No one in Hammond knew anything at all about her.

He had come to a dead end. It was time to go home.

He drove to the nearest pay phone to call Lily. She would be waiting near the phone to hear his report.

"The news is not good, Lily. I just missed Glenda. She's vanished...without a trace." There was no response and he jiggled the receiver. "Lily?"

"I can't talk now, Zach. I'm crying."

"I didn't really expect it to be easy, Lily. We're just getting started. We'll find her. You have to believe that."

"I know...." She sniffed. "I know. I'm just being weepy, that's all."

"I'll be home to wipe your tears in about an hour. Hang on, sweetheart."

After he hung up, he realized he had used his brother's favorite term of endearment for Rose. Like every other bit of domesticity, it felt good. Driving home through the cozy darkness of summer with the high sweet hum of insects coming through his open window, Zach imagined a different life for himself, one with a rambling house in the country and a swing on the front porch and dewy-faced children sleeping in their beds and a tender woman at his side. It was only a dream, of course. But it was a pleasant one.

* * *

Lily was asleep on the sofa when he got home, with Bentley curved around her legs like a pretzel, watching his territory with a wicked gleam in his eye.

Grinning, Zach knelt to pet the dog. Bentley took it as his just due.

"Come on, you little pretender. Let's go check on the young master."

Together they went down the hall and through the nursery door. John Henry lay in his crib as relaxed as a wet dish towel, one arm flung back over his head and the other curved upward so his thumb was in easy reach of his little pink mouth. Zach leaned over the crib to smooth the cover over the baby's fat legs. That done, he lingered, gathering the tranquility to his soul like a warm winter blanket. The scent of baby powder hung in the air, mingling with the sweet, distinctive scent of John Henry's skin, a combination of spring grass and vanilla.

The gentle rise and fall of John Henry's breathing punctuated the silence. His dark eyelashes made half-moon curves on his cheeks, and every now and then the corners of his mouth quirked upward as he dreamed of fishing on the Mississippi River with his Uncle Zach.

Finally, Zach tiptoed from the nursery. Only when he reached the hallway did he realize his cheeks were damp. Unashamed, he wiped the tears away. Then he went into the den where Lily still lay sleeping.

Gently, so as not to wake her, he gathered her into his arms. She made quiet sleepy sounds, like a brook meandering over mossy stones; then she snuggled against his chest. Her purple silk gown trailed across his arms as he carried her into the bedroom.

He placed her carefully on the bed, then lay down beside her, fully dressed. He wanted to hold her while she was totally unaware. Gathering her close, he pressed her warm body to his and let the peace of being with her flow over his battle-scarred soul.

Chapter 12

Lily woke with a start. What time was it? She had meant to be awake when Zach got back from Hammond. Groggily she reached one hand to brace against the sofa cushion—and encountered solid muscle.

She wasn't on the sofa at all. She was in bed on top of the covers, and Zach was curled next to her, asleep with all his clothes on.

She didn't move for a while, but lay very still, listening to the deep, even rhythm of his breathing. When her eyes adjusted to the darkness, she saw his dark hair, tousled over his forehead, and the white scar gleaming high on his cheekbone. His lips were slightly parted, the bottom one fuller than the top.

He had brought her to bed, then fallen asleep still dressed. Her heart wrenched to think of how tired he must be.

She eased off the mattress, then went around to the foot of the bed and began to remove Zach's shoes. That was the least she could do to make him comfortable. She set the shoes side by side on the floor. She studied him once more, then decided to remove his belt. Surely if he rolled over in the middle of the night, the belt buckle would pinch.

Holding her breath, she eased the buckle open and began to pull the belt from his pants. Either he was too exhausted to notice or had developed a certain trust, for he slept on.

Taking a belt from a sleeping man was not easy. It got stuck when she tried to pull it from underneath him. Biting her lips, Lily tugged again. Finally she gave up. At least now it wouldn't constrict his breathing.

He looked so vulnerable asleep, so approachable. Awake, Zach was sometimes so full of fierce energy and mysterious darkness that Lily found him almost formidable.

She leaned down and brushed his hair off his forehead. He sighed and mumbled her name. Was he dreaming of her? Lily smiled at the thought.

With her hand still on his forehead, she whispered, "Good night, Zach."

His hand snaked out and trapped hers. He opened his eyes. "Lily?"

"I didn't meant to wake you."

"I'm glad you did." He held out his arms, and she came to him. "I didn't mean to fall asleep with my clothes on."

"And I didn't mean to fall asleep on the sofa. I wanted to wait up for you."

They smiled at each other in the darkness.

"Now that we're both awake, I have some very good ideas about what we can do," he said.

"Talk?"

"Not for a while."

He slid the straps of her nightgown off her shoulders. His lips were warm and moist as they grazed her skin. As always she was astonished at her own reaction. Why did his hands feel so special? His lips? His body lying next to hers? What particular magic worked to make the touch of one man satisfy like no other touch in the world?

Lily let her feelings take charge. They wrapped around and through and over her until she was bound by tenderness and deep affection and white-hot bands of passion.

Zach still wore his clothes. His hands and mouth were all over her, pleasuring her as they had so long ago in the Monteleone. Lily moved with the feelings that held her captive. She writhed under his touch, moaning her pleasure.

And when she felt that there was nothing better in the world than what she had just experienced, Zach stripped off his clothes and proved her wrong. He took her to the screaming edge of pleasure. There was a power in his lovemaking, a determination that had not been there before. In the fringes of her mind that were capable of rational thought, she decided he must be exorcising ghosts.

Groaning her name, he lifted her hips so that she encased him. There was nothing except Zach—in her and around her and through her. She was completely possessed. As their cries broke loose, she clung to him, wishing she never had to let go. . . .

After his trip to Hammond, Lily and Zach fell into a routine. Early mornings and late nights were for them and the pleasure they found in each other; the days were devoted to John Henry's care and his custody case. Every day Zach checked with Sam to see what progress was being made in finding Glenda Rockman, while Lily checked with the bank to see if there were any problems needing her attention.

Glenda Rockman remained at large, but the frustration was eased by the sense of normalcy that reigned at the apartment on 13 Royal Street. Keeping the world at bay, Lily and Zach almost came to believe that they could go on forever, living together and taking care of John Henry.

On the Rockman estate, Bemus was having better luck with his investigations. He sat behind his huge desk and in his opulently appointed office, listening to Smothers's latest report.

"You were right about hearing that Taylor name somewhere besides oil connections."

"I knew it." Bemus rubbed his hands together, smiling. There was nothing he enjoyed more than being right—unless it was a good glass of wine, well aged, and a good woman, still young. "When I get these gut feelings, I'm seldom wrong."

He walked over to his concealed bar and poured himself a glass of wine to celebrate. "Now," he said, "tell me what you've got."

"Do you remember that girl who was gunned down in Algiers seven years ago? The one who got caught in the cross fire of a drug vendetta?"

"Yes." *Did he remember?* It was emblazoned on his mind. An innocent girl. Beautiful. Blond. Good family. Much like his own daughter. "It was a tragic loss. I didn't even know her, but I still grieved." He took a sip of wine and gazed out the window as if he were seeing the events once more. "Such a waste."

"She was a Taylor—Zach Taylor's sister."

Bemus's hands began to tremble, threatening to spill his wine. He set it on the table and moved back to his desk. It wouldn't do to let Smothers know how much the news affected him.

He pushed the girl to the back of his mind, hoping she'd stay buried there.

"Anything else, Smothers?"

"Not yet."

"Keep digging.... Have you found my daughter yet?"

"Not yet. You know how Glenda is when she wants to stay hidden."

Bemus smiled. "Like father, like daughter, I guess. I have to admire that about her. She definitely has a mind of her own . . . even if it doesn't work right sometimes."

His daughter was giving him gray hairs. Or maybe it was his business. Maybe it was time to think about retiring. That way, he'd have more time to spend with his grandson.

He walked to the French doors and stood looking out. "That will be all, Smothers," he said over his shoulder.

Rose inched down the jetway, hanging on to George's arm. "Are you sure you're all right, honey?" she asked.

"I'm fine, sweetheart. Just great."

To tell the truth, he wasn't really fine. Outside, the temperature was in the nineties. The heat that scorched the tarmac at the airport had multiplied in the jetway. Air-conditioning was almost unheard of in Spain.

He was going home, home to his new baby boy, and that was enough to take his mind off his own aches and pains. There was nothing to worry about, anyhow. His doctor had told him to expect a certain amount of discomfort. There was no cause for alarm.

"I can't wait to see John Henry. Lily says he's the cutest little thing and choosy about what he wears. He hates pink." Rose's cheeks were bright as she settled him into his seat and buckled herself in. "I'll bet I have to get him a whole new wardrobe when I get back."

George reached for her hand. Flying made Rose nervous, and when she was nervous, she always talked nonstop.

"We'll be in the air soon, sweetheart. Everything is going to be all right."

"I know. But I do wish there were another quick way across the ocean besides flying." She shut her eyes as the plane lifted into the air.

George squeezed her hand. It would be a long flight home. And somewhere across the Atlantic, he'd have to tell Rose about the battle for custody of John Henry.

He settled back to wait for the right time.

* * *

Lily and Zach stood beside the crib, watching John Henry sleep. A patch of afternoon sunlight made a halo on his hair.

"He looks like an angel." Lily reached down to touch his head. "I can't believe this is the last time I'll put him down for his nap."

"And the last time I'll walk the floor with him, singing his favorite song."

" 'Misery and Gin' is his favorite song?" Lily smiled at Zach, teasing him.

"He happens to like Merle Haggard."

Zach smiled down at Lily, and they got caught up in each other for a while. Then they turned their attention back to John Henry.

"I'm going to miss this little fellow," she said.

"At least you'll only be across the courtyard from him."

"You won't be all that far yourself."

Zach smoothed the covers over John Henry's legs, then traced the baby's cherub cheek with one finger.

"I'll be another world away," he said.

Another world away, Lily thought. *A world without her.*

"Their plane will be here in two hours," she said.

Zach reached for her hand. "That gives us time to say goodbye."

In the bedroom, Zach picked Lily up and spread her across the covers like a fallen flower. Leaning over her, he lifted strands of her hair and watched it catch the sunlight coming through the window.

"Your hair reminds me of sunsets." He pressed a silky lock to his lips, knowing he would never see another sunset without thinking of Lily's glorious hair spread across the pillow.

She reached up and touched the scar on his cheek.

"How did you get this? You never told me."

"Slaying dragons."

"Another world away?"

"Yes."

He gathered her close and held her so tightly, their heartbeats blended. She dug her fingernails into his shirt, clinging to him. They spoke their anguish without words, rocking together, holding on, not wanting to let go.

And finally the nearness and the steady rhythm created a need that would not be denied. They undressed each other slowly, being careful not to miss a single detail. He memorized her ivory-colored skin, blushed with peach when she got hot. She cataloged the triangle of dark hair on his chest, the way it curled intimately around her fingers when she touched him. He stored away the memory of her heart-shaped face. She memorized the curve of his bottom lip.

When they lay together, naked upon the sheets, Lily hovered over him, her hair spread like a red-gold waterfall on his chest.

"I want to taste every delicious inch of you," she whispered. "Starting here."

Her tongue flicked into the hollow at the base of his throat. Such a small touch. Such an innocent taste. And yet he felt branded.

"More, Lily."

She moved downward, leaving a trail of moist, hot kisses in her wake. When she reached the juncture of his thighs, he arched upward, groaning.

The sun stood still. They were frozen in the erotic, golden moment, with her red hair tangled against his dark curls and her lips berry colored around his pink skin.

He tangled his hands in her hair, urging her to stay. There were hoarse sounds in the room, urgent cries. Zach was too far gone to realize they came from him.

Sensations ripped through him. There was the heat and the moisture and the sweetness of her mouth and the rhythm that carried him the long way around to that mystical place no one else knew. When they reached it, he called out to her.

"Now, Lily, now."

She settled over him, and he slid home in the sweet, deep recesses of her body. They clasped hands, holding on to each other for the fierce final leg of their journey. When they arrived, he exploded inside her and she cried out. For a small eternity, they held on together, rigid, straining, and then Zach rolled onto his side, taking her with him.

They held each other without speaking. He tenderly caressed her back, and she gently smoothed his hair off his face. The burden of their parting was so great, it hung like a funeral pall over the room. And their long journey in the afternoon sun didn't seem to be enough.

"Oh, God, Lily."

Zach pressed his lips against her throat, then he took her breast in his mouth and suckled until she was begging him for more.

He gave her what she wanted. What he wanted. What he would always want. She was fire and satin and honey and musk. He tasted it all, tasted until she was on the screaming edge of control.

He lifted himself over her and drove home in one final, powerful burst. She reached for him, and they lay in a tangled heap on the sheets, their chests glued together with sweat. They didn't speak for a long time. Neither of them wanted to be the first to break the spell.

Finally the practical side of Lily battled its way through the fog of her passion.

"The plane will be here soon."

"Yes." Zach didn't move.

"I have to change the sheets."

"I'll help." Still he didn't budge.

When she touched his face, it was damp. She didn't know if it was from sweat or tears.

"Zach?" she whispered.

He raised himself on his elbows and looked down at her, his eyes very bright.

"Remember me, Lily."

She traced the tiny scar on his cheek. "I'll never forget."

Silently, they left the bed. There was nothing else to say.

Lily and Zach stood together at the airport, scanning the faces of the deplaning passengers. Zach held John Henry in one arm and Lily with the other.

"There they are," Lily said.

Rose spotted them at the same time. "Lily!" She waved both hands and blew kisses in their direction. Tears streamed down her face. "George, honey, it's them. They've got the baby."

"Go ahead, sweetheart. Don't wait for me." Pale but smiling, George gave his wife a little nudge forward.

She raced toward Lily and Zach, her red curls bouncing and her bangle bracelets tinkling. "I can't believe it! I just can't believe it!"

When she was even with them, she stopped and wiped her tears. "The first time my baby sees me, I look like something the cat dragged in." She scrubbed at her face some more, doing more damage than good. "Do I look all right, Lily?"

Lily tenderly wiped the smudges from her sister's cheeks. "You look beautiful. John Henry is going to adore you."

Rose clasped her hands tightly together and closed her eyes briefly, as if she was praying. Then she reached for her baby.

"Hello, little darling. It's your mother."

Zach gently placed John Henry into his mother's arms. The baby looked up at the familiar red hair and cooed.

"He loves me." George reached them, and Rose turned to him. "He loves me, honey. Just look at that little smile." She rubbed noses with the baby. "'Ou wuv 'our mother, don't 'ou, sweetie pie?" She beamed at her husband. "See! I told you he loves me."

Lily wiped her own eyes. She didn't know if she was crying because her sister finally had a baby—or because she had lost one. She gazed with a certain longing at John Henry's tousled blond curls. She had been the one to smooth them down, and now Rose was doing it. Was that actually jealousy that she was feeling? It couldn't possibly be. What kind of person was jealous of her own sister just because she had a husband who adored her and a baby with blond curls and the face of an angel?

She was just tired. That was all. Tired and upset. John Henry was leaving her. Zach was leaving her. Tomorrow her life would be sane again.

"Let me hold him," George said.

"Do you think you should, honey?"

"I just want my son in my arms. If you're worried, you brace his weight, sweetheart."

George held out his arms and Rose carefully braced John Henry in them. Now that George had lost his paunch, he looked more like his brother. Except that he wasn't, Lily thought. His cheek didn't have a distinctive scar and his face didn't have that brooding intensity and his eyes... Oh, God, his eyes. They didn't make her want to melt.

A pain wrenched through Lily as she watched George with the baby. How many nights had she tiptoed into the nursery and seen Zach smiling down at John Henry? How many times had she stood in the den and laughed while Zach sang one of his crazy, made-up songs to the baby? How many times had she watched while Zach rocked the baby, even when he wasn't crying, rocked him because he said babies needed to be rocked?

She realized she was jealous of George, too. On Zach's account. Zach had looked so right with John Henry.

Tomorrow her life might be sane again, but it would be extraordinarily lonely. Already Lily felt separated from them. She even moved apart. Zach let his arm slide off her shoulders and drop to his side. She didn't look at him. She couldn't. She just stood there, staring at the baby and aching.

John Henry looked up at this new person holding him and claiming to be his daddy. He was big like Uncle Zach. And he had a deep, rumbly voice like Uncle Zach. But he wasn't Uncle Zach. John Henry studied the face intently, trying to decide what to do about this new turn of events.

"Look at that, sweetheart," George said. "He's looking at me like he knows I'm his daddy."

John Henry poked out his lower lip and worked up a tear or two. That ought to tip everybody off that he was tired of this new person and wanted to go back where he belonged. Besides, he was ready to be rocked to sleep in that nice chair, and he wanted his Uncle Zach to do it.

"Don't cry, little man," George said. "We'll be home in a minute." John Henry let the tears roll. "I guess he's hungry or something. Did anybody bring his bottle? Let's all just sit over here and let the little man eat."

Four big people hovered over him, getting everybody settled into seats, and he still didn't have his Uncle Zach. John Henry guessed he'd have to show them what he wanted. He opened his mouth and let out his biggest squall.

"Good grief," Rose said.

"Don't cry, now. Daddy's got you." George tried to get the bottle into John Henry's mouth, but he was kicking and screaming so hard that the task was impossible.

"Better let me take him, honey. You're still too weak for this." Rose took her crying baby. He stopped crying long enough to give her a pouty look, then he started in earnest once more. "Oh, my," she said, beginning to cry herself.

Lily and Zach watched in anguish. Finally Zach could stand it no longer.

"Here, let me." He plucked John Henry out of Rose's arms and settled him against his chest. "It's all right, little man. Uncle Zach's got you."

John Henry sniffled some more, just on general principles, then cuddled up to the familiar broad chest, his thumb in his mouth. But not before he gave everybody a triumphant, watery smile.

Lily felt like crying. Kicking and screaming, too. She envied John Henry's ability to express himself so well. She didn't want to leave Zach, either, but she was forced to stand aside and go through the rituals of departure because she was an adult and, therefore, too civilized for such behavior.

"Would you just look at that," George said.

"He'll get used to you," Zach told his brother kindly. "It'll just take awhile."

"Yes," Lily chimed in. "He cried like that with us when we first brought him home."

"Why don't we all go back to the apartment now and get him settled back in. I'll get the luggage and meet you at the car." Zach handed Lily the baby, and she led the weary travelers to the car.

With the warm bundle resting once more in her arms, Lily was content. She could almost pretend that things were going to continue as they had for the past few days—Zach and the baby and the loving. Most of all, the loving.

She couldn't think about that right now. She would concentrate on keeping her tears inside until she was alone.

Back at the apartment, Zach and Lily stayed long enough to settle John Henry down for a nap and to brief Rose and George on the latest findings for the custody battle.

"Now that you're back to take care of the baby, I can concentrate my full energies on finding Glenda Rockman," Zach told his brother.

"And Lily can get back to the bank." Rose patted her sister's hand. "I know how anxious you must be to get back to your work."

As anxious as a Thanksgiving turkey facing the ax, Lily thought. She exchanged a quick glance with Zach, then turned back to her sister.

"I've loved taking care of John Henry and Bentley, but I've discovered I'm not very good at it. It will be good to be back in familiar territory."

"I knew it," Rose said. "Lily's always been the one with potential. We're so proud of her business success," she told Zach.

He said something appropriate, and he and Lily tried not to sneak secret glances at each other while they took their leave. Finally they were both outside the apartment, suitcases in hand, while George and Rose were inside with the baby.

Lily gripped the handle of her suitcase until her knuckles turned white. "Well," she said, forcing a smile. "I guess this is goodbye."

Zach touched her cheek. "No, Lily. This afternoon in my brother's bed was goodbye."

She swallowed the tears that were clogging her throat.

"Lily, look at me." He tipped her face up. "It has to be this way."

"I know," she whispered. "I just wish goodbyes didn't hurt so much."

Zach pressed a tender, lingering kiss against her lips. "Take care of yourself, Lily."

"You, too."

He held her face tipped up to his for a long moment, then released her and strode to his car, not looking back. Lily watched him leave. She guessed she wouldn't hurt so much if she would let it be over without this final agony, but she couldn't help herself. As long as she could see a glimpse of his car, she felt as if he were somehow still in her life.

Finally there was nothing left for her to see except the street, crowded with chattering tourists and musicians heading for their favorite street corners with trumpets and saxophones and harmonicas.

She crossed the courtyard and let herself into her own apartment. The carefully coordinated decor that had always been soothing to her now depressed her. She caught herself looking for torn-up magazines and empty baby bottles. She found herself missing the smell of baby powder and roses.

Lily unpacked her bag and hung her clothes in a neat row in the closet. Her business suits looked foreign to her, as if they belonged to somebody who had lived in the apartment a long time ago. She reached out to touch them, hoping contact would make them real.

It didn't. Nothing in her life seemed real right now. It was almost as if she had gone to another planet for a few days and had come back brainwashed.

Lily poured herself a fortifying drink and carried it to her balcony. Maybe tomorrow she'd feel like her old self again.

Rose was walking John Henry up and down the den floor. Both of them were crying.

"Sweetheart, do you want me to call Lily?"

"No."

"She said she'd be glad to come over anytime we needed her. So did Zach."

"Lily has to go to work tomorrow." Rose sniffed and wiped her nose with a rumpled tissue. "Besides, how can I ever be a mother if I keep handing my baby over to somebody else?"

"I wish I could be more help." George shifted to a more comfortable position on the sofa. "When I get my strength back, everything will be all right."

"He doesn't like you any better than he likes me."

"Nonsense, Rose. He loves both of us. He's just not used to us yet."

"And about the time he gets used to us, old Bemus Rockman is going to take him away." Rose went into a fresh gail of weeping. John Henry cried all the harder.

George reached for the telephone. "I'm calling Zach."

"No. Wait." Rose stopped crying. "I'm going to be brave about all this. I promise."

"Let me call him, sweetheart. There's no point in both of you getting sick." George was worried. He'd never seen such a flood of tears as his wife and baby were making.

"Well, all right."

Rose stopped pacing and sat down in the chair. John Henry was glad. He was tired of all that bouncing. Furthermore, he was tired of crying. Just when he had everything going his way, along came a new set of big people he had to break in. The man who called himself Daddy was right—it was enough to make a baby sick.

Zach was pacing when the telephone rang. He decided to let it ring. He didn't want anything to interrupt his black mood. Everything precious to him had been ripped out of his life once more, and this time he didn't have drug dealers to blame. Who could he blame? Himself? He didn't like that. He had too much to do to get bogged down in self-recriminations. There was Glenda Rockman to find, and the drug kingpin and the evidence to prove Bemus unfit for custody.

The phone continued to jangle. He balled his hands into fists and rammed them into his pockets. He missed Lily like hell. He had no idea that leaving her this time would be like leaving his soul behind.

The loud racket of the phone reverberated through the room. He jerked the receiver off the hook.

"Hello."

"Did I interrupt anything, Zach?" It was George.

"No. Why?"

"You sounded as if you want to bite somebody's head off."

Zach relaxed his fists and made himself smile. "Had my mind on other things, that's all. What's up?"

"I hate to ask you this, but can you come over? We're having a devil of a time with John Henry. And Bentley's not helping matters. He's barking his head off."

"I'll be right over," Zach said. He tried not to be too pleased. John Henry needed him. He hadn't had somebody need him in a very long time. He didn't remember how good it felt.

It was almost dark when Zach reached the apartments on 13 Royal Street. He parked his car and started toward George's front door. Halfway there, he paused. From the courtyard came the rich, sweet smell of gardenias and the liquid murmuring of the water fountain. But it was not his surroundings that gave him pause; it was the strong feeling that Lily was near.

He turned slowly and looked across the courtyard. She was sitting on her balcony, her face turned in profile to him. Her red hair caught the glow of two gaslights on her side of the courtyard. Her face was the color of pale ivory. She was wearing something blue, a soft-looking, flowing garment. Underneath she would be silky to the touch.

Just looking at her made him tight with desire. The ache to touch her was so great, he groaned aloud. Fortunately there was no one around to hear. He was all alone.

He wanted to go to her. He *longed* to go to her. But what would that accomplish? Just another goodbye.

The sight of her was too precious to lose. He stood outside George's door, watching Lily while the darkness spread its veil across the courtyard.

When it was almost too dark to see, Lily turned her head and looked his way. He stood very still. Did she see him? Would she come to him? What would they do if she did?

Her head was up, like an animal that senses a trap. She kept her face turned toward him for a small, breathless eternity. Surely she saw him.

He tensed, waiting. And then, slowly, she turned to go. Zach expelled a long breath. Lily hadn't seen him, after all. Or had she?

He turned toward his brother's door. John Henry was waiting for him.

Chapter 13

"Hi, Lily. Good to see you back."

"Welcome back, Lily."

"Hey, where have you been?"

The greetings followed her through the bank, all the way to her office. Everybody was glad to see her. Lily wished she could be happier to see them.

She walked into her office, hoping for a resurgence of the joy she used to experience every time she entered her private domain. Everything looked the same, the plain gray carpet, the pale-mauve-and-gray furniture, the simple watercolors on the wall, the elegant smoked-glass-and-stainless-steel desk. Even she looked the same—smart navy blue business suit; crisp white blouse; plain pumps; hair in a tight French twist.

The problem was, she didn't *feel* the same. She didn't feel challenged and invigorated by the prospect of work. Instead, she felt a dull, throbbing ache in her head, which could be from too much Scotch, but which was more than likely from too much time alone to think. She'd had all night to think about her current situation.

Basically, she was right back where she had started. She had no dog to care for, no baby to love and no dark-eyed man to hold her through the night. She felt like crying. Plainly and simply, she had an enormous case of the blues. And the only thing she had as a cure for them was work.

She sat down at her desk and opened her briefcase. It was a beginning.

Zach was slumped in front of his computer, watching the cursor blink fluorescent green. He had been working almost around the clock since his brother came home—three days. He felt exhausted and surly and wretched.

Sam sat hunched over a computer at the opposite side of the room, tapping the keys in a never-ending rhythm. He had been faithful, tireless and cheerful. The man deserved sainthood.

There was a sudden silence of the keyboard and a scraping sound as Sam pushed back his chair. Zach shut his eyes, welcoming the silence.

"Zach. Can you come over here?"

Zach left his computer. "What is it, Sam?"

"Take a look at this."

Sam had pulled up a record of one of the first drug busts Zach had engineered after he went undercover with the DA's office. The time was six years earlier. The dealer was Jefferson McLaurin, age 49, male Caucasian. Previous record included bootlegging and accessory to auto theft. Place of arrest, Algiers, Pier 51.

"Three arrests in the last seven years, all at Pier 51," Zach mused. "Hardly enough for a pattern, but maybe too much to be coincidence."

Sam, who loved drama, saved his big card for last. He punched in instructions and the computer screen glowed with information on Bemus Rockman—his place of birth, his address and his holdings that were a matter of public record.

Zach's attention was riveted to one item. "Rockman Warehouse, Algiers, Pier 51. Damn!"

"It could be something," Sam said.

Zach ran his hands over his face. It was rough with beard stubble. He hadn't shaved in two days.

"How could I have missed that?" he said.

"Like you said, three is not enough for a pattern."

"Check it out, Sam. Get somebody inside to talk to those three men. I'll see if we can get a snitch over to work on Pier 51. Let's pull every string we've got. Something might start unraveling." Zach headed to the door. "I'll inform the DA."

"Maybe you should shave first," Sam said mildly.

"I don't have time."

"You look like hell," Rafe McKenzie said. He reached toward the silver service on his marble-topped coffee table. "Sit down. Have a cup of coffee."

"Coffee would be good." Zach left the doorway where he had been lounging and took a seat opposite the district attorney.

Rafe handed him a cup of coffee, black, the way he knew Zach liked it.

"I take it you're back from whatever mysterious business you had."

"I still have some personal business to take care of, but I'm visible again."

The DA laughed. "You'd better shave before you get too visible, or else you're liable to ruin that lady-killer image of yours."

Lady-killer image. Zach thought of Lily, soft and warm under him. The last thing he wanted to be right now was a lady-killer. Donning that persona again was going to be harder than he had ever imagined. Almost, he wished he hadn't given in to temptation. Almost, he wished he hadn't taken Lily to his bed. Almost . . .

"Zach?"

"I'm sorry. I'm tired, I guess. What did you say?"

"I didn't say anything except your name. I was just watching you." Under the guise of drinking coffee, Rafe observed his friend. He didn't like what he saw—the fatigue, the emptiness in Zach's eyes, the haunted look on his face.

Rafe set his cup on the table and folded his hands across the noticeable bulge of his stomach. His wife was always chiding him to do something about that bulge, and he knew he should. He should do a lot of things. Retire, for one.

"Have you ever thought about quitting this undercover business, Zach?"

"Quitting?"

"I'd hate like hell to lose you. You've done the best job of any man we've ever had."

"My work isn't finished yet."

"Take it from me—it will never be finished. There will never come a time when you can sit back and say, 'Now there's no more to be done.'" Rafe picked up his coffee cup again.

"I want to find the kingpin," Zach said.

"You've done a damned fine job of rounding up drug dealers."

"Not good enough. I want the man responsible for supplying them."

"We'll get him . . . eventually." Rafe toyed with his coffee cup. "Did you ever think about getting back to your law practice? About settling down and having a family?" Zach's face became a careful blank. "I don't mean to pry, Zach, but I like you. In fact, I've never told you this, but I take a sort of fatherly pride in you."

"Thank you, Rafe."

"I don't want thanks." Rafe ran his hands through his gray hair. "Hell, I don't know what I want. I guess I'm just an old fool trying to keep somebody from making the same mistakes I did."

"But you have a lovely wife. Sarah—"

"Is the finest woman alive," Rafe said, interrupting him. "I kept her waiting for twenty years before I married her, Zach. Twenty wasted years. By then, we were both too old to have children.... Ahh, hell. Listen to me, going on about something that's none of my damned business." He folded his hands over his stomach once more. "Now, what is it you wanted to talk to me about?"

Zach told him of his latest findings and the plan for further investigation. Rafe nodded his approval, occasionally grunting with satisfaction.

"Anything else you need, Zach, just let me know."

As Zach stood to leave, Rafe put a hand on his shoulder. "Think about what I said."

"I will."

Zach took the long way home, driving by the apartments on 13 Royal Street, knowing he wouldn't see anything except the iron gates that guarded the entrance, but he went that way anyhow, imagining that he might catch a glimpse of Lily as she left or entered. When he got there, he saw nothing except the gates, closed and locked against intruders. The security guard made a dark shadow on the window of his office.

Sad and weary, Zach drove on to the empty house he called home. What a joke. Home should be a place with warmth and laughter and gingerbread baking in the oven. Home should be a place with a wife who smelled like flowers and a baby who smelled like spring grass and vanilla. Home should be a place that filled the heart and renewed the spirit. Home should be— Not Lily and John Henry. He had borrowed them for a short time, pretending the rest of the world didn't exist. But they didn't belong to him, could never belong to him.

He parked his car in the garage and let himself into his house. It echoed with stillness. Even Sam wasn't there. He had a life of his own outside the confines of work. Zach envied him that.

In his bedroom, Zach stripped off his shirt and sank onto the bed to remove his shoes. The telephone sat on his bedside table.

He stared at it for a long time, as if by staring, he could make it come to life, make it ring so that he could be connected with another person. *Lily.* Lily was the one he wanted to be connected to.

He should call her. After all, she was as interested in the progress of his investigation as he was. She had a right to know.

He reached for the phone, imagining how her voice would sound, what it would do to him, what it would make him want to do to her. He drew his hand back.

There was no use trying to fool himself. He didn't want to call her and report on an investigation. He was quite certain that Rose and George kept her informed. His motives were far less pure. He wanted to call and say, "Lily, I'm coming over. I can't stand another night without you."

Angry at himself, at his inability to put the recent past behind and focus on his work, he stripped off his clothes and stalked to the shower. Inside, he turned on the Cold tap, gritting his teeth as the water hit him. He guessed he'd be taking cold showers for a while. Until he got over Lily.

Afterward, as he lay in his bed, he wondered if he'd ever get over Lily.

Two weeks and Lily hadn't heard from Zach—except through Rose and George.

"He has some good leads on Bemus Rockman," George had told her. "Thinks he might be able to prove him unfit for custody."

"And Bemus's daughter, Glenda Rockman," Rose added. "Somebody in Augusta, Georgia, spotted her. We might be close."

Lily sat in her perfect apartment with the moon making a soft glow across her expensive carpet and the absolute silence echoing through her soul like the cries of lost soldiers. The telephone was on the table at her elbow, creamy white, glow-in-the-dark push buttons, streamlined—and silent as a bank vault.

Maybe she should call Zach. After all, she was interested in the investigation. Maybe Rose and George hadn't told her everything. Maybe Zach could shed some new light on the case.

She picked up the phone and held it against her ear, listening to the dial tone. With her right index finger, she reached out to push the first digit of his number.

It has to be this way. His parting words came back to her as clearly as if he had said them only yesterday. Quietly, she set the receiver back in place.

Then she began to pace. Zach was right, of course. They were totally unsuited to each other. He was full of dark, brooding silences and deep mysteries; and she was full of purpose and a hunger to succeed. Until recently.

Recently she had been filled with other needs: the need to put her head on Zach's shoulder; the need to curl against him at night and listen to the even sound of his breathing; the need to share her thoughts with him; the need to share her problems with him. But most of all, the aching need to have him enter her and take her to that magical place that only the two of them could find.

Letting him go was the brave thing to do, the right thing to do. But, dammit it all, she was so tired of doing the *right* thing.

She stalked into her kitchen and jerked open the refrigerator door. Lettuce, carrots, asparagus and broccoli were neatly arranged in the proper drawers. Lowfat milk and salt-free, lowfat cheese sat on the shelf with whole wheat English muffins. She even did the right thing in her kitchen.

"Dammit!" Lily slammed the refrigerator door shut, then kicked it for good measure. It felt good to take out her frustrations on an inanimate object. She clenched her fists and said, "Dammit, dammit, dammit." A variation of primal-scream therapy. She'd read somewhere that such uninhibited screaming was a good way to release pent-up rage. If she didn't feel better tomorrow, she might drive to some quiet road beside the river where nobody could hear her and give it a try.

Staunchly turning her back on her correct kitchen, she marched into the bedroom, taking the pins out of her hair as she went. She remembered how Zach used to take the pins from her hair, how he used to let it filter through his fingers, how he used to say her hair smelled like flowers.

Lily stood for a moment with her own hands in her hair, aching. Then she roused herself to action and took off her suit coat. As she undid the top two buttons on her blouse, she recalled how Zach's hands had felt on her skin. With her hand pressed flat over her chest, she closed her eyes.

"Oh, God," she moaned aloud. She would never get over him. He was forever emblazoned in her mind and in her heart.

Moving slowly, as if she were in a dream, Lily brushed her hair so it was free and wild around her face, the way Zach loved it. Then she applied fragrance, his favorite, he had said. She was going into the French Quarter. But not the way she had four years ago, not to prove to herself that she was a woman. Zach had done that already—twice. She was a woman, all right, and he was the only man for her. Funny how she knew that. Funny how love had crept up on her and she hadn't even known until it was gone.

Not that there was anything she could do about it—or even *wanted* to do about it. She was where she belonged, and he was where he belonged. No, she wasn't going into the French Quarter for love. She was going for food—high-calorie, high-cholesterol food that wasn't good for her body, but was good for her soul.

Lily took a taxi to Snug Harbor, a quaint restaurant tucked into a corner of the old section of the French Quarter. The restaurant was one of New Orleans's best-kept secrets. Because it was off the beaten path, the mainstream of tourists hadn't discovered it. Frequented mostly by locals, it featured good food and good jazz—at reasonable prices.

Lily ordered the most fattening thing on the menu, then topped off her meal with a decadent dessert. Rose would be proud of her. "You don't pamper yourself enough, Lily," she always said.

Lily could almost feel the waistband of her skirt expanding as she ate. Tomorrow she'd be as big as the Bell Tower at the Ursuline Convent. But who would notice?

Still feeling blue and more than a little sorry for herself, Lily slipped into the small showroom adjoining the restaurant and took a chair in a darkened corner near the back. A young woman with a voice like a choir of angels and a build like a hydrangea bush in full bloom stood on the stage, crooning into a microphone, singing the blues. Lily's kind of song.

Lily closed her eyes and let the music wash over her. When she opened them, she was staring straight into the eyes of Zach Taylor.

He was sitting across the room from her at a darkened corner table. She didn't know if he had been there when she came in or if he had come while she had her eyes closed. He was alone.

"Zach," she whispered.

He inclined his head slightly, and she knew that was the only acknowledgement she would get. But he didn't turn away. His dark eyes held her captive. He was very still as he watched her.

His expression might be neutral, but his eyes were not. They were vivid, fierce, penetrating. Lily's breathing became unsteady. Zach was making love to her with his eyes. Unconsciously she touched her parted lips, then slowly ran her hand down her throat. Heat spread through her. With her hand resting at the base of her throat over the wild beat of her pulse and the music swirling around her, she gave herself up to sensation.

Onstage, the singer hovered intimately over the microphone, her voice velvet. The music was appropriate for Zach's mood.

There was Lily, across the room from him, vivid, *real,* and he was chained to his chair, dreaming. If he were young again, young and innocent and unencumbered by responsibilities, he would go to her. He would cross the short distance that separated them and take her in his arms and cuddle her close while the haunting ribbons of music wove around them.

When she touched her lips, he was kissing her as surely as if he had left his chair. When she moved her hand to her throat, he tasted her silky skin, felt her pulse beating against his lips.

He made love to her with his mind. Seeing how she watched him, seeing how her body slackened and her eyes brightened, he knew that she, too, was making love to him in her mind.

Music and passion pulsed in the air. In his perfect vision, Zach pulled Lily onto his lap with her full woman's hips pressing down upon him. Driven by need and emboldened by the darkness, he ran his hand under her skirt. Her skin was warm and silky. He moved his hands over her legs. Her soft whimpering sounds were drowned out by the music. He nudged aside her heavy fragrant hair and pressed his mouth against the side of her throat. His tongue flicked out to taste her. She was a heady combination of down-home sweetness and exotic spices.

He eased aside the wisp of lace that covered her. She was warm and satin slick. The music pulsed and beat around them.

Across the room, Lily's head lolled sideways, as if it were too heavy to be supported by her slender neck. Zach was suddenly left sitting at an empty table with his empty arms and a great yawning void inside him.

Silently he cursed fate. He cursed being an adult and, therefore, being responsible and careful and wise. Watching Lily, he longed for the innocent days of youth when even his wildest dreams were possible and magic was waiting around every corner.

He wanted to go to Lily. He wanted to take her hand and lead her out of Snug Harbor and tuck her into a taxi and take her to his bed. But more than that, he wanted to sit boldly with her in a public place and not worry about putting her in jeopardy. He wanted to walk openly with her in the streets, holding her hand and laughing. He wanted to toast her with champagne at Antoine's and hold hands with her across the checkered oilcloth at K Paul's Kitchen. He wanted to run with her beside the river and stroll with her around Jackson Square. He wanted to share pralines with her until their mouths were coated with brown-sugar crystals.

He wanted to do all that—and not worry that a hired killer's bullet would end it all.

Onstage, the singer crooned "A Nightingale Sang in Berkeley Square." It was an appropriate song for goodbye.

Zach slipped silently from the room. At the doorway, he turned. He had to have one last glimpse of Lily. She was facing him, pale and still, her eyes glimmering with unshed tears.

A knife twisted in Zach's heart, and he realized the price he had paid for his obsession with revenge. Not only had he paid the price, but Lily had, too. Of all the burdens he had to live with, that was going to be one of the heaviest.

"Have you turned up anything on Bemus Rockman?"

Zach perched on a stool in his kitchen, while Sam stood at the counter, making himself a huge sandwich.

"Nothing. Nobody's talking. They're either covering for him or scared or..." Sam shrugged.

"Or there's nothing to tell," Zach finished for him. "Damn."

It had been a week since he'd seen Lily at Snug Harbor, a week of frantic activity. He'd chased down four leads on Glenda Rockman and run into as many dead ends. Sam had worked steadily to uncover Rockman's secrets. It seemed he didn't have any.

"As far as I can tell, Bemus Rockman is Mr. Clean," Sam said.

"Keep checking. There's something about that man that doesn't ring true."

"You've always had good instincts, Zach..."

"But?"

"I don't mean to second-guess you, but I'm wondering if this custody thing is clouding your judgment."

There might be some truth in what Sam was saying, but Zach wasn't ready to admit it. "Emily didn't cloud my judgment," he said.

Sam put his hand on Zach's shoulder. "Sorry, pal. I was out of line."

"We're both testy. Tired, I guess."

"Maybe we're stir-crazy. What we need is a diversion, a good party with lots of wine and a loud band and a couple of wanton women."

The knife that had been twisting in Zach's guts for weeks now dug a little deeper.

"What I need is a breakthrough. Bemus filed for custody of John Henry yesterday. Time's running out." He picked up his own sandwich, looked at it with distaste, then flung it aside. "Keep digging, Sam. I'm going to tap our friend Bemus."

"Zach . . ."

"I know, I don't have anything to go on except coincidence and hunch, but I've played hunches before and they've worked. Who knows what a wiretap will turn up on Bemus, and it might lead us to Glenda."

"When are you leaving?"

"As soon as I can get an interception order. I think I can give Rafe enough on Bemus to convince a judge of probable cause. And if I do turn up something, I want to make damned sure it's admissible in court." He stood up and headed for the door. "But first I have to say goodbye to John Henry."

Chapter 14

Glenda Rockman took vicious pleasure in the cat-and-mouse game she played with her father. Sitting in a motel room in West Memphis, Tennessee, she contemplated her beer bottle. It was almost empty. And it was the last of her six-pack. Soon she'd have to get out and buy some more. Maybe she ought to buy a little food, too. Her head was buzzing.

It would serve Bemus Rockman right if she passed out and died. Maybe she'd go to heaven, where she could look down at her father's discomfort. She'd make the headlines. Sugar Mogul's Daughter Dies in Sleazy Motel. He'd be mortified. That was very important to him—what the rest of the world thought. Never mind that his daughter thought he was a monster and that his wife couldn't stand to sleep with him anymore.

Reeling slightly, Glenda walked to the bedside table and pulled out a piece of motel stationery. It was too far to walk to get back to the chair, so she sank onto the edge of the bed, propped the paper on the Gideon Bible she found, took a pencil stub from her blue-jeans pocket and began to write.

Father Dearest,

I guess your black heart is broken in two now that I took the thing you wanted most from you. Did you think I'd let you get your hands on my baby? I'd see you in hell first.

She signed the letter, "Your Crazy Daughter," in big, bold strokes. Then she added a P.S. "Don't come to Memphis trying to find me. I'll be long gone by the time you get this letter."

She'd mail it on the way to get a hamburger. In the process of writing her letter, she discovered she didn't want to die, after all. She wanted to live so she could make her father suffer.

Lily walked through the deepening dusk toward her sister's apartment. She was going to visit John Henry. It was the only thing that kept her sane these days.

The gardenias had long since stopped blooming, and even the water fountain had a mournful sound, as if it knew summer was coming to an end. One of the sad facts of life was that all good things soon came to an end. Lily decided not to think about that right now. These days there were many aspects of her life she just didn't think about. Sometimes she felt as if she were hanging on to the edge of a cliff by her fingernails and that one more distressing thought would weigh her down so that she would lose her grip and fall.

Lily had always privately thought her Aunt Bonnie Kathleen had been a little bit crazy, living her reclusive life in a big, old house with nothing but cats to keep her company. Lily wondered if she was going to be just like her.

With a determined effort at cheerfulness, Lily put a smile on her face and knocked on her sister's door. George answered. His color was back, and so was his strength. Standing in the doorway, he looked strong and steady and reliable—qualities Lily had always loved in her brother-in-law.

"Lily! Come in." He gave her a bear hug, then stood back to look at her. "You're not getting enough sleep. Are you trying to run that bank single-handedly?"

Her sleeplessness had nothing to do with the bank, but she decided it was safest to let George think so. "You know me, George. A workaholic."

"What you need is a big dose of Rose and John Henry. They're good for the soul." Taking her hand, he led her into the den.

Rose and John Henry were both sprawled on their stomachs on a quilt that had been spread over the rug. A dozen stuffed bears were propped in front of them, and a lively tune from *Sesame Street* played on the stereo.

"You're just in time, Lily," Rose said. "We're having a teddy bear picnic."

"So I see." Lily started toward the sofa, but Rose stopped her.

"Not there, for goodness' sake. You can't take part in the picnic way over there. Besides, John Henry wants you to sit by him." She leaned toward her baby, rubbing noses. "Don't you, sweet darling? Doesn't Mommy's widdle baby want Aunt Lily to sit down here?" She grinned at Lily. "He said yes."

George was enchanted. "See? What did I tell you, Lily? Isn't that the most beautiful sight in the world?"

"It is." Lily's agreement was heartfelt. And she was glad. For a while after Rose and George came home, she had been so jealous and envious that she had feared she'd never be the same with them again. The feelings had passed, and maybe they had merely been a different form of loneliness. Now she was happy for all of them—John Henry, Rose and George.

As she sank onto the quilt beside John Henry, she tried not to think about Bemus Rockman's power to destroy the baby's small, secure world.

"I would join you, but it's still too early after surgery to try to get down on the floor. I might not get back up." George sat on the sofa, laughing. "Besides, if I got on that quilt, there wouldn't be room for Zach."

"Zach?" Lily looked at the doorway as if she expected him to materialize.

"He called a minute ago," George said. "He's on his way over. John Henry will be tickled pink. He still prefers his uncle to me."

"George, honey, you know that's not true."

George laughed. "It's true, sweetheart. But it will change. I'm just giving the little fellow time, that's all."

Lily was only half listening to what they said. Her mind was on Zach. He was coming here, to this apartment. She glanced around the room. They had made love on the sofa late one night after John Henry was asleep. They had made love on the rug with the afternoon sun streaking their naked bodies. She had arranged gardenias for him on the coffee table, and his roses had sat on the table beside George's favorite chair. *Memories.* The apartment was full of memories.

She didn't think she could endure seeing Zach in this apartment again—especially after that evening in Snug Harbor.

"I just popped in to see how everybody's doing." She stood up. "I'll see you all later."

"You just got here," Rose said. "You can't possibly leave. I have a dozen things to tell you."

"Stay, Lily. Zach has some things he wants to tell us, and I'm sure you'd like to hear them."

"I really have some work I need to do at home. You can fill me in later."

"If you don't stay, I'm going to cry," Rose said, and she probably wasn't kidding.

Lily was torn by indecision, wanting to avoid seeing Zach and not wanting to hurt Rose and George—or to arouse their suspicions.

"Besides," Rose added, "I thought you and Zach had become friends while we were in Spain. I even thought you might be sleeping together."

"Rose," George chided.

"It's all right. This is my sister." Rose sat up and scooped John Henry into her lap. "One morning when I called home, it did sound like Zach was in the bed with you."

Lily's cheeks colored. Rather than lie, she said nothing.

"That's really none of our business, sweetheart."

"Now, George. This is family business. Lily and I have never kept secrets, even about our love lives."

Except once, Lily thought. And that was about Zach, too. *Dammit.* Sometimes she wished she had the right to march onto the balcony and shout loud enough for the whole city to hear, "Zach Taylor and I are lovers." Of course, it was all in the past now.

"My love life would bore you to tears, Rose," Lily said, and she meant it. She frequently shed tears over it, herself, but they were not tears of boredom: they were tears of loneliness.

Smiling, putting on a brave front, she moved toward the door. "I'll drop by again tomorrow when I have more time to stay. You can give me a full report."

The doorbell interrupted her quest for freedom. Lily froze. She was caught now, and there was nothing she could do about it.

Rose answered the door, and Zach came into the apartment. He brought the vitality of New Orleans in with him. The fever for excitement burned in his eyes, and the need for action showed in the tense lines of his body. He also brought the city's sensuality. While New Orleans seduced with the haunting strains of jazz and the timeless appeal of the river, Zach seduced with a dark, brooding charm and a quick, sharp gaze that turned liquid when he saw Lily.

She wondered how she would breathe with him in the same room, so close, she could almost touch him. His eyes trapped her and she couldn't have moved if a herd of elephants had been stampeding her. Fortunately Rose and George didn't seem to notice.

"We were just discussing you," Rose said. "Lily wanted to leave, but I wouldn't let her."

Lily gave her sister a look designed to kill. Rose smiled serenely.

"I'm glad you stayed, Lily." Zach started toward her. The heat of him smote Lily so hard, she thought her legs were going to buckle. "It's good to see you."

He caught her hand and held it briefly. But it wasn't his hand that put Lily in a state of upheaval. It was his eyes. They penetrated, probed, mesmerized. She was caught up in his fierce and hungry look, caught up and swept away into a world where nothing mattered except their feelings for each other.

"It's good to see you, too," she managed to say. To her surprise, she sounded normal. She hoped she looked normal, though she doubted that. Surely her love must show. It was shining through her as bright as a new moon. Rose would notice.

Zach moved away from her as easily as if they had never been more to each other than passing acquaintances. Watching him walk away a few weeks ago hadn't been easy, but watching him now was hell. Then she hadn't known she loved him; now she did. Seeing him move to the other side of the room was unbearable agony. Every fiber in her body cried out to touch him. She wanted to put her hands on his face and look deep into his eyes and smile at him in a secret lover's way. She wanted to laugh with him and whisper intimacies to him. She wanted to feel his arm across her shoulder in easy friendship. She wanted to talk with him in the way of people who respect and admire each other.

Lily made her way almost blindly to a chair. Then she folded her hands in her lap and tried to act as if she spent every day in the same room with the man she loved, looking but not touching. Now she understood what writers meant when they described weeping hearts. She could feel the tears in her heart.

Was Zach hurting, too? Surely not, or he wouldn't seem so controlled. If she could look into his eyes, she might guess what he was thinking. But he studiously avoided her gaze.

"What have you heard, Zach?" George asked, leaning forward in his chair.

"Nothing yet."

Rose clutched John Henry to her chest and made a small sound of despair.

"I don't want either of you to be discouraged," Zach said. "It will be weeks before the case gets put on the court docket. That should give us plenty of time. And if we need more, we'll file for a continuance."

"I feel so helpless," George said.

"I'm doing everything that can possibly be done." Zach swung a brief glance at Lily, then looked quickly away.

She hung on to it as if it were a life vest. What had she seen in his eyes? Compassion, certainly. Zach was a kind man. She had also seen that special look between two people who have bonded on some level. The passion was there, burning like a flame in his eyes. Zach was a man with insatiable sexual appetites, and it showed in his eyes.

But the one thing she was looking for was absent: love. She supposed she was a silly romantic to even be looking. He had made no promises. She had gone into their affair knowing how it would all end. The only thing she hadn't counted on was falling in love.

"What about taking out ads? TV and newspaper?" George suggested. "You know, the kind that say, 'Has anybody seen this girl'?"

"If Glenda is running because she knows we're trying to find her, ads could run her farther underground," Zach said.

"What do you think, Lily?" Rose asked, turning to her sister.

Lily felt selfish. Her sister was faced with the prospect of losing her son, and all Lily could think about was the heartbreak of unrequited love. She made herself concentrate on something besides Zach.

"I think we would be making a mistake to rule out any help we can get," she said. "On the other hand, Zach knows more about this kind of thing than any of us. We just have to keep waiting and hoping."

"George..." As always, Rose appealed to her husband when she was troubled. Tears trembled on her eyelashes, but for once in her life she fought valiantly to hold them back. Crying was good for the soul, she had told Lily, but it wasn't too good for John Henry.

"It's all right, sweetheart." George pulled her into his arms. "Zach knows what he's doing."

"Everything is going to be all right, Rose," Zach said. "I promise you. I'm going to concentrate all my resources on finding Glenda Rockman. Sam is continuing to dig into Bemus's background, and I'm going to put a wiretap on him. I have a hunch we're going to get a breakthrough soon."

"Rose and I have the greatest confidence in you, Zach."

"We do." Rose came to Zach's chair, then leaned down and kissed his cheek. "You've never let us down, Zach."

Zach squeezed Rose's waist. "I don't plan to now, Rose."

"Then you're leaving?" Lily asked, struggling to sound casual.

"As soon as I say goodbye to my nephew." He held out his arms to John Henry. "Come here, tiger."

John Henry went to him, chortling and kicking. He had wondered when his Uncle Zach was going to get around to him. In his opinion, it was high time.

Zach walked John Henry around the room, talking the man-to-baby nonsense Lily had grown so accustomed to when the three of them were living in the apartment. For a moment, she spun back in time. It was almost as if the two of them would soon stand over John Henry's crib, their arms around each other, watching him sleep. Then they would stroll together down the hall, arms still entwined, sometimes stopping for a lengthy kiss before they ended up together in the big bed.

She couldn't sit still and watch the comforting domestic scene any longer.

"I have to go," she announced.

Zach caught her eye. "I'm leaving. Let me walk you to your apartment."

Why? she wanted to ask. *It's all over. We both agreed. Why prolong the agony?*

He took her silence for consent. After kissing John Henry, he handed him to Rose.

"Take care of the little tiger for me, Rose."

Then he took Lily's arm and propelled her from the apartment. She didn't even have time to say a decent goodbye to George and Rose, let alone John Henry.

Outside the apartment door, she balked. "What are you doing?" she whispered fiercely.

"Lily, I have to talk to you . . . alone."

"I thought we had said all there was to say."

"I thought so too. . . ." He urged her across the darkened courtyard. "And then I saw you at Snug Harbor."

"I saw you, too."

"I know."

They didn't say anything else for a while. Their footsteps echoed on the stones as they passed by the shadowy trees and the huge urns with their browning gardenias. The smell of sweet decay filled the air, drying flowers and an apple core left behind by the macaw that occupied a courtyard perch during the daytime.

When they reached the stairs, Lily gazed up at Zach. Even in the darkness she could see the determined set of his jaw. Saying nothing, she let him lead her up the steps. If he had said he wanted to escort her to the moon, she would have gone. Love had made her foolish.

"Your key, Lily," he said at her doorway.

She handed it to him. "Am I inviting you in?"

"Yes." His smile was a little ragged around the edges.

He pushed open the door. The cool air, scented with peach potpourri, felt good on their skin after the damp mugginess of the outdoors.

"Nice," Zach said, looking around her room. "Your elegance and sophistication are here, Lily." He smiled down at her. "But where is your fire?"

"Maybe I didn't have any fire when I decorated."

Zach arched one eyebrow. Lily regretted her slip. His hold on her was already too great. It wasn't necessary that he know she had been bland as yesterday's cold tea before he came along.

"Can I get you anything? Coffee? Tea? Scotch?" She tried to move out of his grasp, but he held on.

"No, Lily."

They looked at each other and time came to a standstill. A muscle ticked in the side of Zach's jaw, and the scar on his cheek shone with an unearthly brightness. He seemed larger than life, more powerful, more dangerous.

I love you, Lily's mind screamed. She wet her dry lips with her tongue, then opened them to say the words. No sound came out, and she stood watching him with her lips half-parted.

"Lily. . ." he said, and the moment was lost. He touched her cheek. "I had almost forgotten how beautiful you are." His hand traced her lips. "How desirable." With one finger he rubbed the moist inner lining of her lower lip. "How very desirable."

She closed her eyes. Her world was spinning out of control, and she had no desire to get it back. She wanted to spin, to drift, to fly away in Zach Taylor's arms. There was a small whimpering sound. She made it, she guessed, for Zach released her.

"Damn." He paced the floor, his shoulder muscles bunched and his jaw set. With such a large, restless man moving about, her apartment looked small.

"Lily," he said, stopping in front of her, close enough to touch, but not touching. Close enough to kiss, but not kissing. Close enough to love, but not loving. "I didn't come here to try to resurrect the past. As much as I want you, I have no intention of taking you to bed."

"I didn't ask you to." His rejection hurt. Color flared in her cheeks. "I didn't even invite you here. You invited yourself."

"Now that I have you here alone, I realize my intentions weren't all that noble. I wanted to touch you. I've wanted to touch you all evening."

She held her breath, letting him do the talking. That seemed the safest thing to do.

"All I could think about as I sat there in George's apartment was how we had made love on the rug. Everywhere I looked, I saw you, Lily, saw us, together."

"So did I," she whispered.

"Oh, God, Lily," he said, but he didn't touch her again. Instead, he stood before her like something magnificent and noble carved in stone. She wanted to scream.

Suddenly he spun away from her and walked to her French doors. Looking out over the jazzy, night-glittering city, he began to speak.

"I left you without explanation, Lily... twice. You deserve better than that." Ramming his fists into his pockets, he turned to face her once more. "I shunned you in Snug Harbor... as I will snub you in all public places." His face took on that brooding look she knew so well. "Physically, I shunned you, and yet mentally, I was caressing you, running my hands over your legs, pushing aside your lingerie and bringing you to a climax in a public place. I wanted to do all that, Lily... and more."

And I enjoyed every stolen, secret moment of it. She couldn't say that aloud. He had made it perfectly clear what their future relationship would be.

"I can't tell you what I do, Lily. I can only tell you that I'm not the playboy I seem to be."

"I figured that out weeks ago."

"My work is secret and very dangerous. Serious relationships are impossible for me. I can't involve anyone else in that danger. I want you to understand that. If I can't have your... body... at least I want your understanding."

"I understand." What had he been going to say? *If I can't have your love?* Lily had always considered wishful thinking a sign of weakness. And here she was, a woman of potential, engaged in just that. If Aunt Bonnie Kathleen were living, she would be mortified.

"Lily, if ever a woman has tempted me, it's you."

"Thank you," she said. If she couldn't have his love, at least she had the knowledge that she was tempting to him.

"We'll probably run into each other from time to time because of John Henry."

"I'll try not to, Zach."

"When you see me, think kindly of me, Lily, and know that I'm thinking kindly of you."

"I will."

Raw emotion showed on his face. Lily wondered if it showed on hers, as well. She hoped not. She was trying very hard to be brave—for her sake as well as his.

Desire arced between them, so strong, the air seemed to pulse. They held each other with their eyes, and neither of them was capable of letting go.

From far away in the Quarter came the echo of a blues trumpet, mourning love lost. A sudden unrest in the elements sent a flash of lightning through the sky. Rain soon followed, sounding soulful as it drummed against the windowpanes.

"I won't forget you, Lily."

"Nor will I forget you."

Still they watched each other. Still they couldn't let go.

Later, when she thought about it, she couldn't have said who moved first. But suddenly there was movement and she was in his arms.

"I can't leave without one kiss," he said.

"Yes. Oh, yes...." She laced her hands across the back of his neck and drew him closer. "Just one," she whispered.

They came together with aching hearts, sad in the knowledge that this would be the last kiss they would ever share. That knowledge made the kiss tender and poignant and lingering.

If Zach had deepened the kiss, if he had delved into her mouth with his tongue and raked her hips against his, if he had stoked the fires that were already glowing within her, she would have been his...no matter what the consequences. But he chose to be noble and unselfish, taking only what he had asked for and nothing more—one kiss.

But such a kiss. It would burn in Lily's memory forever.

When it was over, Zach pulled back and gazed at her. There was nothing else to say. He swayed gently for a while, silently rocking her in the bosom of love, and then he let go.

She felt as if everything that was precious to her had suddenly been torn away. She felt raw and naked and bleeding...and afraid.

With his eyes searing into hers, he traced her face with the back of one hand. Then he released her and turned to the door. He left so silently, so quickly, she could almost have convinced herself that she'd dreamed he was there.

But it was no dream. She still felt the heat of him in her body, the taste of him on her lips, the need for him in her heart.

Walking slowly, as if she would break at any abrupt movement, she went to her sofa and sat down. Carefully she arranged her clothes, as if she expected the first lady for tea at any moment. Or Aunt Bonnie Kathleen, back from the dead.

Dead. That was a good description of the way she felt. How many times could she lose Zach and not die?

Zach moved silently and rapidly away from Lily's apartment, trying to concentrate on nothing except getting to his car and getting out of New Orleans. It didn't work. Lily was with him every step of the way. She was in the rain-glistening courtyard. She was in the strains of jazz drifting down Royal Street. She was in his car, in the rich aroma and soft yielding of the leather seats, in the beat of rain against the windows, in the smooth rhythm of the tires against the blacktop.

He was tempted to go back. He was tempted to bound up her steps and pound on her door, begging her to let him come back in. He longed to sink himself into the warm satin of her body, to lose himself in a night of deep soul kisses and whispered erotic words and sweet, hot love almost too good to bear.

He tightened his hands on the wheel and clenched his jaw. He was doing the right thing, the *only* thing. Danger was everywhere he went. To expose Lily to that would be foolish and cruel.

He left the city of New Orleans behind and cruised along the black ribbon of highway that would take him to Bemus Rockman's place. Even with an interception order in his hand, what he had to do was best done under cover of night. Rockman would not take kindly to wiretapping.

But John Henry's safety depended on it. Zach had to keep him safe.... A cold lump of fear settled in the pit of his stomach. He had lost Emily, lost her through carelessness, lost her in a pool of blood on a dirty street.

Sweat stood on his brow. He couldn't lose John Henry. He *wouldn't*.

A vision of Lily came to him as clearly as if she were sitting in the car. She turned her heart-shaped face to him. There were tears in her eyes.

"I won't lose you," he whispered. "I can't bear to lose you."

The sound of his own voice shocked him. Was he going mad? After all these years of living for revenge, was he finally losing his mind?

What in the hell was he muttering about, anyhow? He had already lost Lily. In fact, he had never had her.

You had her. Now he was arguing with himself. Maybe he needed a cup of coffee. He'd pull over at the first all-night diner he saw. He needed all his faculties for the night ahead.

You had her, and you let her go. Zach didn't know if he was hearing the voice of his conscience or the voice of truth. Perhaps they were one and the same. But the simple fact was that he'd had Lily. Not just her body. All of her. Her mind, her heart, her spirit.

And he had let her go. Because he was afraid of losing her.

It wasn't a pretty truth, but it was one he faced alone on the dark road. There was danger, and plenty of it, but he could leave it all behind. He could move to a small, quiet town and take up his law practice again. He could lead a normal life. He could have a wife and children. He could go to the grocery store on Friday and the movies on Saturday and church on Sunday.

If he weren't afraid.

This new truth sat on his heart like a stone. To have Lily...really *have* her...and then to lose her would be a hell he couldn't bear.

The lights of an all-night diner flashed out of the darkness in a curve of the road just up ahead. He covered the distance, then pulled into the parking lot. He would go in and order a cup of coffee.

He wished he could also order happiness.

Chapter 15

Four days after he set up the wiretap, Zach hit pay dirt.

Bemus Rockman's phone rang late in the night. It was his daughter, Glenda.

In his surveillance van, sheltered by a thick grove of trees, Zach overheard the entire conversation. What was more, he had traced the call.

Glenda Rockman was in Hot Springs, Arkansas. In less than twenty minutes, he was headed that way.

When he reached Hot Springs, Zach called Glenda from her motel lobby, if such a cramped space could be called a lobby. It boasted two plastic chairs, a coffeemaker on a Formica-topped table, and enough Oaklawn racing forms to paper the wall. Spending money was not one of Glenda's vices.

As the phone rang, Zach thought about what he would say to Glenda. Afraid she would run, he had concocted all sorts of lies to get her to talk: telling her that she had won a jackpot, saying he was an old friend of her mother's, telling her he was a friend of Angela's. In the end, he had decided on the truth. He would tell her his name and that he wanted to talk to her about the time she spent in the Sweet Angels Adoption Agency.

She answered on the second ring.

"Hello." Her voice was cautious, sullen.

He gave his rehearsed speech, then added, "Please don't hang up."

"Did Bemus send you?"

"No."

"This sounds like one of his tricks to me."

"I swear on my mother's grave. Bemus doesn't know I'm here. All I want to do is talk to you, Glenda."

"Well . . . all right. I'll meet you at McDonald's. Fifteen minutes. And if you try anything funny I'll scream my head off. Your name will be mud, mister."

Zach watched in the parking lot until Glenda left her room. Then he followed her. He wasn't talking any chances. Fleeing was her pattern. If she ran, he would be right behind her.

He breathed a sigh of relief when she pulled in at McDonald's. He went around the block, then parked in an empty space across the lot from her.

When he went inside, she was already sitting at a booth, hunched into a blue-jean jacket as if she felt cold, although the temperature was still in the seventies. Her blue eyes were puffy and her blond hair was scraggly. She wore no makeup, and she looked as if she hadn't had a good meal or a good bath in several days.

Zach stood beside the door observing her unnoticed. Glenda Rockman talked tough, but she looked like a scared, unloved little girl. He would take the gentle approach with her.

"Glenda?" He didn't move in too close, but stood a distance back from her booth, smiling.

"Yes. Are you Mr. Taylor?"

"I am." He had decided to use his real name. The less lying he did to her, the better. "May I sit down?"

"Suit yourself. I don't own the booth."

He slid into the booth on the opposite side of the table, still smiling.

"How are you, Glenda?"

"What do you care?"

Zach refused to be baited. He leaned back in his booth, not pushing, letting Glenda get used to him. He *had* to have her cooperation. He sensed it would only be gained through patience.

"How come you're looking at me like that?" Glenda said.

"Like what, Glenda?"

"Like some stupid private eye." Wariness came into her eyes. "My father hired you, didn't he?"

Zach played a trump card. "I wouldn't work for Bemus Rockman if he were the last man on earth. He is my sworn enemy."

Glenda believed him. She settled back in her booth, some of the sullenness gone from her face.

"You know him?"

"Yes."

"Do you know my mother?"

"I know who she is. I've never met her."

"Can you give her a message for me? Every time I call home, he answers. And he won't let me talk to her. Says it upsets her too much."

"I'll be glad to take your mother a message."

"Tell her I'm not coming home this time."

"All right."

"Tell her..." Glenda paused, twisting her hair around her fingers. "Tell her I'm sorry about the baby... about giving it away, and all, but I just couldn't let Daddy get his hands on it. He'd ruin it like he ruins everything else."

Zach kept his expression carefully neutral, but inside he was celebrating. By broaching the subject of the baby herself, Glenda had made it easy for him. He said a silent prayer of thanks for his good fortune.

"Did you know your father has filed suit to gain custody of the baby he thinks is yours?"

"No!" Glenda pounded her fists on the table. Two young boys turned to look at them, then studiously turned their attention back to their food.

"Would you like to go to a place where we can have more privacy?"

Glenda glanced around the McDonald's, then shook her head. She leaned across the table and whispered fiercely, "He can't have my baby. I won't let him."

Now was the time for the complete truth. "My brother adopted the baby Bemus is trying to claim. I'll do anything I have to in order to keep your father from getting that baby."

Glenda's eyes narrowed and her spine stiffened. "You came here to drag me back to New Orleans, didn't you?"

"No. I promise I won't take you back. But I do need your help."

"I'm getting out of here." Glenda scooted across the booth, her jeans whining on the plastic seats.

"Glenda. Wait." She paused long enough for Zach to add, "Do you want your father to have this baby?" He could see her hesitation. He pressed on. "If you walk out of here, that's what will happen. Bemus Rockman will gain custody of an innocent child. He'll raise the baby as his grandson."

Glenda slumped. "What do you want me to do?"

"Name the father."

"Why?"

It was time for the full truth now. Zach studied Glenda, trying to decide the best approach. For all her defiance and bravado, there was something strangely innocent and very vulnerable about her. She looked like a young girl who had been hurt...more than once. She also looked and talked like a young woman in full possession of her senses.

"I'm hoping a blood test of the young man will prove that the baby my brother adopted cannot possibly be yours."

"If he's not mine, why is my father trying to get him?"

Zach took the long way around with his explanation. He wanted to fully prepare Glenda for the truth.

"Do you remember a young woman who gave birth in the home for unwed mothers when you were there?"

"Yes. We both had boys."

"We believe my brother's baby belongs to that other girl. Bemus wants it to belong to you...so he can have it."

"That's just like him...trying to get something that doesn't belong to him. But why wouldn't he be after my baby instead of hers?"

Zach reached for her hand. She looked startled at first, then allowed the gesture.

"Because your baby is dead, Glenda."

"No! No!" She jerked her hands away and pounded the table. Tears stood in her eyes. "That bastard. That bastard killed him...just like he killed that girl."

What girl? Zach thought he would stop breathing. *Emily?* It couldn't be. The odds were impossible. To be looking for one piece of the puzzle and stumble over another. And yet...the connection was there. On paper. Pier 51.

Glenda pounded the table as if she were driving nails. Tears stood in her eyes, but didn't roll down her cheeks.

Zach covered her hands. Glenda swung her eyes to his face. She looked scared.

"What girl?" he asked gently. She stared at him, but her eyes were focusing inward, seeing things he couldn't see. "You said your father killed a girl, Glenda. Do you remember who it was? When it was? What girl, Glenda?" He kept his voice quiet and even.

"I was twelve years old. I had gone into his study. I wanted to talk to him about the junior high dance. He was late.... I fell asleep on his leather couch." She tensed, as if she was reliving what had happened.

"You fell asleep on the couch," he said, coaxing her.

"It must have been late. I heard footsteps, then the door opened. It must have been late. I got scared. Daddy never let any of us in his study when people came to see him. I rolled off the couch and crawled behind it just in time. Daddy put the lights on."

She bit her lower lip so hard that she drew a drop of blood. It was bright scarlet against her pale skin. Zach's heart pounded. His own private hell tried to intrude, but he pushed it back. *One nightmare at a time,* he told himself.

"I heard them talking...."

"Who?"

"Daddy and a man I didn't know. I peeped around the couch. The man had a huge birthmark on his left cheek. If I ever saw his face again, I'd recognize it."

"Do you remember what they were saying?"

"I'll never forget." She fell silent again. Zach watched her, praying and hoping that she wouldn't stop now. After a long silence, Glenda sighed, then started talking again.

"The man with my father said that Crown Mackey did the job. And he told Dad that the drug dealer wouldn't do any more skimming ... or talking, either."

The hairs on the back of Zach's neck stood up. *Crown Mackey. Emily's killer.*

"Dad then said that's what he paid for... to get the job done." Glenda slumped down in the booth, her chin resting on her chest. Tears rained down her cheeks. "The other man told him a girl named Emily got in the way—and she died."

"You're sure of this, Glenda?"

"Yes. I heard it. All these years and I've never told anybody." She wiped her hands across her cheeks. "They thought I was crazy. I was crazy... with hatred of my own father.''

"I'm glad you told me, Glenda. You did the right thing.'' Zach patted her hand.

She looked up at him with huge, tear-stained eyes. "I want to go home. I want to go home to Mama.''

"I'm going to help you, Glenda. Will you help me?''

"The baby. I forgot about the baby.... You want to know the father.''

"Yes. And more. Emily Taylor was my sister. Will you testify in court to what you heard?''

"Will it put my father in prison?''

"Yes.''

"Good. That bastard.'' Glenda sniffed once more, then pulled a bandanna out of her pocket and blew her nose. Next she pushed back her hair and straightened the collar of her dingy blouse. "Will you buy me a hamburger, Mr. Taylor? I ran out of money yesterday and haven't had time to get any more.'' She gave him a brave, watery smile. "I'm starved.''

"I'll buy you all the hamburgers you want, Glenda. And then we'll go home.''

"I'll be glad to see Mama.''

Zach stood up to get her burger. "With cheese or without?''

"With. And get two.''

He slid out of the booth.

"By the way, my baby's daddy lives in New Orleans. His name is Glover St. Clair.''

"Thank you, Glenda.''

"Thank *you*, Mr. Taylor. If you hadn't found me and told me my baby died, I might have gone on carrying that burden the rest of my life. Carrying that burden and running.'' She raked her hair back again. "It's going to feel good to quit running.''

* * *

Zach was on the road home within two hours...with Glenda Rockman in tow. Now that the burden of her past was lifted, she was lively and talkative. Zach listened, saying an appropriate word here and there. But mostly he drove, clipping off the miles at a fast pace.

When they stopped for dinner, he called his brother.

"It's over, George. John Henry is safe."

"The girl told you who the father is?"

"Yes. And we'll follow through, but we don't even need that information anymore.... She's an eyewitness to Bemus Rockman's conspiracy to murder Sasha and her father. She's agreed to give her statement to the DA as soon as we get back."

"Rockman killed Emily, then."

"Yes. No judge in the world would give him custody of John Henry.... George? Are you there?"

"I'm crying, Zach. I'm crying tears of relief and joy."

Zach realized his own cheeks were wet. "So am I, George."

"Zach...if I forget to tell you this when you get home, I appreciate everything you've done. You're a hell of a man and a damned good brother."

"Thanks. You, too...." His brother's love reached across the miles and touched him. Standing in the phone booth, Zach felt the warm glow. "I'll let you go now. Tell Rose. And George...call Lily and tell her the good news about John Henry."

"Is there anything else you want me to tell her?"

What else could he say? Nothing had changed for them. Not really. Right now Zach was feeling the sweet relief of triumph. He had saved John Henry. He had very likely found the drug kingpin. Only time would tell. Now that one thread was loose, the entire ball of yarn would start to unravel. With Glenda giving testimony against her father, others would start to talk.

But Zach hadn't changed the world. He *couldn't* change the world. There was no way he could stop another assassin's bullet from going astray. There was no way he could stop the muggings, the drug trafficking, the endless, senseless terrors that stalked the city and threatened its citizens. There was no way to ensure that Lily would never be a victim.

And he couldn't live with another loss. He couldn't set out on another seven-year odyssey of revenge. He was too old. He was too tired. He was losing his edge.

Besides all that, his job wasn't over. There was still much to do before Bemus Rockman was put behind bars.

"No, George. I have nothing else to tell her."

Zach replaced the receiver, then joined Glenda. He had suddenly lost his appetite.

It took days to tie up all the loose ends. Glenda gave the DA her statement. A warrant was issued for Bemus Rockman's arrest. Happily for mother and daughter, Glenda moved back home.

Zach tracked down Glover St. Clair, whose blood type ruled him out as John Henry's father. An out-of-court settlement was reached in the custody case.

John Henry, blissfully unaware of all the commotion surrounding him, took full control of the Taylor apartment on 13 Royal Street. He had four doting adults to do his bidding . . . the two he had started out with and the two he had ended up with. Besides all that, he had his very own dog. Sometimes he had a hard time being the boss with Bentley, but that was okay with him. He wouldn't have put up with a sissy dog that didn't know its own mind.

During the rush of events, Lily spent her days at the bank, working, and her nights in her apartment, trying not to pine and trying to stay away from pralines. She had discovered that they satisfied some deep urge within her.

Her skirts were getting too tight. She was going to have to do something about that soon, she decided. Right after John Henry's christening.

The day before the christening, Rose called Lily at work, bubbling with excitement.

"Lily, are you busy?"

"Not too busy to talk to you, Rose. What's the matter?"

"I just realized that's the first question you always ask. You've been fixing things for me for a long time, Lily. I think it's high time I started taking care of my own problems so you can get on with your life."

"Nonsense, Rose. You're part of my life. You know I'll always be there for you if you need me."

"Zach asks about you every time we see him."

"If you called to talk to me about Zach, you've wasted your time. I have work to do, Rose."

"Don't get on your high horse. I didn't call to talk about you and Zach, though I do think something went on between the two of you while George and I were in Spain. Something good, Lily. Something you're either too heartbroken or too proud or too stubborn to talk about...or even *do* anything about. He's a fine man, you know."

Lily gripped the receiver. "Rose...I'm going to hang up now."

"Wait! I haven't told you the good news yet." Rose loved drama. She was silent for so long, Lily wondered if the phone had gone dead.

"Rose? Rose? Are you still there?"

Rose burst into peals of laughter. In the background, Bentley started barking.

"What's going on there? Rose?"

"You're not going to believe this, Lily."

"Believe what?"

"It's simply too good to be true."

"What is?"

"It's a downright miracle."

"I'm running out of patience, Rose."

"I'm pregnant, Lily."

It was Lily's turn to be flabbergasted. Rose. Pregnant. Sometimes it happened. Couples who hadn't been able to conceive for years found themselves expecting a child soon after they adopted.

"I'm thrilled for you and George. Tell him I said so."

"I just found out. I couldn't wait another minute to tell you."

"That's wonderful, Rose."

There was another dramatic pause on Rose's end of the line. Then a sniffle.

"Rose? Are you crying?"

More sniffles, then a muffled snorting as she blew her nose.

"Crying...and thinking. Remember how we did everything at the same time when we were growing up?"

"Yes." They'd had chicken pox together, measles together, even broken arms together.

"Well, wouldn't it be wonderful if it would happen that way this time?"

"Horrible is more like it, Rose. I'm not even married."

"It's because you don't try."

"I'm hanging up now, Rose."

"I'm sorry, Lily. I promised myself not to talk about that again."

"It's all right." Lily twisted the phone cord in her hand. "I'm really excited for you. We'll have double cause to celebrate at John Henry's christening tomorrow."

Rose hung up, and Lily swiveled her chair to look out the window. Two pigeons looked back at her from the window ledge.

The christening. Zach would be there.

Lily closed her eyes, remembering the long, summer nights in his arms. Absently she reached across her desk for a praline.

Wouldn't it be wonderful, Rose had said. The praline dropped from Lily's hand. She sat bolt upright in her chair. Then she began to count the days.

Chapter 16

Lily burst into tears several times as she dressed for the christening. Why hadn't she known? The strange cravings, the too-tight skirts, the afternoon sleepiness? Two missed periods. She'd blamed the first one on the commotion of taking care of John Henry. The second she'd blamed on tension, all that anxious waiting while Zach tracked down Glenda Rockman.

Zach. What would he say? They had been so careful... or so they had thought.

Lily sat on the edge of her bed, clutching her dress in one hand, not caring if she wrinkled it. Zach wouldn't say anything, because she wouldn't tell him. Hadn't he told her more than once that he couldn't make commitments, that his life was filled with danger and he had no room in it for a *woman*—let alone a woman and a baby.

She got off the bed and turned sideways to her full-length mirror. She could already see the thickening in her middle, the slight bulge of her abdomen under her slip. No question about it. Even if the early-pregnancy test hadn't told he the truth, her body did.

She was definitely pregnant.

Back when she had been married to Howard, she used to dream about how it would be. She'd tell him over candle light. He would send her roses and carry her around on a satin pillow. All the women at work would envy her. In the break room she would display her new maternity outfits and her new figure, and they would all tell her how lucky she was—a great job, a wonderful husband and a baby, to boot

Only Howard hadn't been a great husband. There had never been a baby. And now there was a baby and no hus band.

What was she going to do? One thing was certain: she was going to have her baby. She had always been resourceful. She would make plans. They would manage.

But first she had to get through the christening. She had to face Rose and George and Zach—especially Zach. And she had to smile and carry on and be brave and strong. Bu most of all, she had to act as if she weren't pregnant.

As she went into the bathroom to wash her face, she rubbed her abdomen.

"Don't worry, little one," she whispered. "I'm going to take good care of you."

Zach scanned the crowd at the church. Rose and George were there with John Henry. Rose was glowing with the bloom of her pregnancy, and George looked healthier than he had in years, slimmer and more fit.

George's friend and fellow professor, Adam Miller, was in the crowd. So were their neighbors, the beautiful Evangeline Le Chevalier and the eccentric Mrs. Randall Turner. Taylor and Cooper relatives were there by the dozen.

But Lily was nowhere to be seen. It wasn't like her to be late. And she would never miss John Henry's christening.

Fear rose in Zach. Something had happened to her. Something dreadful. At this very minute she could be lying in the street, mugged or run down by a taxi or—

Stop it, he told himself. He was being paranoid, and all because the woman he'd had an affair with was late arriving at the church.

Finally Lily walked through the door. He had never seen her look more radiant. Her hair was down, making a bright frame for her exquisite face. And her face! He had never seen it glow like that, almost as if a candle were burning underneath her porcelain skin.

Her gaze swung around the crowd and stopped when it reached him. A smile touched her lips, and her eyes lit up.

Suddenly he knew. Lily was not just somebody he'd had an affair with. She was the woman he loved. He guessed he'd always loved her, from the moment he'd carried her to the canopied bed in the Monteleone so many years ago. And certainly since those wonderful summer days and sultry nights together in his brother's apartment. Was love always like that? Did it exist unknown until that bright moment when it exploded inside the mind and heart like fireworks?

The newfound knowledge made him catch his breath. Knowing he loved her, he was compelled to be near her, close enough to hear her voice, close enough to touch her skin, close enough to inhale her special fragrance.

He moved through the crowd toward Lily. He had no idea what he was going to do about his love. All he knew was that he had to be near her.

On the fringes of the crowd, she waited for him, her eyes unusually bright.

"Hello, Lily," he said when he was at her side with her silk skirt brushing against his leg.

"Zach." She sounded breathless. Up close he could see that her color was high and that it was not artificial.

"I've never seen you look more radiant."

"You look good, too."

She was a confection. If she had been an ice-cream sun
dae, he would have eaten her with a spoon. As it was, he wa
thinking of more erotic ways he'd like to taste her.

"It's been a long time," he said. "How have you been?"

"Good." Had she hesitated before she answered? H
must have imagined it. "And you?"

"Busy but happy," Zach replied.

How polite they were. Like two strangers. Zach put hi
hand on her elbow, wanting the contact, wanting more tha
politeness, even in the church.

"I haven't seen you to tell you how proud I am of the jo
you did. Without you, we might all have lost John Henry."

"Thank you, Lily." He would have said more if Georg
hadn't interrupted.

"Family and friends..." George held up his hands fo
attention. The crowd became silent. "We are all gathere
here for a solemn and joyous occasion, the christening o
our son, John Henry Taylor."

There was clapping. George smiled down at Rose, wh
was standing in the curve of his arm, holding John Henry.

"But before the christening ceremony begins, Rose and
want to share another joy with you.... Rose is pregnant
We're going to have another baby."

Zach felt a jolt of envy. George had it all—a wife,
beautiful son—and now another baby on the way. Whil
Zach had... What? An empty house. Revenge.

Immediately Zach was ashamed of himself. He guesse
what he really felt was not envy, but sadness that all thos
things were denied him.

He was happy for George, and so was everybody else.

Voices lifted in congratulations. Adam Miller rushe
forward to pump George's hand. Evangeline hugged Rose
Various relatives murmured their approval.

Beside him, Lily didn't move. She was very still, and he
face was carefully composed. Almost too composed.

Zach studied her. Was she feeling a bit of sadness, too? A bit of nostalgia for the way things had been between them this summer and a bit of regret for the way they were now?

"Lily?" He put his hand on her shoulder. "Are you all right?"

"Oh, yes. Isn't it wonderful? Now Rose will have two babies." She turned to him, smiling. But there were tears in her eyes. One of the things he had always loved most about Lily was that she let her emotions show.

Did he? Was his love showing on his face, in his eyes? He didn't dare let it, for love without hope was in some ways more destructive than no love at all.

"And I'll be an uncle twice over," he said lightly. "All the joys without the headaches."

Lily paled and went very still. "Will you excuse me?" She didn't hurry away from him, but she moved quickly enough to give him pause. He watched as she disappeared in the direction of the rest rooms.

Had he and Lily come so far together, only to end up back where they had started? How had they gone from polite strangers to lovers, then to careful strangers once more?

Watching the empty hallway for her, Zach ached. When she came back, she moved to the other side of the sanctuary to stand beside her sister. Zach was struck by how much alike they were today, identical twins with identical radiance. Except one was his sister-in-law and one was his love.

Zach felt as if the world had been rearranged while he wasn't looking and that he was the only one who didn't have a map. For the first time in his life, he was lost and didn't have any idea what to do about it.

While he was pondering his fate, the minister called his name and he went to take his place beside his brother. He and Lily were godfather and godmother to their nephew.

John Henry gave him a smile that was both wise and mischievous. Zach winked at him, then leaned down to whisper, "How are you, little tiger?"

Squealing with delight, John Henry grabbed Zach's nose. Laughing, Zach disengaged himself.

"Ahem." The minister cleared his throat. "Shall we begin?"

Zach straightened up and looked straight into the bright green eyes of Lily. His attention stayed fixed on her through the entire ritual.

She was so close, and yet he had never felt more isolated from her. It was almost as if she had withdrawn behind a mask.

The ceremony ended and Lily leaned down to whisper to Rose. Zach was drawn into conversation with some Taylor kin, and when he looked up, Lily was gone.

He thought she had slipped away to the rest room again, or had gotten sidetracked and carried away by a relative. In the fellowship hall, he kept looking for her to return.

But Lily never came back. Feeling more lonesome than he ever had, Zach made his apologies and left early.

He had no place to go, no destination in mind. All he knew was that he had a lot of thinking to do.

It took Lily only two days after the christening to make her plans. At the bank, she asked for an extended leave. Next she arranged to sublet her apartment. The last thing she did was go across the courtyard to say goodbye to Rose and George and John Henry.

After she got back to her apartment, she packed her bags into her car and drove off into the night.

In the days after the christening, Zach reached for the telephone several times to call Lily. But each time he let his hand drop to his side. There was nothing he could say.

As much as he wanted to see his nephew, he stayed studiously away from his brother's apartment for fear of accidentally running into Lily. He hated the feeling of uncertainty in himself. He was becoming a man in limbo, a man who didn't belong anywhere. His house felt alien to him; his work felt empty. Lily's apartment might as well have been in another world, and his brother's place was strictly off-limits.

Sam called him to task.

"Are you going to wear a hole in the carpet, or are you going to do something about whatever the hell is eating at you?"

"I'm that bad, huh?"

"Yes. You're that bad. Anything I can do, old pal?"

"Not unless you can work miracles."

"I can't work miracles, but I can give a piece of advice.... You've served your sentence in hell, Zach. It's about time you gave yourself permission to go free."

What Sam said was true. Zach stood in the middle of his richly appointed den, thinking of his seven years of hell. The danger, the denial, the fear, the loneliness. Unless he made some changes, he was consigning himself to that same hell for the rest of his life.

Such a future was not only bleak, it was intolerable.

He crossed to Sam and put a hand on his shoulder.

"Thanks, pal."

"Anytime."

"There's one more thing you can do for me. Call Rafe. Tell him I'm on the way to see him."

When Zach left his house, he walked straight into the bright sunshine of a glorious autumn day. He looked straight into the sky, letting the sun warm his face, before he got into his car and drove to the DA's office.

Rafe was waiting for him in his sun-room.

"Zach." He clapped a hand on Zach's shoulder and led him to the glass-topped table. "Have some cookies. Sesame seed. Damned health food my wife insists on. But they're good." He poured two glasses of mint tea, then sat in a chair facing Zach. "Now, what brings you here?"

"I'm quitting, Rafe. Getting out. It's time to let a younger man do the job."

"Good. You don't belong undercover anymore. You belong up front, doing *my* job." Rafe gave him a sly grin. "Ever think about running for the DA's office?"

"The only thing I'm going to run for the next year or two is a good fishing spot on the river."

"You're not getting out of law?"

"No. I thought I'd hang out my shingle in some small, quiet town far away from New Orleans. I need a change of scene."

Rafe nodded. They ate their sesame-seed cookies and drank their tea. As Zach was leaving, Rafe shook his hand.

"Good luck, son. You can quit knowing you've beat them. You got the kingpin."

Zach left Rafe and went straight to the cemetery. Two enormous stone angels guarded the Taylor family mausoleum. Zach approached slowly. It was the first time he'd been back since the day they laid Emily to rest.

The sun warmed him as he studied her name: Emily Susan Taylor.

"Emily, I just came to tell you that you and Sasha have been avenged. The man who did this to you is going to pay. It's all over."

The bitterness and hatred he usually felt when he thought about Emily's death were replaced by a kind of peace. From a live oak tree in the corner of the cemetery, robins sang their simple, joyous song. Down the street, the sound of children at play rang out as they challenged each other at hopscotch. A lizard slithered through the grass and disappeared behind the mausoleum.

Even in the midst of death, life was everywhere around him, a veritable parade of joy. Zach was ready to join the band. There would always be evil. There would always be pain. There would always be loss. But he was ready to take the risks again. He was ready to love . . . and not be afraid.

With the birdsong and the children's laughter fresh in his mind, Zach drove to Loyola to see his brother. George was sitting in his cluttered office amidst science journals and chemistry books and his dusty collection of antique marbles. Bertha, the skeleton, stood in the corner, grinning her permanent grin.

When George saw his brother, he sheepishly closed his bag of potato chips. "Don't tell Rose."

"I thought you had given up the junk food." Zach straddled a straight-backed chair facing his brother's desk.

"I have...mostly. Usually I eat an apple or an orange, but sometimes I get this craving for food that's not good for me." George grinned. "I guess it's because we're pregnant."

"Rose is the one carrying the baby, not you." Zach chided his brother mildly. Nothing could spoil his mood.

"I know, I know." George wadded the bag and tossed it into the garbage can. "I'm not going to do anything to jeopardize my health. Too many people depend on me."

He picked up a pen and began to doodle on a pad. "What brings you here, Zach? You don't usually come out until dark."

"I'm through with all that." Zach told his brother of his decision to leave his undercover work and resume his law practice.

"I'm damned glad to hear that. Rose and I have been worried about you. We would both like to see you settle down, get married, have children."

"I plan to...if Lily will have me."

"Lily!" George dropped his pen and stared at his brother. "Well, damn," he said softly. "Rose was right."

"Right about what?"

"She's told me all along that something was going on between you two."

"I'm in love with Lily, George. And I have reason to believe she feels something for me." Restless, Zach stood up and began to pace. "You know, it's funny. I have a reputation for being a ladies' man, yet I don't have the first idea how to court the woman I love. I'm seven years out of practice."

Zach turned toward his brother. "I thought I would call first, while she's still at the bank. Or maybe I'll wait until she gets home and surprise her. Maybe I should get the ring first. What do you think about the ring, George, or is that taking too much for granted?"

George assumed his thinking position, staring into space, fingers laced together over his stomach. Zach waited, knowing his brother never came to a hasty decision and wouldn't be hurried into one. Although why he had to spend so much time thinking about the ring was a mystery to him.

Finally George unlaced his fingers and looked up.

"Lily's gone, Zach."

"Gone? On vacation?"

"No. On an extended leave. She left a few days ago."

"Why? Where?"

"She didn't tell us why, only that she needed some time away and she would be back in touch with us in a few weeks."

Why had she gone? Was she sick? Was she in trouble? Old habits died hard. Zach's initial reaction of expecting disaster threatened to swamp him. He rammed his fists into his pockets and clamped down on his fear.

"Did she say where she was going?" *God, please let her have told them where.*

"The Cooper family has a cabin on Lake Pontchatrain...."

"Is that the same one I went to a couple of years ago with you and Rose?"

"That's the one."

"Thanks, George."

"Good luck, Zach," his brother called, but Zach didn't hear him. He was already out the door.

* * *

Since coming to the lakeside cabin, Lily had discovered that digging in the dirt helped her relax. Dressed in jeans and a loose shirt, her hair tied back with a blue ribbon, she knelt beside the flower bed. Her gardening paraphernalia was scattered around her—trowel, bags of peat moss, planting instructions, tulip bulbs. Early next spring when her baby was born, the earth would be sprouting with color. It gave Lily a deep satisfaction to know that she was creating something beautiful, both inside her body and inside the earth.

She placed a hand over her abdomen. Already she was showing a little. That was a trait with the Cooper women, carrying their babies proudly out front for all the world to see.

The sun warmed her and she leaned back on her heels to wipe a streak of sweat off her forehead. Although the calendar said autumn, the weather said summer. As usual, cool fall temperatures would come slowly to the South.

She dug another hole and reached for a bulb.

"Lily."

Her hand froze in midair. Zach's voice. It couldn't be.

"Lily."

She turned in slow motion, as if she were in the middle of one of her dreams.

Zach was standing off to the side and slightly behind her. He was darkly handsome and extraordinarily self-possessed. In one swift motion, he knelt beside her and took her hand.

In a gesture both courtly and tender, he lifted her hand to his lips, dirt and all, and placed a kiss in her palm. Lily trembled. In the solitude and isolation of the cabin, she dreamed a lot. Some of her fantasies were about her baby, what it would look like, whether it would be a girl or boy, whether she would be a good mother. But most of her fantasies were about Zach. Like any good hero in the books she had read as a child, he would find her and claim her. He would declare that he'd given up his kingdom for her, that they were going to live happily ever after.

Of course, she was too mature, too wise, to think that any of that would happen. Real life wasn't like fairy tales.

Zach's eyes sparkled as he looked at her over the top of her hand. Although it was far too early, she imagined the baby recognized his father and quickened within her.

Lily didn't want to believe in things that weren't true, and yet, with Zach's lips still warming her palm, how could she not?

"Why are you here, Zach?"

"Because I love you."

She closed her eyes, letting his words sink in. They sounded so simple, so pure. With the bright sun shining down and the wind whispering in the pines like a benediction, it seemed to Lily that the rest of her life might be as simple and lovely as Zach's declaration.

She wanted to believe.

"I love you, too," she said.

His laughter was pure joy. He caught her to him and pressed his face in her hair. Kneeling together in the dirt, they rocked back and forth.

"I was prepared to scale mountains and fight dragons to prove my love to you. I had planned how I would wear down your resistance."

"How?"

"With chocolate and roses. With wine and candlelight. With emeralds and diamonds." He laughed again, holding her closer.

"My love is free to you. It always has been."

Zach leaned back to look at her. "I've come to take you back with me, Lily."

Her heart sank. Was that all he wanted? Her back in New Orleans, back in his bed, waiting for the brief moments of pleasure they could share when he wasn't off doing whatever dangerous, mysterious work he did?

"I can't go back, Zach."

"If it's because of all the things I've told you, or *not* told you, about my work, you can forget that. I was working undercover for the DA's office, Lily. I've given that up."

"Why?"

"I had collected too many ghosts, sacrificed too much. I realized that I couldn't go on living in isolation and loneliness." He cupped her cheeks. "There will be no secrets between us anymore. No masks, either real or symbolic."

Fear squeezed Lily's heart. She was carrying the biggest secret of all. Was that why Zach was here? He was damned good at finding out other people's secrets. Had he found out hers? For that matter, Rose was an expert at reading Lily's mind, and being pregnant herself, she might have noticed and guessed the truth. If she had, she would surely have told George.

"Did Rose or George tell you why I'm here, Zach?"

"I didn't see Rose before I left. George told me where you were, but not why you had gone. Only that you are taking an extended leave. Why are you here?"

She closed her eyes, gathering courage. The truth had to be told, no matter what the consequences.

"Because I'm carrying your child."

Zach looked as if someone had knocked the wind out of him. He was so still, so silent that even the leaves sounded loud as they rustled in the trees. In the small eternity before he spoke, Lily died a thousand deaths. What if he hated her for not telling him about the baby? What if he wanted her as a lover and nothing more? What if he felt trapped?

"You're carrying my child?"

"Yes."

Slowly he placed his hand over her abdomen.

"My baby," he whispered. "My baby."

All the wonder and the joy he felt shone in his face. Lily recalled how he had looked bending over the cradle where John Henry slept. She remembered him sitting in the rocking chair, singing his dear, funny, made-up songs. She remembered him unashamedly brushing away the tears when he told John Henry goodbye.

How could she have doubted him?

"You're not angry at me?" she whispered.

"For not telling me?" Rubbing his hand back and forth over the small protrusion that was his child, he smiled. "I suppose I should be. I suppose I should think of some appropriate punishment...such as keeping you prisoner in my bed until you beg for my forgiveness."

"That's no punishment," she said, laughing, partly with relief, but mostly with joy.

"How could I be mad, Lily? I've waited seven years before reaching out for love, for a family. And now I discover that I'm getting a wife and child both at the same time. No waiting and wondering. No counting backwards and hoping. No calling my office to say your temperature has risen...."

"What office?"

"My law office. I'm going into private practice again. In a small town somewhere...." He grinned. "One that has a good gynecologist."

"Is this a proposal?"

"I'm on my knees in the dirt, Lily. What does it look like?"

"I'm on my knees in the dirt, too, Zach, and I'm not sure I can get up without help."

"I think I'm supposed to take you over the threshold."

"That's after the wedding."

"How about if we practice before?" He helped Lily up, then scooped her into his arms. "I recall a very good feather bed in this cabin."

He carried her up the steps and through the door, kicking it shut behind him. Although he hadn't been in the cabin in two years, his instincts were good. He carried her straight to the bedroom and laid her on a patchwork quilt. She sank deep into the feather mattress, her hair fanning around her face.

Zach lay down beside her and began to unbutton her blouse. "Do you think my baby will mind?"

"He'll love it, and so will his mother."

When her breasts came into view, Zach touched them gently. Her nipples were darker, fuller. They tightened at his touch.

"I've missed you, Lily. I've missed us together."

"So have I."

He continued his slow unveiling of Lily, murmuring his delight, as if he had never seen her before. The gentle curve of her abdomen fascinated him most. He pressed warm kisses over the soft bulge, then put his cheek down on the soft flesh as if he was trying to hear the baby growing inside her womb.

"Hello, there, little one," he whispered. "This is your father talking. I love you."

Smiling, Lily tangled her hands in his hair. She and Zach had come full circle, from the silk-draped bed in the Monteleone four years ago to a simple feather bed in a cabin in the woods. It seemed as if all her life she had been waiting for this man and this moment, this golden moment with the sun pouring through the window and his love pouring through her heart.

"Lily," Zach whispered, lifting himself on his elbows so he could see her face. "My Lily. I love you. I will always love you."

"I love you, too. Now and forever."

She lifted her arms and he came to her. He filled her body as surely as he filled her heart, filled her with warmth and tenderness and passion, filled her with hope and joy and love.

She welcomed him with soft cries of delight. She turned her head to glance at the mask on her bedside table. The single diamond winked at her.

Lily winked back.

Epilogue

John Henry liked his new house. It had high ceilings that echoed when he yelled. It had a big backyard full of wonderful things his daddy had made for him—a sandbox and a little swing with a seat so he wouldn't fall out and a new red doghouse for Bentley. Bentley turned up his nose at the house and refused to set a paw inside, but John Henry liked it. If he got down on all fours, he could wiggle through and sit inside and pretend he was a king inside his fort, fighting off dragons. Bentley made a good dragon. He stood outside the door, barking and looking fierce. John Henry guessed he just wanted somebody to come out and play, but still, he could pretend Bentley was breathing fire and snorting brimstone.

His new house had a staircase, too. John Henry liked that most of all. He couldn't go up it yet, although everybody told him how smart he was to be walking at his age. Shoot, he already knew that. He liked to get down on all fours and scoot backward down the stairs as fast as he could go. His mother and daddy laughed and applauded. They thought everything he did was bright and cute. They told him he was special and wonderful.

He already knew that, too. Now, of course, he had a new baby sister, and they told her the same thing. But that was all right with John Henry. He guessed she needed all the cheering up she could get, as ugly as she was. Her face was all puckered and red, and she spit up on herself all the time. Daddy said that was because she was a newborn, and that she'd learn manners just like John Henry. She wore pink, too. John Henry couldn't abide pink. He guessed it was all right for her, though, since she was a girl. He sort of liked having a little sister. When she got big, she'd probably think he was the finest thing in the whole world. Well, he was.

"John Henry." His daddy came into the room that was all John Henry's own and plucked him from among his nest of teddy bears. He'd been pretending they were dragons. "It's time to get cleaned up. Uncle Zach and Aunt Lily are coming."

John Henry liked the way his daddy dressed him, no-nonsense, just straightforward pulling off the dirty clothes and putting on the clean. He loved his daddy. He loved his mother, too, but when she dressed him, she still sprinkled baby powder all over him. Baby powder was for babies. And he was nearly one-and-a-half years old; almost a man.

"They're bringing your little cousins," Daddy told him. "Isn't that nice?"

He didn't know what cousins were, but he guessed he'd find out. About the time Daddy got his shoes tied, the doorbell rang.

"I'll get it," his mother called.

"Upsy daisy." His daddy always said that when he put John Henry on his shoulders. He liked riding tall. He could see everything.

He and his daddy went down the stairs, laughing, and who should be coming in the door but Uncle Zach and Aunt

Lily. They were both carrying little bundles in their arms; Aunt Lily a blue one, and Uncle Zach a pink one.

"Come meet your new cousins, little tiger."

Uncle Zach still called him that. His daddy carried him across the room, and he was glad to be up high so he could get a better view of what everybody called his cousins. They didn't look like much to him. The one wrapped in blue had red hair and a fierce scowl, and the one wrapped in pink had dark hair and a funny little heart-shaped face.

"What do you think, little tiger?"

Uncle Zach and Aunt Lily looked so pleased that he didn't dare tell them what he really thought. He didn't want to hurt their feelings.

"Baby," he said.

"How about that," his daddy said. "My boy's a genius."

"John Henry's brilliant," his mother said. She was holding his baby sister, but she was smiling especially for him.

"How's everything in Lake Charles?" his mother asked Aunt Lily and Uncle Zach. She was making small talk. John Henry didn't think it was very interesting. He'd much rather be going down the staircase backward.

"Great." Aunt Lily looked like she meant what she said. "Zach's law practice is thriving, and the twins are keeping me busy. We love it."

Uncle Zach put his arm around Aunt Lily and kissed her. If things were going to get mushy, John Henry was leaving. He began to squirm and wiggle in his daddy's arms.

"I'm so glad you're both happy." Tears stood in his mother's eyes. She always cried when she was happy. She cried when she was sad, too. But that was all right, and nobody had better tell John Henry any different. Mostly his mother laughed, and she was the best mother in the whole world.

"We owe it all to John Henry," Uncle Zach said.

John Henry quit wiggling. If the grown-ups were going to say nice things about him, he wanted to stick around and hear.

"We might never have gotten together if we hadn't had to move into your apartment with him," Aunt Lily said. "I fell in love in that old apartment at 13 Royal Street."

"So did I. And mostly because of John Henry. The little tiger taught us both how to love."

Aunt Lily and Uncle Zach got all sparkly eyed, then kissed each other. His daddy leaned over and kissed his mother, too.

Love must be something wonderful. John Henry guessed he'd invented it.

*   *   *   *   *

INTIMATE MOMENTS®
Silhouette

Ever since the appearance of Linda Howard's
incredibly popular MACKENZIE'S MOUNTAIN in 1989,
we've received literally hundreds of letters, all asking
that same question. At last the book we've all been
waiting for is here.

In September, look for MACKENZIE'S MISSION (Intimate
Moments #445), Joe's story as only Linda Howard
could tell it.

And Joe is only the first of an exciting breed here at
Silhouette Intimate Moments. Starting in September,
we'll be bringing you one title every month in our new
American Heroes program. In addition to Linda
Howard, the **American Heroes** lineup will be written
by such stars as Kathleen Eagle, Kathleen Korbel,
Patricia Gardner Evans, Marilyn Pappano, Heather
Graham Pozzessere and more. Don't miss a
single one!

Welcome to Conard County, Wyoming, where the sky spreads bold and blue above men and women who draw their strength from the wild western land and from the bonds of the love they share.

Join author Rachel Lee for a trip to the American West as we all want it to be. In Conard County, Wyoming, she's created a special place where men are men and women are more than a match for them.

In the first book of the miniseries, EXILE'S END (Intimate Moments #449), you'll meet Amanda Grant, whose imagination takes her to worlds of wizards and warlocks in the books she writes, but whose everyday life is gray and forlorn—until Ransom Laird walks onto her land with trouble in his wake and a promise in his heart. Once you meet them, you won't want to stop reading. And once you've finished the book, you'll be looking forward to all the others in the miniseries, starting with CHEROKEE THUNDER, available in December.

EXILE'S END is available this September, only from Silhouette Intimate Moments.

Take 4 bestselling love stories FREE

Plus get a FREE surprise gift!

TAKE A WALK ON THE DARK SIDE OF LOVE

October is the shivery season, when chill winds blow and shadows
walk the night. Come along with us into a haunting world where
love and danger go hand in hand, where passions will thrill you
and dangers will chill you. Come with us to

In this newest short story collection from Silhouette Books, three of
your favorite authors tell tales just perfect for a spooky autumn
night. Let Anne Stuart introduce you to "The Monster in the
Closet," Helen R. Myers bewitch you with "Seawitch," and
Heather Graham Pozzessere entice you with "Wilde Imaginings."

Silhouette Shadows™
Haunting a store near you this October.